INTERI

CW00997042

NIRUPAMA SUBRAMANIAN was born in Chennai, grew up in Delhi and has worked all over India. She is now a freelance consultant, corporate trainer and executive coach. Her fiction, travelogues and articles have won awards and have appeared in several publications. She won the Commonwealth Short Story prize in 2006. Her first novel, *Keep the Change*, was a national best-seller. She lives in Gurgaon with her husband, daughter and a cupboard full of books.

INTERMISSION

Nirupama Subramanian

HarperCollins *Publishers* India
a joint venture with

New Delhi

First published in India in 2012 by
HarperCollins *Publishers* India
a joint venture with
The India Today Group

Copyright © Nirupama Subramanian 2012

ISBN: 978-93-5029-323-2

2 4 6 8 10 9 7 5 3 1

Nirupama Subramanian asserts the moral right to be identified as
the author of this work.

This is a work of fiction. The names, characters and incidents portrayed in
this book are the product of the author's imagination. Any resemblance to
actual persons, living or dead, events or localities, is entirely coincidental.

All rights reserved. No part of this publication may be reproduced,
stored in a retrieval system, or transmitted, in any form or by any means,
electronic, mechanical, photocopying, recording or otherwise,
without the prior permission of the publishers.

HarperCollins *Publishers*
A-53, Sector 57, Noida 201301, India
77-85 Fulham Palace Road, London W6 8JB, United Kingdom
Hazelton Lanes, 55 Avenue Road, Suite 2900, Toronto, Ontario M5R 3L2
and 1995 Markham Road, Scarborough, Ontario M1B 5M8, Canada
25 Ryde Road, Pymble, Sydney, NSW 2073, Australia
31 View Road, Glenfield, Auckland 10, New Zealand
10 East 53rd Street, New York NY 10022, USA

Typeset in 11/15 Adobe Jenson Pro at
SŪRYA

Printed and bound at
Thomson Press (India) Ltd.

For Rajesh
The not-so-middle-aged man in my life

1

ON THE BALCONY of his seventh-floor apartment, oblivious to the swirl of midsummer dust, the rasping April breeze and the faint voices of his household that rattled behind the French windows, Varun Sarin pretended to read the newspaper. He felt the familiar knot within, an uneasy anticipation which he tried to ignore as he gazed at the pages of the *Hindustan Times*. He vaguely registered the fact that the Opposition party had staged a walkout in Parliament and that a family in a nearby village in Haryana had poisoned their only daughter and slaughtered her lower-caste lover; fifteen pieces of his body had been found in a mustard field. The state of the nation and other people's lives did not interest him, at least not at this time of the morning.

He glanced at his watch. 7:30 a.m. Ten minutes late. Through the great wrought-iron gates of Trafalgar Towers, the daily passage of human and vehicular traffic had begun. The security guards in their blue uniforms, charged with controlling the influx of the outside world and regulating its outflow, had come into their own. They scrutinized the visitors, prepared gate passes on small pink slips and followed with their eyes every vehicle that left the building.

Varun noticed a few schoolchildren heading towards the bus stop in front of the building, the smaller kids flanked by mothers or maids, the teenage boys hitching up their baggy trousers and the girls tossing their hair with studied nonchalance. The iron barrier in front of the gates swung up to let out a large gold-coloured car. A herd of drivers – thin men of average height, their clothes drooping, their faces heavy with the drudgery of the day ahead – trooped in. A few of the younger men looked aggressively hopeful in bright T-shirts that bore the logos and cheerful slogans of the companies their employers worked for. They gazed furtively at the maids who flocked in twos and threes, like colourful birds in their red yellow orange saris, calling out to one another in animated Bengali. Splashes of vermillion blazed on their bright faces, red and white bangles encircled their wrists.

An old man in a white kurta pyjama plodded along the walking path and three middle-aged ladies wearing sneakers and flowery salwar suits marched along like grim warriors fighting a losing battle against weight and age. The lawns were a patchwork of green and brown. In some places, where the grass had been worn thin by children playing football or cricket, it resembled the tonsured head of a child with a week's growth of scraggly new hair. A young couple froze and unfroze their limbs in the various poses of the Suryanamaskar on yoga mats spread out on the lawns.

He saw her then. Rounding the curve of Tower 1 and stepping onto the path that circled the park, pausing for a second to adjust the ipod strapped to her arm. Varun felt the knot in his chest unravel. She was in a bright-red halter-neck T-shirt that scooped her breasts into a rounded prominence, and black track pants. He took in the jaunty arc of her long ponytail, the dip of her waist and the determined swaying of her narrow hips. Her face was indistinct from this distance but he had an impression of delicate bones, a smudged mouth and buttery skin. Of something pure and wholesome within her. It seemed to him that she was being borne along in a shiny bubble, in this world and yet not a part of it, and he wondered, as he had done for the past three weeks, if she was only a part of his imagination.

He watched her disappear, then reappear from behind the semicircle described by the four peach-coloured towers of Trafalgar Towers. As he watched her, he tried to recall the moment when he had first noticed her, when he had changed from a dispassionate onlooker to an interested observer to an avid watcher. He wondered who she was, what she did in the twenty-four hours between the morning walks, who were the people she claimed as her own. And he wondered why he, Varun Sarin, forty-four-year-old successful entrepreneur, faithful husband and competent father of a sixteen-year-old boy, a man with the stolidity of half his life behind him and the certainty of what lay ahead, should wait every morning for a glimpse of this girl, like a teenager in the first throes of an infatuation.

He would have liked nothing better than to stand there observing how long she walked and where she went afterwards but his morning routine dictated otherwise. He stepped back through the windows and plunged into a different world. Gayatri, already showered and dressed, juggled a Blackberry and a piece of multigrain toast between her fingers. They had an established morning routine: Gayatri had to be dropped off at her office, which was on the way to his own, the specific time of departure set for 8:45 a.m. – absurdly early for him but just right for her.

'Varun, aren't you ready yet? We're going to be late. I have an early morning meeting with Jai. I told you yesterday that I had to leave by 8:15 today. If you aren't ready in ten minutes, I'm leaving.' He didn't know if it was a plea or a threat; he read both in her voice.

'Then leave. I'll go later.'

'Fine.'

'Tell Jagdish to come back here after he drops you.'

'Fine.'

The words, spat out at him like cherry pits into the wind, carried a faint whiff of accusation. Gayatri grabbed her handbag, her laptop, lunch bag, Blackberry and sunglasses and slammed out of the apartment. For a moment, Varun was tempted to resume his scrutiny of the park but he was conscious of the presence of the cook, Jhumpa, who had emerged from the kitchen to ask him if he would have some breakfast. The cleaning maid, Bulbul, moved towards him on her haunches, inscribing impatient sloppy circles with a grey mop on the floor, a certain tilt of the head indicating that he should clear the way and allow her to get on with her work.

Solitude in this apartment was a luxury, he had begun to realize in the past few weeks. He seemed to be always surrounded by people. His workday was an endless series of meetings and at home his family and staff hovered around him constantly. He was caught within an orbit of people wanting, needing, giving, taking, sharing, complaining, arguing, doing things that often did not concern him. He wanted nothing more than to be by himself and contemplate the girl in red, to meditate in peace upon the parts that made her glorious whole.

Later, as he stood in front of his bathroom mirror, shaving, he looked at his face, his body, the parts that made him whole. He felt fit, the weekend golf and occasional tennis keeping his midriff in check, though of late he had begun to watch for signs of an incipient paunch. Running a razor through his day-old stubble, he reflected that the contours of his face were not unpleasant. No one would call him handsome, but he wasn't ugly either. He wondered how the girl might describe him to her friends. That is, if they ever met and if she ever talked to her friends about him.

Varun knew he was growing old, though he didn't feel it. He joked about the increasing threads of silver that coloured his hair: he was glad, he said, that he still had some hair left and was not growing bald like some other men his age. A few weeks ago, his ophthalmologist had suggested reading glasses but he had deferred the decision of acquiring spectacles. When he compared himself to the Varun Sarin in the wedding photograph on the bedside table, he could see the difference even though he couldn't identify exactly how he had changed. He knew that he had aged well but the external signs of ageing always took him by surprise, more so as he sometimes recognized in himself the inchoate stirrings of a sixteen-year-old boy.

It amazed Varun sometimes to think that he owned and managed a company that employed over two hundred people, that he had sustained a marriage for seventeen years and was father to a teenager. The mural of his life, when he was inclined to think of it that way, was full and vibrant; there were strokes he was thankful for and splashes of colour he could look upon with some pride. Yet the picture as a whole seemed to lack something. It seemed to him that there was a part missing that he was only beginning to be aware of.

2

VARUN AND GAYATRI had been invited to a party by the Sharmas on the twenty-first floor of Tower 2 in Trafalgar

Towers, Phase 6, Gurgaon. The Sharmas were a wealthy, generous couple in their early fifties who were known to throw lavish parties, especially during Diwali, when the poker stakes were said to run into lakhs. Every once in a while they invited an assortment of friends and neighbours to dinner. The selection of guests seemed to be random: very few knew that the Sharmas had a secret checklist against which prospective guests were measured for their physical beauty, their place in the pecking order, their entertainment value. Varun Sarin had a nodding acquaintance with Pramod Sharma. This was the second invitation the Sarins had received since Varun's photograph had appeared alongside a short article in the *Economic Times* –TECHKNOWLEDGE TO RECEIVE ADDITIONAL FUNDING FROM BLUESTONE PARTNERS: AN INTERVIEW WITH TECHKNOWLEDGE CEO VARUN SARIN. They had declined the first but felt obliged to acknowledge the persistence and graciousness of the Sharmas with their presence and a bottle of Californian Merlot from their diminishing wine cellar.

Gayatri did not care to attend parties thrown by people she did not know well but she had a strong sense of the neighbourly obligations that made such interactions essential to life in a condominium. Varun was ambivalent. He would have preferred to stay home and watch a tennis match on TV with Anirudh. But after a couple of Single Malts, he usually felt kindly towards his fellow human beings. Gayatri knew that he would amuse the other guests with stories of how they had struggled with Gurgaon after many years in Fremont, California; the stories never failed to evoke laughter. If he was in the mood, he would be charming to the ladies and lavishly praise the hostess for her culinary efforts. He often said it was the least he could do for those who provided food and drinks and created a semblance of entertainment for him.

He had another reason for agreeing to come to the party: he carried a faint hope that he would get some news of the girl in red from their neighbours. At the same time, he worried that any new information would force him to confront the reality of her existence in ways that he did not wish to. Over the past few days he had built a fragile relationship with her: she had innocently offered herself for his contemplation and he had taken that offering in good faith. He watched her daily, not with the salacious gaze of a voyeur but with the wonder of a tourist who had come upon a majestic work of nature and was content to spend a few minutes in its presence without any desire for possession. If she was real, and if she turned out to be a nineteen-year-old college student with a nasal voice and ambitions in the area of fashion modelling, it would destroy the tenuous bond he had forged with her.

He stood on the balcony of the Sharmas' elegantly decorated penthouse apartment, swirling whisky in a crystal glass and listening to the men talk about the stock market, real estate prices, newly launched automobiles and the amazing deals they had cracked at work. Their conversation rarely revealed anything about their lives, but their opinions on matters of global importance were voiced in unequivocal tones, as though they had fashioned these events themselves. They weighed each other up silently, the measures being their ability to generate wealth and leverage connections with people of consequence. Each personal revelation was designed to offer some information that would tip the scales in their favour but the competitiveness was convivial, without malice.

Gayatri sat on the plush brown sofa in the living room and listened to the other women talk about the health and accomplishments of their children, the quality of schools, their constant efforts to lose weight, the audacity of the maids, and the recent purchases they had made at the malls. Each one sought to simultaneously arouse empathy and envy among the others. All of them were married, most of them appeared to be comfortably settled: they segued from the smugness of newly-weds to the resignation of grandmothers. Gayatri didn't know any of them well and didn't feel like furthering their acquaintance either. There was a trio of giggling women perched on the sofa in front of her. Roma was the next-door neighbour she bumped into occasionally. The other two had been introduced to her as Ragini and Garima but she was unable to match the names to the faces. She had seen them in the park, chaperoning a gaggle of small girls. The women, in their mid-thirties, seemed to derive great amusement from one another's company and formed a charmed semicircle that excluded the rest of them. She could overhear their conversation, which now centred on the doings of a neighbour in Tower 4, a lady newly returned from the US who was paying her maid an exorbitant sum of money for 'just jhadoo ponchha' and spoiling the market for others. The discussion then moved on to a new diet that Roma was trying hard to follow; it had been recommended by the famous Dr Makhijani, who advocated eating seven small meals every day and swearing off sweets till eternity. The others pitched in with their own stories and theories of weight loss.

Gayatri was squeezed in between two women, one of whom wore a blue salwar kameez and shimmering fuchsia lipstick and resembled a minor character in a television soap opera – a well-meaning sister-in-law or a distant cousin perhaps, who shines like tinsel briefly, for a few episodes, before she is ejected from the story. The lady on her right was a little older and had the sleek, satisfied look of a well-maintained cat. She seemed to be the kind whose eyeliner never smudged, whose hair retained the immaculate look of a recent blow-dry even at the end of the day. She wore an expensive-looking pink tunic with a deep V-shaped neckline embellished with small pearls, and a pair of dark trousers. Her earrings matched the diamond pendant that knocked against the door of her cleavage. Gayatri herself was dressed in a demure raw-silk churidar kameez. She had never managed to figure out the appropriate wear for these dinners. In Fremont, parties were usually casual boisterous affairs, mostly potluck, with people sauntering in wearing jeans and T-shirts and helping afterwards with the cooking and clearing up. She remembered children running around the yard, men brandishing skewers over barbecue grills, and lots of laughter. She hoped that at one of her outings in Gurgaon she would meet a woman who could become her friend, a friend with whom she could talk about her life, exchange notes on the state of their respective marriages, even go out for a Saturday lunch. She still missed Harini and Sheetal, the lazy lunches at Santana Row, sipping wine at a roadside café under a clear Californian sky, then some shopping, a shared ice-cream at Ben & Jerrys, and driving back home on the freeway listening to Kishore Kumar songs in the car. But none of these women seemed her type. She couldn't say what she was looking for in a friend but she doubted that she would find one here.

'So which flat are you in?' asked the older woman sitting next to her.

'We are on the seventh floor, 207 D,' Gayatri replied. She was still getting used to hearing the word 'flat' after years of saying 'apartment'.

'Aap job karti hain?' enquired her other neighbour.

'I work with a company, Goodricke Dickson. They make medical equipment.'

'Oh . . . what do you do there?'

'I head finance. I am the CFO.' Gayatri couldn't help feeling satisfyingly superior every time she said it. CFO. The syllables rolled off her tongue. The job was important to her, she liked the title. She felt special in this group of women, most of whom appeared to be housewives.

'What do you do?' she asked.

'Oh, I am a homemaker,' said the woman. 'It's a full-time job, really. The kids need to have their mother around even though they are in high school Their father travels so much. He is the regional head of sales and marketing at MicroLan. I also volunteer with the Literacy Project – we teach underprivileged children every Saturday. It's so satisfying.'

'Me too,' chimed the other lady. 'So much work at home. Kuch aur karne ke liye time hee nahin hain.'

Gayatri immediately felt guilty for being a CFO, wretched about neglecting her child and her social obligations. An uncomfortable silence hung over them as she stared into her white wine, her second of the evening. They all ignored the plate of cocktail samosas on the table in front of them.

'How long have you been here?' Gayatri felt compelled to say something to the older woman, Shalini. She thought she might have a little more in common with her than with her other neighbour, whose tendency to lapse into Hindi made her feel a little awkward, even foreign. She wasn't snobbish but she was unwilling to go out of her way to get to know people who she sensed were different from her. Shalini was not unpleasant and something in her posture suggested that she was inclined to continue the conversation.

'In Gurgaon? Almost four years, though we moved into this apartment a year ago. Before that, we were in Singapore. Where are you from?'

This was a question Gayatri had encountered more times than she could remember since they had returned to India.

She sensed in it the questioner's need to pin her down to an easily identifiable geography which might provide a map for further excursions into each other's lives. In the beginning she had taken the trouble to explain herself: 'I am a Tamilian but I grew up in Bangalore. I am married to a Punjabi and we are American citizens.' But the answer was far from satisfactory, the roots messy and too tangled to provide the connections that the other person wanted so badly to establish.

'California,' volunteered Gayatri, aware that she had drawled the 'r', said it with a Californian accent, unlike many Indians who stressed the 'o'. As though she felt a need to offer proof of her life before Gurgaon, and disown any claims that this place might have on her. Sometimes she extended her 'a' sounds and slurped the hard consonants so that she sounded more American. In Fremont she had switched seamlessly between the accented American at work and the Indian English that she used with other desis. When she spoke to her mother-in-law over the phone in a mixture of halting Hindi and English, she took particular care to sound Indian, rooted.

'Where in California?'

'Fremont.'

'Oh, we have a cousin in San Jose. I believe it's quite nice there.'

'It's beautiful. The weather is wonderful throughout the year. We stayed in a really nice area, just off Mission Boulevard. We had an amazing view from our house. On a clear day, you could see up to Mission peak. And it was gorgeous during the Fall, when the colours would change the hills and the trees all around. The roads were broad and clean, so driving was easy. We were in a good school district and there were so many Indian stores that we didn't miss anything at all. Really, it was the best of both worlds. I had such great friends there.'

'So how do you find it here?'

'Quite chaotic. The traffic is so bad and the roads so terrible that I can't drive here. There is no sense of time or urgency, and everyone is so rude. You can't get anything done unless you shout and get aggressive. Also, I can't believe there's so much garbage on the streets. Some days, everything is a struggle, managing people, the weather. I don't think I've adjusted to it yet. I really miss Fremont.'

This was something Gayatri had said many times before. She spoke with such nostalgic passion, such evocative longing for a time gone by, and displayed such obvious hatred of her present condition that the listener was prompted to ask the question, the question she waited for.

'So why did you move back?'

Her husband, looking at Gayatri through the clutch of men on the balcony, knew what came next from the set line of her lips, the flaring of her nostrils and the agitation that gripped her body.

'My husband wanted to move back to start his own company in India. Initially we thought we would move to Bangalore. My parents are settled there, so I was okay with the move, though I never really wanted to leave Fremont, my job, my friends. But I thought, my parents are getting older and I should be there for them, closer, just in case. I thought maybe it would be good for Anirudh, our son. Then suddenly Varun's plans changed, just after we had sold our house and even found a school for Anirudh in Bangalore. There was some problem with the office space. I had no idea we would end up in Gurgaon.'

I had no idea we would end up in Gurgaon. Words that could be said in so many different ways: with a high little laugh at the end, hinting at amusement at the predicament she found herself in; an indifferent shrug indicating a reluctant reconcilement to the idea of ending up in Gurgaon; with a sense of wonder at finding herself in the Millennium City, amidst gleaming new concrete structures in the heart of India shining; with stoic calm, with sorrow, with tender indulgent love for a place that she now called home.

But for Gayatri the words were stones, each one weighing her down with a terrible feeling of having been betrayed, cheated of a life she had loved, fooled into accepting one she could never come to terms with. She sank deeper with each word and by the time she finished, she felt herself drowning in a sad pool of self-pity and helplessness. Gurgaon could never be home. She felt out of place in this brash city that bristled with guiltless consumerism, that was urgently mutating into something unrecognizable, that allowed the uneasy, edgy coexistence of extreme wealth and acute poverty. She disliked the concrete clutter, the condominium life that permitted her actions, entries and exits to be subject to the scrutiny of strangers. Home in India had always been Bangalore, the quiet part of Jayanagar, where her parents lived amidst tree-lined avenues and gentle people who spoke in low tones. Varun, she thought, could live anywhere in the world; he was able to merge with his environment and yet be detached from it, not letting the surroundings impinge on his state of mind. He 'managed', making do with whatever was thrown at him. She, however, had taken a while to adjust to the American way of life and just when she had found her rhythm there, just when it seemed that Fremont was home, she had been forced to move.

Her distaste for her new home had been triggered partly by an incident that occurred in their very first month here. She was not yet employed with Goodricke and was busy with the process of settling down, a process that seemed to be taking a long time. One morning, she had set out to pick up some groceries from Le Marche at a nearby mall. Though she had handled a Honda CR-V with considerable ease on the wide orderly roads of Fremont, she had been apprehensive about driving in Gurgaon. She was hunched over the wheel of their brand-new Toyota Corolla, peering at the road ahead in a state of tense anticipation, when suddenly a pig darted out from the undergrowth at the edge of the road. The large sow, slick with mud and dirt, and the pair of piglets that emerged from behind to follow their mother onto the road, threw her completely. She swerved to avoid them and then, seeing that she was headed straight towards a large pothole in the middle of the road, braked with all her strength. It might have been funny, to be caught between a pig and a pothole. She could have narrated the story later with a mixture of exasperation and amazement. But in the instant after she pressed the brakes, she fell forward and her head hit the steering wheel.

She sat still for a minute, in shock, unable to fathom what had just happened, and then realized that she had been rammed by a vehicle behind her. She expected the driver to come up to her. In a civilized world, there would have been mutual apologies, an assessment of insurance, an exchange of numbers. But as the black Scorpio pulled up beside her, she saw that there were two men in it, young, well-muscled men in tight T-shirts, and something in their expression was louche, the way they leaned out of the window was insolent. They shouted at her, the words not very clear, but there was no mistaking the derisive tone. They said something about her driving skills, about women at the wheel and then a word, a gaali, a gesture, which she did not understand though she grasped the insult that was intended.

They sped away then, their vehicle only mildly scratched; it did not occur to her to note down the licence number. Her own car had not been severely damaged but she was shaken, her sense of self dented. That night she could not sleep, she still heard those voices, saw the black Scorpio driving off, the mocking scrawl of the words 'Gujjar Boy' on its back window.

The women around her could feel her misery, the deep sense of having been wronged, and it seemed to awaken something similar in them. Two of them turned from their own conversations to register her presence. Gayatri was suddenly aware that she was connecting with them. She saw their faces shine with compassion and understanding. We too are martyrs, they seemed to say, sacrificed on the altar of our husband's ambitions and children's well-being. But from that pyre we rise as good wives and good mothers. It is this knowledge of our own goodness, the absolute goodness of our selfless sacrifice that keeps us alive day after day. They were angels, these women, they fanned her with their diaphanous wings and whispered to her, Courage, Courage.

Gayatri looked down at her empty glass and wondered if she'd had too much wine.

3

THREE WEEKS HAD gone by since Varun first saw the girl. She had become part of the morning routine but there was nothing mechanical about the way he lay in wait for her, watched her and memorized the minute details of her appearance. After she had completed her walk, he left the balcony, got dressed, called for his car and left for work.

Work. Work was the reason Varun and Gayatri had given up their lives in Fremont, uprooted Anirudh 'Rudy' Sarin from the soil he had come to believe was his own and relocated their family within a four-bedroom (with servant's quarter) apartment in a Gurgaon condominium. Work was what brought the maids from Bangladesh, the housekeepers from Jharkhand, the drivers from Bihar, the cooks from Nepal and the construction workers from Rajasthan to live under asbestos roofs and cardboard walls in the slum clusters and shanty towns that made up a large part of Gurgaon. Work was what induced Korean and Japanese salarymen, Croatian pilots, German consultants, Russian engineers, Tamil accountants, Malayali nurses, Manipuri telemarketers and returning non-resident Indians from Singapore, New York and London to live in the multistorey apartments, art-deco villas and town houses with Italian marble flooring and 100 per cent power back-up, that made up the rest of Gurgaon.

For Varun, his work was the realization of a dream he had nurtured since his days as an engineering student at IIT. The idea of having his own company had played through his life like a recurrent background score all through business school, through his first job, then later with Infosys and Innovent Inc, till it built up to a crescendo during his last days there. When his boss at Innovent ordered him to abandon a project that he and his friend Sambasivam 'Sam' Ramanathan were working on and move on to something that would 'impact the bottom line in the near term and not a hundred years later', Varun began plotting his escape. He wrote a business plan, found a venture capital firm willing to back his idea for a business intelligence and knowledge management company jointly owned by him and Sam, and announced his resignation. The dream of managing his own company did not stem from any desire to leave a legacy for his child or accumulate enough wealth to retire to the Bahamas or be recognized as Entrepreneur of the Year by popular newsmagazines. It was just a new challenge that seemed exciting at the time.

Varun had always welcomed the idea of change; the new, the unexplored, held a strange fascination for him. As army kids, he and his younger sister Shweta had moved five cities, four small towns and two remote army camps in the course of their childhood. The constant moves had made him self-confident, given him the ability to adapt and connect with different kinds of people, and imbued him with a certain optimism that things would turn out all right.

Now TechKnowlEdge was his life, it had become a part of his identity and an extension of his personality. He was almost always at work: meeting his team, talking to clients in the US at odd hours, solving other people's problems and getting things done. The work fed him, fuelled him and propelled him from one day to another.

For Gayatri, work was serious business. She had been brought up with a strong work ethic. Her father had been a professor at the Indian Institute of Science, acknowledged as brilliant by his community. But though assiduous, and meticulous about his duties, he could never summon up the ambition to distinguish himself in any significant way. In his retirement, he was a consulting editor with a scientific journal and continued as a guest faculty at the Institute. Her mother had shown early promise as a Carnatic musician and had even sung on All India Radio and performed at local concerts in Chennai. But after marriage she had given up her desire to be a professional singer, had moved to Bangalore and settled down to housekeeping and child rearing. She had contented herself by giving music lessons to children but Gayatri sensed that there was some sense of regret deep inside her, a silent sorrow at the voluntary suppression of her ambitions. She had instilled in Gayatri the need to have a career, something of her own, and had been fiercely supportive of her decision to continue working after becoming a mother.

Though it gave her a sense of satisfaction, Gayatri did not expect joy or demand fulfilment from her job. She was hard working, her bosses admired her diligence and she had moved up the corporate ladder by displaying unquestionable integrity and prudent decision making. In Fremont she had worked out of necessity, to pay the mortgage on their house and maintain a decent standard of living. She had derived a certain pride from her job and a sense of having found her place in the world but it was only a part of her identity, interwoven with the other roles she played. Now in India, as CFO of Goodricke Dickinson, she saw her work as escape from boredom and insurance for the future.

Varun and Gayatri claimed to welcome the weekend and complained about the working week ahead but they knew that Monday mornings were the markers that tracked and measured their lives.

4

VARUN RETURNS HOME early from work with a headache. He has scheduled a call with a client in California at 10:30 p.m. IST and would like to rest before that. As he waits in the lobby of Tower 2, the elevator door opens and spills out an old lady in a stiff white sari and a young woman who clutches in her hands the chubby wrists of two identical little girls dressed in identical pink satin frocks, each holding a gift wrapped in shiny silver paper. The little girls are talking at the same time.

'Mamma, I want to eat chocolate cake.'

'Mamma, mujhe noodles chahiye.'

'Noodles are yucky. Like worms.'

'No, they are not.'

'Badey pyare bachchen hain. So sweet,' remarks the old lady, pausing to pinch one of the little girl's cheeks. The girl glowers at her but the mother smiles politely. The old lady is in the mood to carry on the conversation. She starts by asking the names of the little girls.

As the mother struggles with the questions, her daughters' demands, the gifts, her handbag and the mobile phone which has just beeped a message, she looks at Varun Sarin for a moment. Her mouth moves in a half-smile. Her eyes are the colour of new honey. This is his girl, he realizes with a start, the girl he has watched every morning for three weeks. It is a moment he will relive for the rest of his life, the moment when he realizes that he will no longer be content to view her from a distance.

The ladies move on. Varun has missed the elevator and is alone again in the lobby, free to rewind the past few minutes. He is not surprised that he did not recognize her immediately. It's a little like meeting one's dentist in a movie theatre or seeing the security guard of the building out of his uniform, crossing the road.

Varun is distracted for the rest of the evening. He tries to recall the details of her appearance. She was dressed in dark blue jeans, a snug white top and white open-toed sandals. A faint memory of her perfume remains. The rest of her is a blur. He knows now that she is not a nineteen-year-old college girl, she is a married woman, a mother of two little girls. But for now, he sets that aside.

He wishes he had more details to linger over, vivid details that would sink her image more firmly into the recesses of his mind from where he can dredge it up at will. His headache has intensified and he feels the familiar knot in his chest. He tries to sleep but cannot. The maid has retired to her room, Anirudh is out at soccer practice and Gayatri has not returned from work. The solitude is a blessing. He flips open a can of beer and puts on some music. Ella Fitzgerald croons 'You go to my head' and he smiles at the delicious aptness of the song. As he opens his laptop and prepares to reply to emails, he decides that he will get to know the girl better. A gentle move along the continuum from strangers to acquaintances who know each other's name and greet each other, and carry on conversations like 'Hey, how are you doing?', 'Fine, and you?', 'Oh, great!' when they meet in elevator lobbies. He does not know when he will begin and how and where it will end but the knowledge that he is ready to move things along quickens his heart.

He chugs through 201 unread messages and cleans up his mailbox with startling efficiency. Anirudh, returning home, finds his father in a cheerful mood. They talk about soccer, which Anirudh enjoys; cricket, which despite several months in a cricket-crazy nation he does not understand; and school work, which he does not care to discuss in detail. They never talk about girls, never reminisce about the days in Fremont and now, after more than a year, Anirudh no longer asks, 'When will we go back?' Varun hopes that the soccer practice, the acquisition of a good friend – Ved is his classmate at school and shares his passion for soccer – weekend excursions to the malls with his gang and moderately good grades at Hillview

International School are signs that his son has made peace with life in Gurgaon. As he watches Anirudh saunter away to his room, tracking mud across the marble floors, he feels a rush of concern, a desire to protect his child from all harm, which mingles with the realization that he has no clue about what goes on in the mind of a sixteen-year-old boy.

Gayatri, returning home at 7:30 p.m., is surprised to see her husband and son sitting in companionable silence in front of the television. They greet her absently before returning to the soccer match that claims their attention. Afterwards, Varun suggests an early dinner. In Fremont, they had dinner together every night at 8 p.m., with clearly allocated duties for each of them. Gayatri would get the food ready, Anirudh would lay the table and Varun was in charge of clearing up. Gayatri was particular about the time and their duties and any deviations were met with an annoyed comment. 'Why don't you come on time? Do you think this is a hotel?' Here, she sometimes feels like she lives in a hotel. The family eats whatever they want, whenever it suits them. Gayatri prefers a light meal at a quarter to eight. She has been on some diet or the other for the past two years and is firm about leaving a gap of at least two hours between dinner and bedtime. Varun, arriving home between 8 and 10 p.m., is served rotis and vegetables by the maid, who believes that the master of the house needs to be provided with hot nourishing food. He has often told Jhumpa to retire for the night and leave his food in the casserole but she prefers to wait up. Anirudh places his order with Jhumpa when he returns from school and eats when he feels hungry. This is one luxury that he greatly enjoys though sometimes, he tells Gayatri, he misses the conversation and convivial atmosphere of their family dinners at Fremont.

'How was school today, Rudy? Did you submit that history project?' Gayatri asks as she places a roti on his plate.

'Yes, Mom.'

'What happened to the soccer team selection? Wasn't that supposed to happen this week?'

'The coach told me I am in, though they haven't put up a list yet.'

'That's great, Rudy. I'm proud of you.'

'Thanks, Dad.'

'How come you're home so early?' Gayatri asks Varun.

'I have a call at ten thirty.'

'Oh, don't you take your calls in office usually?'

'Yes, but I had a headache, so I thought I'd rest for a bit.'

'Better now?'

'Yeah, fine. How was your day?'

'Fine.'

'Will you call the plumber? The tap in our bathroom seems to be leaking.'

'I'll do it tomorrow. If you are leaving later, you can call him. The office number is 2903. And you need to write a cheque for the building maintenance. It's due this month.'

'Okay, I'll drop it off at their office tomorrow.'

'Rudy, have some more daal and vegetables. I don't know what junk you eat every day. How is the lunch at school these days?'

'Okay.'

The words bounce harmlessly off the walls. Beneath them lurks a subterranean world of things unasked and unsaid. Gayatri feels that underworld call to her, its voice rich, dark and mossy. 'We are trapped here. Come, lift us and throw us into the world,' the rocks seem to say. Gayatri is wary of the voice; she shrugs it off with an imperceptible shake of the head. She knows that heeding it could set off a tremor in the fragile structure of their lives, which has taken so many years to build. She is not ready to see it tremble and topple over.

Varun seems to be listening to his family but he is thinking about the right time to take the elevator, a time when he might accidentally meet his neighbour. He will have to be on the lookout, prepared at any moment to be unnerved by her shining beauty. The simple act of stepping out of the house has suddenly become fraught with adventure.

5

AFTER THAT DAY, the morning sightings both calm and disturb Varun. Each passing day reminds him of wasted opportunities and stirs a new urgency. He thinks of ways to engineer other chance encounters and dismisses all of them as imprudent or impractical. He does not want to make radical changes to his routine. Nor can he think of abandoning his mission. In the middle of a work-filled day, the idea that he has something to look forward to causes the blood to rush to his head.

After marriage, Varun has been friendly with several women – Gayatri's friends, his co-workers, wives of his colleagues – but the interactions have always been courteous, cautious, never crossing boundaries. He had on a few, very few occasions, considered the promise some of them had held out to him. Five years ago, he remembered, he had been to Vegas for a conference with a group of coworkers. In the bar at the Bellagio, one of his colleagues, a tanned blonde Californian beauty, wide-eyed and aroused after several glasses of wine, had smiled up at him and asked, 'Do you want to come up for some time?' He had noted her generously proffered breasts, the little black dress sliding across her thighs, the unconcealed invitation in her eyes, and had gently refused. Vera did not recall, or pretended not to recall, the incident when they met in the conference hall of the hotel the next day. They treated each other with courtesy but he noticed a certain coldness in her that had not been there before.

Varun had been to strip clubs and peep shows with other men, men who slapped the bottoms of gyrating dancers and took pleasure in the display of female flesh. Although he had joked with the others and laughed at their innuendos, the women had left him largely unmoved. Sometimes while crossing the road, at a crowded restaurant, at an airport lounge, he had noticed interesting women. Women who were not just physically attractive but who carried about them an air of mystery, a hint that they had stories to tell, a possibility that they could be good company on a rainy day. He allowed them to pass him by with little regret.

The last time he had felt a spark of passion had been almost three years ago. Gayatri, Anirudh and he were on the BART, taking a last train ride to San Francisco, a city they all loved and knew they would miss. He had noticed a woman sitting a few feet from where he stood. The luxuriant black hair, the smooth olive skin, the slightly arrogant curve of her splashy red mouth were probably vestiges of old Spanish aristocratic blood. She wore a red summer dress and was talking on the phone with a fondness usually reserved for a child or a lover. When she finished talking, she looked up at him, and he felt a sudden frisson of excitement. But then the train pulled to a stop and his family gathered around him as they moved to the exit. He never saw the woman again.

In the early days of marriage, Varun enjoyed making love with his wife. There was a feeling of mutual discovery, a sense of novelty, for Gayatri had been inexperienced and eager to learn. Later, after the birth of Anirudh, which was unplanned but welcome, the levels of excitement waned and he reconciled himself to the monochromatic pattern of marital sex, which was more a reaffirmation of their relationship than an act of passion. Sometimes he wonders what it would be like to make love to another woman just for pleasure, but he has never taken any steps to translate the thought into reality. Monogamy, as far as he is concerned, is not so much a natural state as a necessary condition for the sustenance of his family. Though he often feels that absolute truth is overrated, he is essentially an honest man who takes measured risks; adultery, with its attendant deceit and the possible dismantling of the carefully cultivated structure of his life, does not seem worth it.

As Varun Sarin stands waiting for the elevator to take him home, ten days after he first saw the girl in his building, he thinks of the various women he has seen and met and asks himself why this particular girl has claimed his attention. When she silently joins him in the wait, he is unprepared. It is almost 8 p.m., he wasn't expecting her to be there. He experiences a sudden light-headedness, a constriction in his throat, but he schools his face to a polite smile. She smiles back.

'The elevator seems to be taking a long time,' he ventures.

'Yes. There seems to be some problem. The lifts haven't been working properly for the last two days.'

Her voice is sweet and low, the words uttered in slightly accented convent-school English, her teeth small, white and a little uneven.

'Have you moved here recently?' Varun asks.

'About two months ago. We were in Delhi before. This is our own house.'

'I live on the seventh floor.'

'We are on the seventeenth, 217 D.'

'I am Varun Sarin.'

'I am Sweety.'

Sweety! A part of him baulks at the name. He waits for an explanation, for surely she has another name, probably a long one, not this childish nickname, a banal endearment with which gangsters beckon hard-faced ladies of the night. In the next instant he feels that the name becomes her. He likes the unapologetic way she announced it, without a trace of embarrassment. Sweety.

They are joined by other people. When the elevator door opens, they step in without looking at each other. He steps out on the seventh floor. Despite the presence of a delivery boy from Pizza Hut and a Japanese executive of uncertain age, it is as if they have shared the intimacy of a small closed space. He does not want to part from her.

The meeting is a precious gift which he unwraps at leisure. He recalls how she looked: the sheen of her hair in the dull light, the soft roundedness of her shoulders, the glinting honey of her eyes, which for a few moments held his reflection. He sifts through their brief conversation, hoping to glean some tiny speck of gold, something that he can keep for himself. He remembers the way she offered her address, 217 D, and feels oddly elated that there are only ten floors of steel and concrete between them.

And that sweet lozenge of a name that he swirls around in his mouth. How the simple offering of a name changes

us. It pulls off a layer, humanizes the anonymous. It is a
token of trust, an invitation to move closer. A stranger's
blurry face moves into sharp focus, doors to another world
slowly open, memories can be created. In those few seconds
when they exchanged names, he felt a desire for connection,
a slight signal, maybe an answering echo to his silent call.
Maybe.

Sweet, sweet Sweety.

6

AFTER FINISHING HER morning walk and sending her
daughters to school, Sweety Singh watered the potted plants
in her seventeenth-floor balcony. She was humming a
popular Hindi film song of the season. The May sun, even
at 9:30 in the morning, was cruel and some of her plants
were wilting. Sweety couldn't distinguish between the shade
lovers and the hardy foliage that would withstand the
summer heat. She had bought the plants for their aesthetic
appeal: a small champa tree with waxy pink flowers, a ficus,
a clump of ixora, some crotons, and two mottled orange
terracotta frogs spilling bunches of fern from their gaping
mouths. She was thinking of getting a pair of garden chairs
and a table for the small alcove that had been created by
extending the balcony. She imagined herself reclining on a

chair, opening her face to the mellow winter sunshine and reaching for a cup of hot tea while nibbling a biscuit.

She had been busy settling down but even after two months, there was a lot to be done in the house. Curtains: their colour, texture, drape and sheen; designs for sofa upholstery; the relative merits of an Aqua Guard versus an RO system for clean drinking water; the dimensions of a side table; the best way to arrange a set of four charcoal sketches on the textured wall of the dining room; sizes of bathroom mats and towels – these things had consumed her. They seemed like small steps towards securing for herself a place to call her own.

Sweety had moved straight from her parents' modest two-bedroom house in Janakpuri to the three-storeyed bungalow in Green Park where her husband Amandeep stayed with his parents, two brothers and their families. It was a joint family that seethed with minor grievances, petty jealousies, zealously guarded territories, unspoken grudges and contradicting loyalties. All these were kept in check by the formidable force of blood ties, the burden of mutual dependence and the bond of shared secrets. To the world the family presented a united front; they indulged in displays of affection and concern, sometimes genuine, sometimes necessitated by circumstance. In those first few days of marriage, Sweety had been beguiled into believing that this was indeed a model family straight out of the movies.

After five months, she had wanted to move out. There was nothing obvious that she could point to, no overt animosity that she experienced, no incidents of humiliation or exploitation. She lived instead with a constant feeling of being smothered with a soft satin pillow. There were plenty of servants, her mother-in-law and sisters-in-law took care of the meals and chores; the house already had a rhythm of its own to which she contributed very little. She was expected to fall in line, be thankful for her good fortune and graciously accept any small favours that came her way.

Amandeep's elder brothers were in charge of the family business which included interests in real estate and construction, a factory that made spares for automobiles, and an auto accessories shop in Green Park market. When Amandeep wanted to start something on his own, he had been allowed to set up an export-import business. This meant travelling around the country to source material, and across the world to scout for buyers and attend trade shows. He was rarely at home and Sweety felt abandoned every time he went away, sometimes for weeks. She would retreat into their bedroom and weep every night, feeling alone in a house with twelve people.

When the twins were born, twenty months after their wedding, she welcomed them. Despite the chaos and disorderliness they brought into her life, motherhood gave her a sense of purpose, a timetable by which to live her daily life. In the beginning, she had felt that having many people in the house would give her some respite, that her sisters-in-law and mother-in-law would be happy to take over the care of the babies for a while, but she found that their interest was short-lived, their contribution limited to unsolicited advice and enquiries. It took four years of constant cajoling, artful persuasion and careful plotting to get Amandeep to voice the subject of separation and take the final step of cleaving away from the joint family. Amandeep was not averse to the move, he wanted to get away from the shadow of his father and brothers, stop being the baby of the family and take his place as the man of the house, but he could not summon up the nerve to proactively commit an act of disloyalty to his family. When he was offered a stake in a garment export factory in Gurgaon, it gave them a legitimate reason to move. But it was Sweety's persistence that caused him to make the final declaration.

His parents had given the money for the deposit for the house – Amandeep's rightful share, Sweety had insisted, not a favour they were doing them. They had taken a loan for the balance amount. Sweety believed that her sisters-in-law envied her, her mother-in-law resented her and her father-in-law lived with the fear that their departure would trigger a similar move for separation by the other brothers.

When she first saw Trafalgar Towers, the pale peach towers topped by narrow green spires, the tapering archways in the New Gurgaon Gothic style, the manicured lawns, the red-yellow-green seesaws and slides in the miniature playground, she felt a sense of homecoming. The towers beckoned to her and spoke to her of a new life. The apartment complex had a sparsely equipped gym, an oblong turquoise swimming pool, a grocery shop called All Needs and a tennis court. It was self-contained and gave its residents automatic admission into a community. To Sweety, the apartment block looked like a palace; in one of its 3200 sq. ft flats was her throne. She couldn't wait to take her place there.

Not that she was not fond of her in-laws, she explained to her friends, they had been so helpful with Sanya-Manya – the twins always spoken of as a single hyphenated unit – but it was really nice to have some privacy. The girls were growing up and they needed space. Mummyji had been so concerned that she would be on her own, with Amandeep away so often and for such long periods, but she had assured them that the security in these condominium complexes was excellent. They had guards everywhere and no one could get in without a detailed scrutiny at the main gate. They even had surveillance cameras in the main areas. Also, they were barely a thirty-minute drive away and they would be seeing each other every week. *I am sure I will miss you so much that I will come over every day*, Sweety had told her mother-in-law on the day she shifted to Trafalgar Towers. It was over two weeks since they had met but she was scrupulous about talking to them on the phone every other day.

As she watered the plants, Sweety thought of what the day had in store for her. Sanya-Manya were safely in school for the next five hours. Amandeep was away on work. Sweety had her list ready, of things to do for the day. She

looked forward to driving her little red Alto. She would
stop at Spencer's for groceries, then move on to the malls
on M.G. Road to look for bed linen. She had to pick up a
new water bottle for Sanya and then maybe go on to
Ghitorni to scout for a pair of cane chairs that might sit in
the balcony. She had become adept at driving. The potholed
roads didn't bother her and she had been lucky when it
came to parking spaces. She already knew three other
mothers of young girls in their building, there were
invitations to birthday parties for the children and plans
for lunches and movies with a kitty group. She wore what
she wanted without eliciting any comment, did not have to
report where she was going, whom she would meet and
when she would be back. She planned her own meals; some
nights, she ate only Maggi noodles for dinner. She could
talk to her parents on the phone without being overheard
and did not have to retire to the bedroom to complain to
her husband. She loved the newness of Gurgaon, the tall
shiny buildings, the comforting anonymity of the air-
conditioned malls, the frequent sales with tantalizing
bargains, the proximity to all necessities, the fact that she
was close to Delhi and yet away from it. Gurgaon was a
place where she could breathe. When others complained
about dust and pollution, she was surprised. The air was
alive with possibilities, the days filled with small luxuries,
and Sweety savoured each one eagerly.

7

THE WEATHER AS a topic of conversation might be the refuge of the unimaginative but between the months of April and June in the National Capital Region, it is the glue that binds people together in a web of shared misery. People discuss the heat with passion. Every year, they remark with the same degree of amazement about how the water in the taps is boiling hot even without the geyser being switched on. They exchange remedies for heatstroke and strategies to prevent dehydration. If someone mentions that they could make rotis on the walls of their house, they radiate so much heat, another complains that walking across the floor is like stepping on hot coals. In the high-rises of Gurgaon, power bills spiral as air-conditioners are switched on through the day and in homes without 100 per cent power backup, the residents pray for the long life of their inverter batteries. They cannot even imagine how people in the slums survive without fans and running water. Milk curdles on its own, fruits ripen with alarming haste, children wither.

Many of the residents have left Trafalgar Towers for cooler places. Most schools have closed for the summer holidays and the playground is deserted. The expatriates have chosen to take home-leave and the residents who remain prefer to stay indoors for most part of the day. It is too hot to go out for a walk even as early as 7 a.m. And Sweety for one cannot leave earlier since Najma, her maid, arrives only at five minutes to seven.

Varun Sarin, unaware of these domestic constraints, is disturbed and worried because he has not seen Sweety for over a week. The Sarins have no plans for the summer since Hillview International will not close for the summer break till late June. Each morning, as he braves the emerging sun in his balcony, Varun wonders about Sweety's absence. Has some feminine instinct warned her about his distant obsessive gaze? He feels like going up to the seventeenth floor and knocking on her door just to reassure himself. He is grouchy, easily irritated, inattentive to the people around him. He finds little joy at home or at work. He blames the heat, he admits to work-induced stress.

He finally sees her again as he waits for Jagdish to bring the car to the porch of Tower 2. He leaves for work at different times these days since he has established that he will never bump into her if he leaves at the usual time with Gayatri. That is one of the perks of being the CEO; he does not have to report in at a particular time though he is conscious of the need to lead by example. His people know that he is always at work, even if physically absent. He sees Sweety disembark from a car, almost in front of him. He feels relief at first, followed by delight, then an all-pervasive sense of well-being.

'Hello,' he offers quickly before she can disappear into the building.

Sweety considers him for a moment, slots him into the space marked 'neighbour' and smiles at him.

'Hello! How are you?'

'I'm good. But the heat seems to be getting worse.'

'I know. This year is quite bad. Last summer was cooler, I think.'

'Yeah! This must be what they call global warming. I am still getting used to it.'

'Oh, where were you before?'

'In the US. California.'

'Oh! That must have been different.'

'Quite different. But it's good to be back. Except for the summer. Are you planning to go away for the season? Most people seem to have left Trafalgar Towers.'

'No. We will be here only. My husband is away on work and I have lots of things to do in the house. I have left my children with my in-laws in Delhi for the day. The painter and carpenter are coming to do some work in the house, so I have to be here.'

'Oh. Busy day . . .'

'Mmmm . . .'

'Ah! My car seems to be here. See you then . . . Sweety, right?'

'Right . . . er . . . er?'

'Varun.'

'Haan. Varun. Bye.'

Varun Sarin is a contented man. He experiences a sense of accomplishment, as though he has made definite progress along the continuum. On his way to work, he sifts through the bits of information he has gathered and analyses their implications. The husband is absent most of the time; she is going to be in the building for the summer; she knows his name; she is alone in the house for the present. He wonders what will happen, what could happen, if he went up to the seventeenth floor and rang her doorbell. He could offer to put up nails, paint her walls. He has an image of her in a pair of dark overalls, holding out a cup of coffee to him, wiping a blue smudge off his face as he puts down the roller and turns to her. How absurd his thoughts are. He should be thinking about the interview he has scheduled this morning with a candidate for the position of operations manager. He needs to talk to Ravi, the head of human resources, about the compensation package they should offer. Then there is the mail he needs to send out to all employees with the quarterly update. So many things to be done, and it doesn't help that Varsha is getting a little disorganized these days. He might need a new personal assistant. Someone like Sweety. The mere thought of having her at his workplace, on call, a gently hovering presence outside his cabin, is alluring. Varun Sarin reaches his office and plunges into his work with renewed vigour and a greater sense of purpose than he has felt in a long time.

8

IT SEEMS TO Varun that his life is running on two parallel tracks: one that comprises his domestic life, work and all other relationships, and combines the illusion of frenetic action with the lack of any real movement; the other, on which the story of him and Sweety moves along slowly but with a sure sense of progress, even though the destination is nebulous. They have met a couple of times more in the elevator lobby and exchanged the basic details of each other's lives. He sees her walking on certain days when the sun is less harsh, but only for a few minutes.

One evening, as Varun returns home from work, he notices a scatter of people in front of Tower 2. An ambulance with an ominous unblinking red light, a couple of hospital orderlies and the dull, drawn faces of the people around indicate unpleasant news. He feels a rush of foreboding but his initial apprehension that something has happened to his son is assuaged when the security guard informs him that the old man who lived on the sixteenth floor has died. He was in a coma for several days and passed away that afternoon. They were waiting for the body to be taken for cremation.

The proximity of death, even that of a stranger's, unsettles

Varun. He has never seen a dead body and has never had to deal with the urgent aftermath of a death. He thinks of his father and wonders if there was a knot of people like this at their home in Chandigarh. The air in the building smells of rotten flowers, sickness and camphor. He struggles to breathe, his head feels ready to explode. Sweety, entering the lobby at that moment, becomes aware of the situation, of Varun's distress, and the difficulty of reaching the elevator through the crowd of mourners.

As if by mutual consent, they step out of Tower 2 and retreat to the park.

'Did you know him?' Sweety asks.

'No, not at all. Did you?'

'No. I think he lived just below our flat. I heard from my neighbour. They are Bengalis, I think. An old couple staying by themselves.'

'I heard that he was in a coma for some time.'

'Haan. He was very old. Eighty-seven or eighty-eight.'

'My father died very suddenly. He was only sixty-seven.' Varun does not know why he says this. He never speaks of his father's death to anyone. He does not even allow himself to think of it too often.

Sweety's face looms before him, soft, suffused with concern.

'I am sorry. How?'

'I was in Hawaii attending an offsite. He had an aneurysm that caused a massive haemorrhage. He was watching TV. It was all over in a few minutes.'

'Oh God! So sad.'

'When he was dying, I was playing beach volleyball. They couldn't reach me on time. They couldn't keep a dead body for two or three days. I wasn't in time for the funeral.'

Varun's tone is flat, his face deadpan; he could have been reading out a medical report. But Sweety can hear the bitterness in his voice, see the regret in his drooping shoulders, and something stirs in her and calls forth her own memories of death and pain. In the faint light of a sinking sun, on a stone bench half hidden by a spreading champa tree, they are in a different world, and in this world she can reach out and touch the hand of her neighbour. Her touch is healing. Varun feels something leave his body and a giddy ascension of lightness to his head.

'Is that why you came back to India?' Sweety has removed her hand but he can still feel the light, warm pressure of her fingers. Her question disturbs him. He has not consciously connected the death of his father to his return but it has hovered all along as a reason he is not willing to accept.

'I . . . I don't know . . .' Varun shrugs, suddenly realizing that his relocation is in reality an atonement. It was the exigency of guilt rather than professional compulsions that propelled him towards his home country. No one had accused him of negligence, relatives had murmured sympathetically that it was the will of God and there was nothing he could have done but Varun had felt the weight of the silent accusation in his mother's stricken look and his sister's reproachful eyes. He had let them down, he had not performed his duty as the only son of aging parents.

'It's all right. Don't blame yourself.' Her words are an absolution and for the first time since his return to India, Varun feels a little of the burden lift from him. He is moved by her kindness, pleasantly surprised that she is more perspicacious than she looks, and a little alarmed at how quickly he has bared a hidden part of himself to a stranger.

Sweety is unaware of her part in this moment of epiphany but is touched by his display of vulnerability. It has awakened a sense of responsibility in her, the kind one might feel for a person one has rescued from certain death, an interest in their continued well-being. She wants to let him know that he is not the only one who can be transformed by the death of another. She tells him about her friend Neha, who was run over by a Blueline bus on a busy Delhi road as she was returning from the market where she had gone to buy the week's stock of vegetables. Neha had been her classmate in school and they were married within three months of each other. After marriage, they had been consumed by the demands of their new households and, once the children came along, submerged in motherhood. They had kept in touch through sporadic phone calls and had planned to meet at some unspecified future time. Neha had left behind a husband and a two-year-old boy. Sweety had mourned her friend but in the absence of any tangible impact on her own life, had relegated her to a corner of her memory.

'A year after Neha's death, I saw her husband at a function. He had married again. Her son was calling his new mother

"Mummy", the husband was fussing over his new wife. It was as if Neha never existed.'

Varun has temporarily forgotten his own anguish. Sweety's story and her telling of it have drawn him into her world and he is fascinated by her eyes flashing indignation, the flutter of her pale hands and the tremulous lilt in her voice.

'Life goes on, I guess,' he offers.

'I know. But then I started thinking, what if something happened to me? Would my family forget me so quickly and just move on? I was so worried about keeping my in-laws and husband happy, taking care of my children and doing what everybody wanted.'

'So, what did you do?'

'I wanted to live my life the way I had dreamt it. You know, live more for myself. So I insisted that we move out of the joint family and get our own place.'

'That couldn't have been easy.'

'It wasn't. I had been thinking about it for a while and my husband and I had been discussing it, but it was only after I saw Neha's family that day that I told him, "Either we move out or I move out with the children." He couldn't understand why it was so important to me but in the end he managed to convince his parents.'

'Are you happy now?'

'Yes. You know, it was always a dream to have my own house and do it up my way, to be more independent.'

Varun Sarin looks at her hopeful face lit by her small

dream of happiness. It's as though they have been through a tunnel together and have just stepped out into the sunshine.

Later that night, as he lies in bed unable to sleep, he can still feel the touch of Sweety's fingers searing his skin. The memory of her open, smiling face warms him. He realizes how fragile and transient this happiness of hers is and fears that he is going to play a part in changing the simple design of her life.

9

MRS SARIN WAS visiting her son. She arrived by the convenient Shatabdi express from Ludhiana and was met at the station by Varun. This particular visit had come about due to the engagement ceremony of the daughter of a relative of the Sarins who lived in Maharani Bagh in Delhi. Mrs Sarin had brought with her an assortment of delicacies made with her own hands – homemade mango pickles, a vegetable dish made of bitter gourd that she had prepared in the morning and pinni made with pure ghee – tangible proof of her culinary abilities and fondness for her family. These were duly displayed to Varun and Gayatri, who made appropriate sounds of appreciation.

The moment Mrs Sarin stepped into her house, Gayatri

knew that she would spot a stray cobweb in a corner of the ceiling, a tea-cup stain on the table, slivers of dust on picture frames, an unwashed spot behind the water closet. Her kitchen would be found to be inadequately stocked, her meals lacking in wholesomeness and the growing boys, Varun and Anirudh Sarin, would appear to be neglected and undernourished. After recovering from the initial shock of her husband's death, Mrs Sarin seemed to have acquired a new personality. Her natural forceful self had been kept in check by the brigadier's turbulent nature but after his passing, she had come into her own, marshalling her domestic troops, commanding her kitty party group, admonishing errant vendors for quoting exorbitant prices and drilling anything that was askew or inappropriate into its rightful place.

After the apartment had submitted to her scrutiny, Mrs Sarin enquired about lunch.

'We can make whatever you want,' offered Gayatri.

'I will have whatever you have made. Your maid still does not know how to make kaali dal properly. We can have the karela that I've brought with me. Maybe for the night you can make something simple, just some daal, paneer and aalu gobi.'

She bustled past Gayatri to the guest bedroom with the air of one who felt very much at home.

Over the last seventeen years, Gayatri and Mrs Sarin had arrived at an uneasy coexistence, without any overt animosity but also without much affection. Though she no longer craved her mother-in-law's approval, during each of Mrs Sarin's visits Gayatri felt appraised and found wanting. That she was the chief financial officer of a Fortune 500 company and earned as much as her husband had no value in Mrs Sarin's eyes. Though Mrs Sarin had got over the stupidity of her son rejecting Pooja Malhotra, daughter of Major General Malhotra, long-time family friend and hence worthy of being father-in-law, for a dark-complexioned Madrasi, she was yet to come to terms with the fact that Gayatri could not effortlessly churn out soft round rotis for a family meal. Gayatri, in the first flush of marriage, had tried to please Mrs Sarin by learning to make kaali daal, paalak paneer and gaajar halwa, Varun's favourite dishes, but she could never master the art of rolling out a chapatti while simultaneously tossing another over the flame. In Gurgaon, she rarely entered the kitchen, leaving all the cooking to Jhumpa, who despite a tendency to use too much oil and spoonfuls of garam masala, turned out meals that were acceptable to the family.

As they sat down together for lunch, Mrs Sarin related snippets of family news. She admired her daughter Shweta's ability to maintain a spotless household, her son-in-law's generosity in allowing her a car and driver whenever she required them and lovingly described the scholarly accomplishments of her grandchildren Karishma and Karan. She remarked repeatedly on how lucky she was to be able to live just two streets away from Shweta in a comfortable city like Ludhiana. She then enquired after Anirudh. Mrs Sarin doted on Anirudh as her first grandchild and bearer of the illustrious family name, though the credit for his existence went entirely to Varun.

'Anirudh is at a soccer match in school,' Varun informed her.

'And you? Sab theek toh hai, beta?'

'Yes.'

Usually relaxed and amiable when his mother visited, Varun now felt the need to be on guard. His mother had the knack of knowing when he was up to something. Even though he was almost forty-five, there were times when he felt that to her he was still a little boy incapable of deciphering the world around him on his own. She felt that she owed it to him to interpret the actions and intentions of other people, usually in distinct shades of black and white.

Varun had not seen Sweety since they met in the park. He was unsure of how to initiate any further contact. He knew that he could not make any moves under the watchful gaze of his mother. Under different circumstances, he felt that she might have approved of Sweety. He wished he could tell her something, receive some advice, but he knew that despite her lack of attachment towards Gayatri, she believed strongly in the sacred institution of marriage.

Mrs Sarin had begun to describe her health issues. A niggling pain in the lower back, a sudden bout of giddiness, probably stones in the gall bladder. Gayatri forced a look of polite concern but she was seething inside. The contrast between the bustling Mrs Sarin and the frail, faded form of her own mother was stark, almost painful. Her mother suffered from rheumatic arthritis, a crippling pain in the joints, and was often exhausted due to low blood pressure. Every visit from Mrs Sarin was a reminder that she needed to meet her own parents more often. Gayatri began planning a trip to Bangalore and made only terse contributions to the conversation. Varun was distracted through the discussion and finally suggested that a long nap in the afternoon would help his mother.

The six days of the visit seemed to pass slowly. Though he urged his mother to stay longer, Varun and Gayatri were both relieved when Mrs Sarin left for Ludhiana.

10

ON A SUNNY Saturday morning in June, two monkeys enter the heavily guarded gated community of Trafalgar Towers. They leap over the balcony grills and invade the kitchens of two apartments in Tower 4. They are seen opening refrigerators, smashing eggs, shredding bread, stuffing their faces with aalu parathas extracted from a casserole. One of them scampers away with a young maid's dupatta, another steals a mobile phone. As the news spreads, several people secure their homes and make their way down to the lawns to bear witness to the simian outrage.

Glancing out from his window, Varun Sarin sees Sweety standing on the lawn with her daughters. The girls are jumping up and down, pointing upwards. Varun calls his son and they head down to the park. After a year in Gurgaon, Anirudh is now comfortable with the sudden appearance of a herd of lugubrious cattle in the middle of a busy road; he is used to seeing stray dogs in marketplaces, and the sight of an obese sow lingering at a roadside garbage dump with a litter of piglets no longer elicits remarks of surprise. This is the first time he will be seeing monkeys though.

'This is why India is so amazing,' Varun says to Anirudh. 'You just never know what's going to happen next.'

'Yeah, I can't imagine what we would have done if monkeys were spotted on Riverside Drive.'

'The cable TV networks would have been out in full force.'

A motley crowd has gathered in the park in front of the building. Some people are shouting directions to two security guards who are ineffectually trying to shoo away the monkeys with long-tailed mops. Varun sees a flash of pale brown fur. A monkey has just jumped from a balcony in Tower 4 to one in Tower 3. They are rhesus monkeys, common in this part of the world but exotic specimen to Anirudh, who has seen monkeys only in zoos.

'Arrey, why are you chasing them? They are avatars of Hanumanji. They will go away on their own. Let them be,' an old lady admonishes the guards.

'Auntyji, they are dangerous. One of them bit a child in Hamilton Court,' a woman in a blue salwar kameez retorts, holding on firmly to the hand of a small boy.

Anirudh has found a boy he knows and they are chuckling together. Varun makes his way towards Sweety.

'Hello. It's quite a picnic here.'

'Oh, hi! Yes. Like a mela.'

The monkeys savage a potted plant on another balcony. An unseen hand flings a banana towards them and one of the creatures lopes downward towards the fruit.

The children emit happy squeals. They are dressed in denim shorts and matching pink tops, their long brown hair, exactly the same shade as their mother's, arranged in two braids topped with pink plastic butterflies. The adults smile at each other.

'How are you?'

'Fine. Busy with the house and, you know, the children are at home. So I have my hands full.'

'Right. Amazing how you handle two at a time.'

'It's all right most of the time. The good thing is they play with each other, so I don't have to worry about keeping them occupied. How have you been?'

'Good. The usual work. Keeping me on my toes.'

Varun senses something different about Sweety today. There is a certain familiarity in her manner, her face is unguarded, and the angle of her body seems to suggest that his presence is not unwelcome. Between the commonplace clichés they offer each other, there seems to run another conversation pulsating with words they really want to say.

They talk about the weather, the delayed monsoon, the deforestation in Gurgaon that has caused the inevitable clash between man and nature, the quantity and quality of urban construction, and their plans for the weekend.

The monkeys have disappeared from view. It is possible that they have jumped to the adjoining building, Exotica Deluxe, and therefore beyond the jurisdiction of the guards at Trafalgar Towers. The children have already lost interest in the animals and are claimed by new urgencies. Varun knows that his encounter with Sweety will soon come to an end.

'I hope the monkeys don't cause any damage. I heard that a child was attacked.'

'I think we will be quite safe if we lock our windows. I don't think they are harmful.'

'Look, why don't I give you my number? In case of any emergency, please don't hesitate to call. We are just a few floors away.'

'Oh . . . okay. You can give me a missed call and I'll save your number.'

The exchange of mobile numbers successfully managed, Varun feels jubilant, it's almost like the adrenalin rush he gets from closing a new deal with a customer. He is encouraged by her offer of her own number. In this modern courtship ritual he sees the opening out of new possibilities.

Anirudh, accompanying his father back to their house, notices his good humour and smiling face and figures that his father at least is happy here. He wishes his mother had been home to see the monkey. It might have cheered her up.

His mother, at that moment, is in another part of Gurgaon, enjoying a massage at the Orchid Blossom Salon and Spa. The spa lays claim to an authentic Thai massage experience. The masseurs are young girls from Arunachal Pradesh and Mizoram who dress in batik sarongs to achieve a more oriental look. Gayatri loves the fragrance of patchouli and herbal oils, the silken voices of the girls, the touch of their soft hands on her skin as they stretch and smooth her tired muscles. She feels all the worries and weariness of her daily life fall away from her like old skin. This is the one luxury she truly enjoys in Gurgaon. For a few hours she can pretend that she is far away, in a benevolent world where her body is tended to with compassion.

Over the past two years, Gayatri has become more conscious about her looks, constantly confronted as she is with women who are perpetually well groomed and well maintained. She sees gaggles of young women at the school bus stop in the morning, wearing lip gloss and crisp clothes as though they are setting out for the day. The malls seem to be full of women with glossy veneers and svelte figures who move like fashion models. The women of her class here have more time on their hands, she thinks, and self-indulgence is less expensive and more accessible.

She knows that if she can't salvage her body at the age of forty-two, she won't be able to do so later. A part of her finds this new obsession with the exterior self repugnant; it is unlike her, it is an insult to her intelligence, but she can't help herself. She is drawn to advertisements for slimming clinics and signboards for beauty salons, and obsessively reads articles which dole out easy weight-loss tips. She is not unattractive but there are days when Gayatri feels fat and ugly. Occasionally, she contemplates cosmetic surgery. She doesn't share these feelings with anyone. Instead, she embarks on a regimen of self-care. She experiments with various diets, goes for yoga classes at 6 a.m. every Tuesday and Thursday, does ten laps of the Trafalgar Towers pool on all the other days in summer, follows a meticulous cleansing-toning-moisturizing regimen and makes regular visits to the beauty salons; maintenance work, she calls it.

Gayatri believes that her husband no longer looks at her with desire. She doesn't expect him to either. She isn't doing all this to rekindle a lost romance, nor does she desire the attention of other men. What Gayatri really wishes for is to have other women gaze at her with admiration. She wants to look in the mirror and feel a sense of satisfaction. She wants to find some resemblance to the young girl she used to be, to recapture some of the naïve excitement she felt as a twenty-year-old when life seemed full of promise and pleasant surprises.

So while her husband procures the phone number of their neighbour, Gayatri is getting a special platinum advanced aromatherapy massage designed to open up the energy lines and clear the blocked chakras of her tired body.

11

VARUN WAITS FOR what he believes is a decent interval after their meeting to call Sweety. He realizes he has no reason to speak to her — apart from a terrible urge to hear her voice — and agonizes over the decision a dozen times. Wary of scaring her off, afraid of a rebuff, he worries that the reason he furnishes for the call will be deemed flimsy, a front for dubious intentions. He cannot have her think that he is just another middle-aged man scratching a seventeen-year itch. At the same time, he cannot let go of the feeling that if he doesn't talk to her soon, something will be lost forever. Finally, when he has a few minutes to himself between meetings at work, he dials her number.

Sweety, on her part, has wondered about Varun and their brief encounters with a certain curiosity. The idea that they could be anything more than friendly neighbours has not crossed her mind. She is not completely indifferent to his interest but this she takes as her due, a tribute to her attractiveness. She is comfortable with him, finds his gaze unobtrusive, and instinct tells her that he means no harm.

Sweety Singh studied in a convent school under the vigilant eyes of nuns who lectured their students on the evils of waywardness and the perils of a loose character. At

Jesus and Mary College in Delhi, where she completed her undergraduate studies, interactions with the opposite sex were limited. She was aware of the male gaze and took the usual precautions to insulate herself from eve-teasers on the Delhi roads. When men looked at her with desire, it alternately flattered and repulsed her. Her husband is the first and only man she has been intimate with, and only after marriage has she felt a certain degree of freedom in her interactions with other men. Marriage and motherhood have given her respectability, a certain inaccessibility; she wears her married status like a protective armour. It gives her license to interact with other men while remaining above reproach.

Sweety is surprised to get a call from Varun but it is not entirely unexpected.

'Hello. I hope I am not disturbing you.'

'No. It's okay. Is it an emergency?'

He detects a smile, a teasing note in her voice, and is encouraged to carry on.

'Not exactly. Actually, one of my customers from the US is visiting us tomorrow and is keen to see Delhi. Since you mentioned that you are from there, I thought you would be the best person to ask about the places I could recommend.'

This is not entirely true. There is a customer from the US but she has only expressed an interest in seeing the Taj Mahal in Agra. She has no desire to roam the streets of Delhi on a hot summer day.

Beguiled into recounting the attractions of Delhi, Sweety

takes her role as local expert and travel advisor seriously. She describes the merits of India Gate and Rashtrapati Bhavan versus the old-world charm of Red Fort and Chandni Chowk (very beautiful but so hot and crowded this time of the year, especially for foreign tourists). For shopping, one could go to Khan Market but Dilli Haat might be better for ethnic handicrafts. Connaught Place is no longer a preferred destination though as a college student she often shopped at Janpath. She and her friends from college would also go to Sarojini Nagar market, which offered excellent bargains, and she loved the samosas at Mahendra Sweets but it may be too hot now; she herself doesn't go to these places any more, preferring the air-conditioned malls in Gurgaon. The Mughal Gardens are beautiful but closed at this time of the year. Once, during a school trip, she saw an enormous black and orange butterfly there, almost as big as a cauliflower.

Varun listens, delighted. Her voice is soothing, the little details she reveals about herself endearing, and he asks her the right questions, more to continue the conversation than to get any useful information. It is only when Varsha knocks on the door of his cabin that he remembers he has a meeting with the research team at 3:30 p.m. Reluctantly he brings the conversation to a close, thanking her politely for her time and patience.

They speak to each other almost every day during the week. The calls are initiated by Varun who, after the first two conversations, does not feel the need to explain himself. Sweety responds with moderate enthusiasm. They do not discuss their spouses – there doesn't seem to be any reason to do so. Sweety shares her observations of the day, her surprise at seeing a beggar pull out a mobile phone from his filthy pants and type a text message on it, her inaugural ride on the metro at Gurgaon ('It was so clean I thought I was in a foreign country'), how proud she was when Sanya-Manya came first in the three-legged race on sports day. She listens carefully when he explains some part of his work, his views on a particular news item and his thoughts on the world around him. She is curious to know more.

'How is America?' she asks one day. Varun struggles to answer the question for he has come to realize that it is not easy to describe in a few sentences a country so large and so varied. He had lived in Chicago for a while, travelled extensively to other parts for work and leisure, and finally settled down in California. Each place seemed different to him. It used to be the same when Americans asked him, 'What's it like in India?' during his early days there. There was no single India story that he could narrate, nothing that would encompass all the cumulative experiences he had of his country.

'It's difficult to describe,' he says to Sweety.

'In one word?'

'Big,' he says finally. 'Everything is big.' That is what struck him first when he visited, the fact that he could barely finish a milkshake at McDonald's and that 'tall' was the smallest size for coffee at Starbucks.

'For India, the word would be crowded. There are so many people everywhere,' Sweety offers.

'You are right,' he agrees.

Sweety says wistfully, 'I would like to visit America. I have only seen it in movies. I went to Singapore once, before Sanya-Manya were born. Everything is so clean in Singapore. Why do you think we can't keep it clean here?'

To Varun, her questions suggest an intelligence not fully developed, perhaps due to a limiting education. Her voice fills him with delight. He can't wait to talk to her. By the end of the week, Sweety has begun to look forward to talking to Varun, constantly reassuring herself that he is only a well-wisher, a good neighbour, someone she can count on as a friend.

Amandeep is expected back on Monday. When Sweety mentions this to Varun, she knows he will understand that they can no longer talk freely. She will be so busy with frequent trips to visit friends and family with her husband that they might not be able to talk at all. They might stay in Green Park for a day or two, she tells him, maybe even take a week off to go to the hills for a family holiday.

12

VARUN SARIN FEELS bereft. Though her presence in the same building did not mean proximity, he feels Sweety's absence strongly. In the coolness of the early morning air, along the curving walking tracks, in the slanting sunlight that glinted off the windows of Trafalgar Towers, he feels an emptiness, a jagged tear in the fabric of his life. Every time the elevator door opens, he hopes to see her. Every time his phone rings, he hopes that it might be her. How strange, he thinks, that this girl whose existence he had been unaware of two months ago should so affect the cadence of his life, with such little effort on her part. He knows he is in the grip of a strong emotion that he had not expected to feel at this stage of his life but he still hesitates to call it love. *Love.*

Varun remembers the fact of love but not the feeling. His mind goes back to Julie, perky, pony-tailed Julie, the class queen with mother-of-pearl skin and emerald eyes. He recalls with some embarrassment that he had sent her a card adorned with red roses and plump hearts, emblazoned with the words 'I love you'. Julie Fernandes, who had been used to boys in her class serenading her with the words of a popular song '*Joooooleeeee, I . . . laaav youuu . . .*' had not reciprocated his affections. She already had a boyfriend, a tennis player called Alfred Roberts with whom she went for dances and motorbike rides. She was the first girl who evoked any response from him but after twenty-eight years Varun cannot recall the exact emotion he had felt at that time. He has a vague recollection of excitement tinged with a certain embarrassment, a strong notion that he had made a fool of himself.

The first serious relationship he'd had was with Sushmita

Sarkar. They had met during the last year of his engineering days at IIT. Sushmita was doing a doctoral program in physics. They had seen each other in the library, across a pile of books, and moved quickly towards a furtive relationship founded on the needs of the body rather than the demands of the heart. She had always taken the initiative. Varun spent several restless days waiting for the summons to her hostel room. They would make love without any preamble on an old mattress on the floor and he would slip away afterwards to cope with the rigours of his student life. Initially, Varun had felt inept, unsure of himself, as though he were floundering in unknown waters. Gradually, they had established a pattern that satisfied both. Each time they shared a slow cigarette after a ferocious session on the mattress, he sensed that she derived some comfort from his presence.

Sushmita had been recovering from a relationship with a married professor which had left her bitter and bruised. Varun had given her the confidence to go out into the world again. She, in turn, had given him a sense of having become a man, the knowledge of how to be with a woman. He remembered declaring his love for her, her bemused look, and her calm explanation that they had no future together. She still cared for the professor. He had felt hurt at that point of time, but later he could see that it was only his ego that had been dented. He had not heard from her in several years and now thought of her with detached affection.

He must have been in love with Gayatri once, he supposes.

There could have been no other reason for defying parental strictures, overcoming barriers of caste and community and committing to a lifetime together. He had been attracted by her obvious intelligence, her large dark eyes and air of reserve which he soon realized was only a way of hiding her innate shyness. They had interacted first as classmates in business school, thrown together by the necessity of group assignments. There had been another boy in their group who he suspected had an interest in Gayatri, though she herself seemed ignorant of it. Dolt had been too shy to make any overt moves and had retreated quietly when Gayatri and Varun started spending more time together. They were fond of old Hollywood movies, which they procured on videocassettes and watched on a small television along with other members of Flicks – the movie club. She was one of the few who stayed back to discuss the films. Varun remembered that Gayatri had not enjoyed *Casablanca*, dismissing it as too unrealistically romantic whereas he had been moved by Ingrid Bergman's cool beauty. During a heated debate that followed a screening of *Gone with the Wind*, Gayatri had vigorously defended Scarlett as a truly emancipated woman while Varun had accused the heroine of every feminine vice. Somehow they had drifted together to the little café outside the campus, where they continued the argument and had their first unofficial dinner date.

He cannot remember when they went from being just classmates to good friends to something more. Their movements had been noted in the campus gossip rag, a hastily assembled cyclostyled two-pager tacked on to noticeboards and shoved under the dorm doors. 'GM considering possible merger' said a blurb with a clever cartoon of Gayatri Murthy shaking hands with Varun Sarin. There had been an instant demarcation of them as a couple among their batchmates; they were invited together to dorm parties, included together in group outings, and expected to know each other's whereabouts and accept the good-natured jokes that followed all campus couples. Even though they themselves had not a put a name to it, they did not deny a relationship, tacitly understanding that they were meant to be together. Over the next two years, they became accustomed to each other's moods, whimsies and routines.

After Varun's stormy relationship with Sushmita, Gayatri seemed like the calm shore he could come home to. He sensed a certain restlessness within himself, which he discerned could only lead to chronic dissatisfaction. He knew he needed an anchor to settle him in the life he had chosen. He wanted to be in a relationship where he knew exactly where he stood and had some degree of control. He could sense Gayatri's determined attachment to him and he felt at the time that she would stand by him, no matter what he did. As he went out into the world, she was the one person he wanted in his corner.

After they graduated and moved to different cities with different employers, he missed her – more than he had expected to. Within the year they had spoken of marriage, for she was at an age when her parents were beginning the search for a suitable boy. When she mentioned that someone was coming to see her during the week, Varun had been stunned. It seemed absurd that she should spend the rest of her life with a stranger when they had such a good relationship.

'Why are you even seeing someone?' Varun had asked. He had never declared his love for her, nor let her think that they would be together at some point of time. Yet he felt cheated when she spoke of marriage with another man.

'What do you expect me to do?' Gayatri had countered.

'We should get married,' he had proposed without thinking.

'To each other?' The words seemed to have been uttered in jest, but he sensed the relief and hope that lay behind them.

'Yes!'

'Okay.'

'Okay?'

'Yes. I think we'll make a good team.'

Despite the constraints of geography, objections from each other's families and their own unspoken concerns about the future, they had been married within the year. Varun quit his first job to join Infosys in Bangalore. They found a small apartment close to Gayatri's maternal home and embarked on life as householders. They were comfortable together, as friends and partners. When the news of the move to Chicago and Gayatri's pregnancy came within a week of each other, they were both happy and apprehensive. They looked forward to a life together, they could face the world and triumph.

They had been a couple for so long that Varun cannot quite remember when the uncoupling began. But seventeen years into marriage, he finds himself thinking about love, whether it had been there at all and where it had gone.

13

A FEW HUNDRED kilometres away, at a family picnic outside the Lake View Resort in Nainital, Sweety Singh spreads green mint chutney on slices of white bread and handed them to the children who cluster around her on the maroon dhurrie which is slowly becoming damp as it absorbs the dew from the grass under it. Her mother-in-law instructs her to open a packet of potato chips, a sister-in-law asks her to add ketchup to the chutney for her son and her husband says, 'Oye Switty, zara Pepsi dena.' As she hands him a paper cup with the drink, he hums *'Switty, Switty, Switty, tera pyar chayeda.'* The rest of the family laugh indulgently. Her mother-in-law looks at Sweety as if to say, 'You don't know how lucky you are to have a husband like my son.' Amandeep slurps down the drink, leaving a few brown drops glistening on his moustache. Sweety turns away.

Sweety can only vaguely recall how she came to be Mrs Amandeep Singh. She knows that she was spotted by her future husband at the wedding of a relative. Struck by the sloping line of her fair neck, the lightness of her honey eyes, and the graceful way she moved her body to the music, Amandeep had an immediate desire to stake claim to this beauteous creature before anyone else could. He was at an age where marriage was expected to be the natural outcome of any relationship he had with a woman. Many of the candidates lined up by his family as potential wives had been rejected after they had provided him with their photos. Not one of them had conformed to the image he had of a wife. He was not particular about the financial status, sub-caste, family background or any of the other demographic characteristics deemed critical for a marriage by the elders of the community. He wanted a beautiful wife with a pleasant temperament who could provide him with amiable company and ensure domestic harmony.

Enquiries had been initiated through appropriate channels. Sweety's parents, gratified to acquire a groom from within their own community who also happened to belong to a well-off, respectable family, hastened the proceedings. Amandeep's parents were initially wary of marrying their son into a humble middle-class family; Sweety's father had only recently been promoted as the branch manager of a public sector bank. But Amandeep's mind was made up and the elders could see no real obstacle to the marriage: the girl was fair and pretty, her character was universally acknowledged as being above reproach, the inferior economic status of her family would make her a suitably submissive bride.

Sweety's request that she be allowed to complete her BA degree was acceded to, provided she got engaged immediately. Her parents were relieved that they would not have to go through the process of finding a suitable match for her; their energies could be focused on settling her younger brother Bobby. Bobby, who had fared badly at the Class 10 board exams, did not display any sense of urgency or ambition for his own future. Her parents hoped that Sweety's marriage would open a few doors for Bobby in the future. Sweety had a vague notion of doing something useful with her life, of acquiring fame and fortune through some respectable but as yet unidentified means. She had contemplated a career in hotel management, fashion designing or advertising but nothing stirred her interest enough to induce concrete action. Marriage and children were the only certain parts of her future. Though she was gratified to be the first among her friends to receive a marriage proposal, the idea of marrying Amandeep was not as exciting as she had imagined.

Amandeep Singh was of average height and had a wheatish complexion. His body was slightly rounded with a tendency to fleshiness; there was a suggestion of a life of ease. His moustache and beard were luxuriant and well kept, his clothes were a little too tight and a slight sag of stomach hung over a well-stretched belt. The expression in his round large eyes was usually genial. Sweety was flattered by his attentions and a little in awe of his family's status but could feel no stirring of the heart at the prospect of being joined to him in matrimony. Given the pressure from her family and their eagerness to accept Amandeep's proposal, it did not occur to her that she could refuse him. Marrying him would please everyone; in fact, their extended family would compliment her on making an excellent match, she would be held up as an example to younger female cousins who might be inclined to mutiny or waywardness.

Sweety combined a romantic predisposition with a strong streak of practicality. Her ideas of love and sex were derived from all the Hindi movies she watched and the Mills and Boon romances she read sporadically. Love happened, but mostly to other people in distant places. She saw little signs of the desperation, the longing and the passionate declarations that signified true love in the prosaic world she inhabited. In her world, love was subordinate to family honour and the wishes of elders. She had been expected to be a virgin bride and give herself to her husband, who then became the lawful custodian of her virtue. She had dreamt of falling in love, of finding a soul mate, but had not expected to actually find one. During her engagement, she tried to convince herself that it had been love at first sight for Amandeep. He spoke to her regularly, was solicitous of her well-being and that of her family. He gave her no cause for complaint but a part of her wanted to be wooed, won over and not be treated as a fait accompli. She could not imagine

Amandeep as the anonymous saviour from her dreams but she knew that marriage would be a way to save herself and her family from an uncertain future. As the object of his affections, as his intended wife, she felt obliged to return his attentions.

For a few months after the wedding, she believed that she was in love. During their honeymoon, she was introduced to the terrain of physical pleasures and she explored its texture, its secret smells and urgent demands with curiosity. It was not unpleasant. Later, she submitted to her husband's caresses and bore his heaving weight without active involvement or complaint. She came to accept the physical aspect of marriage as a necessary part of the institution, but not essential to her own fulfilment.

Amandeep was proud of his wife's physical attractiveness. That she still drew appreciative looks from other males bolstered his pride but he was also quick to mark his territory with a touch, a casual arm around her shoulders, especially when they were in public.

Amandeep was attentive to her but Sweety sensed that his good humour would last only as long as she acceded to his needs. As the youngest of the family, he was a little spoilt, used to getting his own way, and Sweety had realized early on that direct confrontation with him yielded no results. Anger and reproach turned him off. She had learned to influence him with appeals to his good nature and wisdom, by maintaining a façade of good humour and resigned martyrdom which assured a speedy resolution of her problems. She did not make any unreasonable demands. He was generous with money, gregarious, trusting of strangers, and a fond father to their daughters. Sweety had never questioned the nature of her relationship with her spouse. There was affection and harmony; she felt she could handle her husband. Certainly, she could not imagine an alternate existence. She was not unhappy with her life, especially since moving to Gurgaon.

But in the middle of the family picnic, in the midst of her extended family of eight adults and six children, Sweety thinks of Varun Sarin. She wonders if he will call her despite her injunctions. She had glanced at her phone several times over the past few days. She misses talking to him. She wants to tell him about the things she has seen, heard and felt over the past few days. She wants to go back to Trafalgar Towers and see him. She does not think about love, not yet.

14

WHEN VARUN SEES Sweety in the elevator, nearly twenty days after their last conversation, he feels a strong desire to take her in his arms and kiss the pink crescent of her mouth. The force of the desire surprises him; he recognizes in it something primeval, something that lies at the heart of human creation. They are alone in the narrow space and he can reach out and touch her face, the face that smiles at him with what seems like genuine joy. Instead, he puts out a hand tentatively, a little awkward, but when the hand is accepted and he feels the soft pressure of her fingers, the handshake grows more confident.

'Welcome back.'

'Thanks. It's good to be back. You know, I actually missed Trafalgar Towers.'

'And Trafalgar Towers missed you.'

'Umm . . . So, how have you been?'

'Ah, well, you know, the usual routine.'

As their brief journey together comes to an end, Varun panics. He will be sucked into his work, she will be consumed by other demands. She will be lost to him again and he will continue to struggle with the uncertainty that has become a part of his life.

'Busy today?' he asks.

'Not really. My husband is away. The girls are in school. So I am back to my routine. I am going to pick up some vegetables and should be free after that till Sanya-Manya come home.'

For a moment, Varun Sarin is utterly happy. In the same moment, Sweety realizes that she has extended an invitation. For Sweety, this is when something changes between them. Varun Sarin is no longer a kind, inoffensive neighbour but a man she wants to invite into her life. She does not know what the invitation entails but the feeling she has is akin to the thrill of standing on the edge of a forest, looking at the dense cluster of mysterious trees ahead. She senses danger but instead of flinching from it, she thrills to it; there is an inexorable desire to forge ahead.

At the Safal vegetable shop, Sweety sorts through a pile of potatoes, absently tests the tomatoes for firmness and snaps the edges off thin green fingers of okra. She cannot concentrate and is glad that she can get through the chore without much exertion.

Varun Sarin smiles through a meeting with his team. He is indulgent with a subordinate who has missed a deadline, not as sharp as usual with Varsha, who has not yet made a flight booking for a business trip, and very efficient in signing the papers put before him. He calls Sweety just before noon.

Through the crackling air space, they find an opening. A simple telephonic conversation becomes suffused with magic. Their voices conjure up a new world in which there are only two inhabitants. This secret world gives them a liberty they cannot take in public, a license to whisper words that Varun has only thought about and Sweety never dreamt that she would want to hear.

'I missed you. I waited for you to get back,' he says.

'Me too.'

'Strange.'

'Why?'

'I don't really know you but I feel so comfortable talking to you. That day, in the park, I told you things I had never shared with anyone. I hope it wasn't uncomfortable for you.'

'No. It wasn't. I feel comfortable with you too.'

'I just want you to know that I don't want anything from you. I mean . . . I know you have responsibilities, other people to take care of. I don't want to impose on your time or anything.'

'It's okay. We are just talking, na?'

'Right!'

Even as he says this, Varun knows that he wants more than 'just talking'. Some days he is aroused just by her voice in his ear. Sweety knows that they are not 'just talking', that this is the beginning of a courtship that cannot have a conventional ending.

They keep telling themselves that they do not intend to deceive. But concealment is a given in what they have begun to share. Nobody knows about their conversations. And they are careful not to let these interchanges impinge on their other lives. They maintain a silence on the nature of their marriages. Both are aware that the real topography of a marriage is known only to the two people who traverse its rocky terrain and sometimes they themselves are confronted with unknown, unexpected twists and turns. Varun is careful not to probe too deeply the small details – how often do they make love, who initiates it, do they fight about money, who says sorry first. Sweety unwittingly discloses some of this in the course of their conversations and this is how Varun interprets the nature of her relationship with her husband. He satisfies himself with the assumption that she is not very happy, she is not loved in the way she deserves to be, but she is a loyal, dutiful wife.

He is aware that he has given the impression that his relationship with his wife is distant, that the ardour of the early days of their marriage has cooled off. Sweety does not question it further. They maintain an amicable but casual façade if they see each other in public. They schedule their conversations, forgive each other's lapses in answering or returning calls and, despite the inherent restrictions of the medium, build a connection that transcends the words and sentences that ebb and flow through the lines.

Varun dreams of making love to Sweety. He imagines himself touching her skin. He knows they will be wonderful together. If and when they do make love, it will be more than an act of physical intimacy. It's not the mere act of possession that he desires but the chance to express himself in the language of the body, to use the vocabulary of touch and feel.

'This isn't enough,' Varun says during one of their conversations.

'What more can there be?' asks Sweety. She can guess what is on his mind, but she can't still openly acknowledge that there could be anything more between them. She has managed to console herself that they are not doing anything wrong. So far.

'Can't we be together for just a while? So that I can see who I am talking to? So that I can look at you properly?'

'No, no. That is not a good idea. If anybody sees us outside, they . . . they won't understand.'

'I know. I know. What can we do?'

'I am going to Jaipur next weekend for a friend's wedding.

Just me. I am leaving the girls with my parents. Jaspreet . . . Jessie, who lives in London, is getting married to this British guy and they want a traditional Indian wedding in a palace. I haven't seen her in a long time and it's not too far away. There are three of us going from here, college friends. We are planning to take a Volvo bus or a car.'

'How long will you be there?'

'Three days. We thought we'll have a good time, you know, do some general masti, away from our family responsibilities.'

'I see.'

It is at this moment that Varun decides to schedule an offsite visit somewhere nearby for the top team at TechKnowlEdge. He calls an impromptu meeting and tells them they have been working too long and too hard and need to go to a different place to think about how they can take their company to the next level. Strategic thinking happens best when you remove yourself from day-to-day tactical work and retire to a scenic secluded spot. He can think of no place better than Jaipur.

15

THE MONSOONS HAVE been kind this July in Jaipur. The rains have driven down the temperatures without affecting normal life. Peacocks call to each other in the gardens of the Rambagh Palace Hotel. The trees glisten a newly minted green and flowers droop gently. Through the huge glass windows of the room in which the TechKnowlEdge team is meeting, Varun looks out on a scene that resembles an impressionist painting and tries to bring his mind back to the discussions his team has been engaged in.

He has studied NASSCOM reports, industry trends and the presentations they have prepared. They argue the relative merits of focusing solely on knowledge management or analytics, starting a CRM business and integrating analytic and information technology. Should they focus more on predictive analytics? What do customers really want? Is there a segment where their organization can offer a compelling value proposition? What could be a game changer? How will the development of the semantic web affect them? What are the prospects for catastrophe modelling? Varun is able for a while to engage in this world; it is a world he is familiar with. His business runs on the premise that data can be mined and that knowledge can be decoded and deciphered to enable logical decisions about the future. He makes money by helping people cope with uncertainty, his people design software to manage a variety of risks. He should by reason have every tool available with him to predict the evening, yet he really has no idea if Sweety will meet him at the hotel at 5:30 p.m. as they had decided earlier. If she does come, he cannot predict what will happen. His planning stopped with their meeting.

Meanwhile, Sweety Singh is dancing to the throbbing beat of '*Munni badnaam hui*' at the wedding ceremony of her friend Jessie and wondering if Varun Sarin will kiss her when they meet. Ever since she mentioned the wedding at Jaipur to him, she has known that both of them are thinking the same thoughts. She wonders how far she might go, what he will think of her if she accedes too readily to his obvious desire for her. She imagines herself in his arms and is surprised by how appealing the image is. At 4 p.m. Sweety gets ready to make her excuses to her friends and snatch a few hours for herself. A part of her is still undecided, she knows that she can still back out, make some excuse to Varun, even though she has replied 'I will try' to his text message giving her the venue and time of their meeting. Another part of her resolves to move ahead. This part is fuelled mostly by curiosity. She has never known the touch of another man apart from her husband and the fear that she might live her life without full knowledge of the pleasures that she believes must exist supersedes the fear of being discovered. She is abashed at her lack of self-control, her eagerness to meet someone her mother would term 'paraya mard', someone else's man, someone who is out of bounds. She knows that she will regret it if she goes to meet Varun, she fears that she will regret it even more if she doesn't.

She comes to him in the low light of the evening. He sees her under a curling arch at the edge of the hotel lobby. She could be a princess in her flame-coloured lehenga, her face lightly veiled, her hands patterned with mehendi. There is a wedding at the hotel and there are several similarly dressed women around, so she does not seem out of place.

'I don't know what I am doing here,' she whispers as Varun approaches her.

'It's all right. You can go back if you want. We can just have coffee and talk at the restaurant.'

'No. It's okay. Can we go somewhere else?'

Varun leads her to his room. It is only when the door shuts behind her that he allows himself to look at her face. Her skin is translucent. Her eyes are troubled. When he takes her into his arms, he feels her trembling. She closes her eyes and leans against his shoulder.

'You are so beautiful.' His mouth moves against her skin.

'We are crazy.'

'You make me crazy.'

They speak the language of lovers, whisper the words lovers have used through the ages, each feeling that they have discovered something special, that they are the only two extraordinary people in the world to feel the way they do. Sweety allows herself to be led to the bed, the lehenga to be pushed up to her hips, the dupatta to be moved aside. She kisses him back, restrained at first and then with passion as something moves and burns inside her.

Varun discovers her body, tracing the outline of her waist, kissing the tiny mole at the base of her neck, stroking the pale green vein on her wrist. He is surprised at the rush of tenderness he experiences at the sight of an old scar on her knee, surprised that he can be so aroused by the way a woman slips a blouse off her shoulders, that he can feel such a rush of anticipation at the prospect of an act he deemed less and less important in his life. He feels the weight of her breast in his hand, tastes her salt-sweet skin, and inhales the moist lemon lavender scent across the length of her body. All his senses are on fire. He holds back; he gives in. Afterwards, when he lies spent within the circle of her arms, his head resting in the arc between her neck and shoulder, he is amazed that their imperfect assortment of blood, bones, flesh and skin can be a source of such pure pleasure. He is dizzy, grateful and more content than he has been in a long time. Sweety is quiet. He feels her stillness, a sudden withdrawal, even though they are still entwined under the sheets.

'Are you all right?'

'Yes.'

'Did I hurt you? Was it okay?'

'It was . . . fine. Wonderful. I didn't know it could be like this.'

He lifts her wrist and kisses the lines on her palm, the life line, his fate line. 'I love you.'

Sweety sighs.

'I don't know . . .'

'It's all right. You don't have to say anything.'

'This . . . you and me, everything is really good but I feel bad. I shouldn't have.'

'Sweety, listen to me.' He sits up and is strangely comfortable in his nakedness. 'You are a good person. You

are a caring mother, a good wife, daughter-in-law, daughter.
This does not make you a bad person. We can work things
out.' It sounds like a rehearsed speech but he means it. He
is sure of her essential goodness, less certain of his own
limits.

'How? What is there to work out?'

'We can't plan this. I don't know what we will do but I
can promise I won't do anything that you don't want me to.
If you tell me that you never want to see me again, I will try
to live with that. I only want your happiness.'

'I am happy.' She smiles, and he is relieved.

'Good. Then don't worry about anything. Let the future
be.'

She puts herself back together, ties up her hair and
paints her mouth into an auburn arc. He watches in silence,
knowing that separation will be the defining aspect of their
relationship.

16

GURGAON WAS OVERFLOWING. The monsoon had been
unusually munificent. A few hours of rain had left the city
waterlogged. Sewers disgorged their contents, cars sank
into gaping potholes, creating traffic jams that made the
roads heave and shudder, umbrellas remained wet and

unfurled through the day. Mothers searched for raincoats, worried about dengue, bronchitis and other unnamed diseases. Residents muttered darkly about global warming and complained about seepage problems in their houses.

Gayatri did not like the rain. She could bear it in small doses at most, preferably in the night when it did not disturb the rhythm of her day. The house smelled of damp clothes and a small moist patch had formed on the bathroom ceiling, where the plaster was flaking like an open sore. The sky was the colour of cold steel. Gayatri's spirits sagged. Gurgaon seemed to have become uglier. The city that was in a perpetual state of construction had slowed down: deadly iron rods lined the roads, large heaps of rubble congealed in vacant lots, migrant workers sat sullenly under blue tarpaulin tents.

During a brief respite from the rains one morning, Sweety stepped out for a walk. A weak sun had emerged through the cocoon of grey smog that enveloped the tall towers, lazily wiping away the remnants of the previous night's downpour. As she circled the blocks, she looked up at the balcony of the seventh floor of Tower 2. Varun Sarin, gazing down at the walking path, had seen her. He felt her smile, felt something smooth and fiery slide down his throat like neat whisky and wished that he could hold the moment forever.

They had not seen or spoken to each other for a week. He knew that Amandeep was home and her family had the first claim to her time. It had been difficult to stay away but he had managed to go through the routine, pausing often to root among the memories they had created and willing himself to wait. When he turned back to face his own world, he felt kindly, poetic, predisposed to find beauty in everything around him. When Gayatri summoned him to breakfast, he was in a good mood.

'Doesn't Gurgaon look pretty after the rains? Like a young girl in a new green dress.'

'More like a whore whose make-up is getting ruined.' Gayatri did not share her husband's light-heartedness.

'What's the matter?' he ventured.

'Nothing.' The nothing was heavy with meaning. It meant that something was wrong. It begged further investigation. Normally, Varun would not have probed any further.

'Is everything all right?'

'Yes. Nothing serious. Work pressure.'

'Do you want to talk about it?'

Gayatri was surprised. His voice did not have the tinge of irritation or sarcasm she usually heard in it. When she looked into his eyes, they were kind. But it was the kindness of a stranger, the impersonal concern we show while listening to somebody else's sad story.

'No. I can manage. Thanks.'

Things had been rough at work. Gayatri and Jai were in disagreement over a matter of incentives for the sales staff. Rajiv Bhandari, the head of sales, who had only recently moved from the global headquarters in Connecticut and was a smooth talker who made impressive power-point presentations glowing with graphs and charts, had proposed a dramatic increase in sales commission for the representatives who sold medical equipment to hospitals and clinics. He believed that people performed well if you threw enough money at them. Gayatri had not warmed to him. His smooth bland face, the way he sprinkled his conversations with jargon, his fidgety, restless energy put her off. The incentives he had proposed made no financial sense. She knew these people, they would never produce the results Rajiv demanded, and in the end there would be greater dissatisfaction and lost productivity. Vivek Mansukhani, the head of human resources, did not seem to have a strong opinion on the matter. He tended to go along with whatever Jai proposed and was carried away by Rajiv's promise that this new incentive structure would dramatically increase employee satisfaction. Jai had almost always heeded Gayatri's advice in the past, she was spoken of as his right-hand woman and others envied their professional camaraderie. But even Jai favoured Rajiv's proposal.

Gayatri was uncomfortable with the manoeuvring and machinations that the corporate world sometimes required. She was not good at lobbying for support, was reluctant to woo important people, form camps and play people against each other. She knew that Varun was better at playing the game. He too had a distaste for office politics, but he played to win and, as far as possible, he played by the rules. In the early stages of her career, she had often talked to Varun about office gossip, the petty jealousies of her colleagues, her promotion prospects and the idiocy of inept bosses. He was good at offering solutions to her dilemmas and even if she didn't abide by his advice all the time, he provided a sounding board and often she would do the same for him. She couldn't recall when the change took place, who stopped talking and who stopped listening. The current pattern of their relationship did not allow for a display of weakness or any sign of neediness on her part.

She was also worried about Anirudh. There were days when she felt that her son was lost to her. He was absent from most meals. School work, soccer practice, friends – online and live – took up most of his time. She checked on his grades at school, ensured that most meals were well balanced, but rarely entered his room. She had not enrolled him as her friend on Facebook, wanting to be an involved but not intrusive mother. Anirudh was usually polite, rarely displaying overt antagonism or adolescent rebelliousness, yet Gayatri felt that she knew very little of what went on in his life. There had been rumours of a boy of the same age in another school dying of a drug overdose at a party, another of a boy who had sneaked his girlfriend to a quack for an abortion, of boys who were rich, crazy and got drunk behind the wheels of their parents' fancy cars. She saw little sign of the Indian values that some of her friends had said Anirudh would imbibe in India. The friends he hung out with seemed no different from the teenagers she had seen in Fremont. They all wore the same baggy ill-fitting clothes, tinkered with ipods and mobile phones and spoke in a language that made sense only to them.

Three days ago, she had heard him talking softly on the phone. She could make out a 'yes, baby, 'me too' and 'I really like'. His young face seemed open and vulnerable, his tone was an entreaty.

'Who were you talking to?' she asked and his face shuttered down.

'A friend,' he mumbled

'A girlfriend?'

'No, Mom!'

'We've trusted you with a mobile phone but I don't want you to waste time talking on it endlessly.'

'Relax, Mom. It's nothing.'

'Rudy, you can tell me, whatever it is. I don't have a problem. But you know this is not California. You have to be careful. Many girls here still come from conservative families and their parents would not like them to have a boyfriend. Do you know that in Haryana there are still honour killings? I don't want you getting into any kind of trouble.'

Gayatri sounded paranoid even to herself. She heard her voice taking on a strident hectoring tone. Her son withdrew from her as though she was an obnoxious interloper. How easy it had been just a few years ago, when he used to hold her hand while crossing the road, when he rushed back from school to tell her how his day had been, when she could heal a hurt with a band aid and a kiss. She saw him changing before her eyes, his childish features hardening and showing signs of the man he would become; his voice had cracked, his mind had become a black box. She had searched the Internet and perused parenting magazines for tips on dealing with teenage boys but they were full of dim warnings about rampant teenage hormones, wet dreams and excessive masturbation which made her feel even more helpless. When she spoke to Varun a while back about her misgivings, he had seemed too casual, almost dismissive. Leave him alone, he will be fine, he had said.

Perhaps she would have handled a daughter better, Gayatri reflected. She would have gracefully explained the significance of menstruation, giggled conspiratorially about bra sizes and discussed the immaturity of boys. They would have been girls together. She was not sure what to do with a teenage boy.

Anirudh joined them for breakfast. Jhumpa was frying puris, which needed to be consumed immediately, while they were still soft and airy. Anirudh was partial to aloo puri, he could polish off a dozen without counting.

'You missed the soccer match last night, Rudy. It was superb.'

'Yeah, Dad. I saw a bit at Rohan's place but not the whole match.'

'Big party?'

'No, just some of us from school hanging out.'

'Were there girls?'

'Yeah. Classmates.'

'So, do you have a girlfriend?'

'No!'

'You mean, not yet!'

'Ha! I mean like *not ever*.'

'So, she doesn't like you?'

'Hmm . . . it's not that . . .'

'You know, Rudy, when I was about your age, I had this huge crush on a girl in my class.'

'Really?'

'Really! Her name was Julie. She was cute, with long brown hair and big green eyes. I guess all of us boys were a little crazy about her.'

'So, did you . . . like . . . date her?'

'No. I did send her a mushy card on her birthday but she never said anything to me. I don't even know if she got it. She already had a boyfriend.'

'Wow! I didn't know people did that sort of stuff in your time.'

'Rudy, people have been doing that sort of stuff for ages! It's quite normal. Let me know if you want to talk about anything.'

'Uh . . . uh . . .'

'Including girls. At your age, girls start becoming interesting.'

'Girls start becoming totally weird. I have no idea what they are thinking.'

'Right! After all these years, I still don't know what your mother is thinking.'

Gayatri, who had been listening to this exchange, realized with a start that even after seventeen years, large tracts of her husband's life remained unexplored. She felt excluded from their talk and yet relieved that Anirudh was talking to at least one parent. She allowed herself a smile, grateful to be given an opening into the conversation.

'So, Varun, what was the problem with Julie? What happened? You never told me about her.'

'Didn't I? Actually, nothing happened with Julie. That was the problem.'

The Sarins laughed together. It started raining again. Varun knew that Sweety must have returned to her home.

17

THE RESIDENTS OF Trafalgar Towers usually celebrate Independence Day on the morning of 15 August with a flag-hoisting ceremony in the lawns, followed by the singing of patriotic songs. The flag is hoisted by the senior-most resident, an elderly gentleman of ninety-two, who wheezes his way through a brief Independence Day speech exhorting the residents to uphold the values of the freedom fighters. The patriotic songs are provided by a group cobbled together by a few enthusiastic parents. Availability and willingness rather than musical talent are the criteria on the basis of which twelve children have been selected to sing '*Saare jahan se achha*'. Tricoloured burfis are distributed to those present and everyone joins in for the national anthem. For about half an hour the residents of Trafalgar Towers set aside their usual routine and experience something akin to national pride.

A private Independence Day party has been planned by Ranvir Bhatia, senior partner with Marcus Reilly, an international executive search firm that has set up operations in Gurgaon. Ranvir wants to meet his new neighbours, network and establish a set of contacts that is critical to his line of work. The Independence Day theme – dress code: national colours – was thought up by his wife Juhi. She has taken pains to ensure that the food is in keeping with the theme, preparing elaborate platters of carrot, radish and cucumber, a starter that comprises broccoli, cheese and cherry tomatoes impaled on a toothpick, along with white dhoklas with green and orange chutneys. The dinner is an assortment of dishes from across the country, national integration served hot on the dining table. Sweety Singh, friend of Juhi Bhatia, who has a daughter the same age as Sanya-Manya, has been invited to the party. Ranvir Bhatia had met Varun Sarin recently at a local networking event organized by the Gurgaon Development Council. On discovering that they are neighbours in the same condominium complex, he has extended an invitation to him as well.

Ever since she returned from Jaipur, Sweety has been alternately nervous, eager, excited, ashamed and confused. Sometimes she yields to the drama of love; she feels the tender pain of separation, a burst of intense longing to be with Varun and sudden silly pleasure when he calls her. She finds herself recreating each minute of her time with him in Jaipur, adding and removing details, toggling between memory and imagination. She recalls the sensation of his mouth on her skin, the shiver that ran through her body. How loving and gentle he was. Everything around her speaks to her of love. All the film songs she hears seem to have been written for her; even the most inane ones that speak of pyaar, ikraar and intezaar make absolute sense and she sighs in empathy with the heroine mouthing the lyrics as she watches the songs on Channel V. This is what she always wanted to feel, this blooming and wilting, this opening and closing, this new clarity about the meaning of words like passion and desire.

On other occasions, while surrounded by her daughters, serving dinner to her husband or talking to her in-laws on the phone, she is overcome by shame. When Sanya-Manya kiss her goodnight and say 'I love you, Mamma', she feels she would give anything to erase the incident in Jaipur. How low she has fallen, abusing the trust that her family has placed in her, how cheaply she has behaved, like a common whore, leaping into the arms of a man she barely knows. He had probably slept with hundreds of women in America. He must think she is desperate, her husband will hate her if he finds out, her children will be snatched away from her, she will have to kill herself. If only she could remove it from her memory, it would be as if it never happened. She doesn't remember what happened. Maybe it never happened.

She will never see Varun or talk to him again. It is wrong. She has to see him soon. She can't bear it if he doesn't call. She cannot believe that this is happening to her. She is a respectable married woman, mother of two girls. She is a girl in love for the first time. Life is amazing. Life is unfair. Life is beautiful. Life is hopeless.

A few days before Independence Day, when Varun phones her, she does not take his call. She ignores his messages. She calls him a day later, contrite, full of love.

'I am sorry. I don't know what to do sometimes. I want to talk to you but . . .'

'It's all right. I was worried that something had happened to you. If I could just talk to you for a few minutes, listen to your voice and know that you are well, that's enough for now.'

'I sometimes think it's like in those old movies, you know, Meena Kumari ke time ke films. My mother and I used to watch them together on TV sometimes. They used to talk of shamma parwana and I never used to understand it.'

'My Urdu is quite pathetic. I still don't know which is which.'

'Shamma is the candle and parwana is the stupid moth which is drawn to the light.'

'Ah! I see. Obviously you are the candle and I am the stupid moth.'

'No. I am the stupid moth. Nothing happens to the candle but the moth gets burnt.'

'So you think nothing is happening to me. I haven't recovered from Jaipur yet. I think I still have burn marks.'

'You are laughing at me!'

'No, sweetheart. I am laughing at myself. I am a forty-four-year-old man and here I am, behaving like a lovesick teenager. My son appears more mature.'

'Hmmm . . . *dil toh bachcha hai ji . . . thoda kachcha hai ji . . .*'

'Right! I haven't heard this song though. You sing well.'

'It's from *Ishqiya*. By Gulzar saheb. Very appropriate for you.'

'Now you are laughing at me. Okay, I'll listen to it. Or you should just sing it for me.'

'Someday.'

'Soon. I wish I could see you. We have been invited to some Independence Day party. I just don't feel like going out and meeting anybody else.'

'Oh? I am also going to one. My friend Juhi, who lives in Tower 1, has called us over.'

'Is her husband Ranvir Bhatia? He is with an executive search firm. I met him last week professionally and he mentioned that he also lives in Trafalgar Towers.'

'It must be the same party. Come, na.'

'I want to see you but I don't know . . . in front of everyone, our families. It might be awkward.'

'It won't, it will be fun. Please come.'

'Okay. I will. I haven't seen you properly for a while. Will you spend the evening by my side?'

'Don't joke! Just come.'

The process of getting ready for the party, the very prospect of the party has changed for Sweety. She is no longer Mrs Sweety Singh accompanying her husband on a social outing. She is a woman going to meet her lover. Even though there is little chance of a union, there would certainly be a sighting, a feasting of the eyes, the possibility of a light touch of the hands – the idea of proximity in a public place is intoxicating. The outfit she had decided on earlier, a white chikan salwar kameez accessorized with a crushed orange dupatta, now seems too plain, too dull. There is a stiff starchiness about the kameez, the colour does not flatter her pallor. She tries on a black dress that she bought a long time ago but has never worn. It falls on her like a sheath, the material is shiny, scaled like snake skin with a deep neck and a low back, an all-woman dress that stands out like an exclamation mark. She smears on a dark shade of lipstick, puffs an imaginary cigarette, blows out imaginary smoke and attempts a seductive smile at her reflection. She could be a vamp from a seventies' movie, a Helen or a Bindu desperately seeking the attention of the hero, who is intent on chasing a virtuous heroine dressed in pastel shades. No, the dress is too bold, too much an attention seeker, the mirror reflects an unrecognizable woman. She does not want to violate the dress code for the evening. National colours it must be. She pulls out a moss-green chiffon sari studded with small gold buttis, with a slim gold border. The blouse is cut deep and knotted at the back, forming a plump tempting bow. She had dismissed it as being too dressy but now she sees that it must be the one.

Later, after a quick dash to the salon to style her hair, she applies her make-up with great care. The curl of the mascara, the curve of the lipstick, the brush strokes on her cheeks, every single action is deliberate, purposeful. She is the *sajjika nayika* of the classical dances, a woman dressing for her beloved. Every mudra speaks of anticipation, longing, a desire to please the lover. When she surveys the end result in the mirror, she is satisfied. The drape of the sari shows off the dip of her waist, the knot of the blouse is perched along the line of her spine, the mysterious slash of her navel is dimly visible through the translucent chiffon. Gold drops glitter on her ears. When she emerges from the bedroom, Amandeep, who has been waiting patiently, is sufficiently impressed and gratified. This glorious apsara from the heavens is his, his wife to hold and keep and show to the world.

18

VARUN AND GAYATRI arrive precisely forty-five minutes after the stated time of 8 p.m. Over the past year they have realized that parties in Delhi never commence on time, guests are expected to be late, there is no precise time for serving dinner, there is usually more food than required. Scanning the throng of people, Varun realizes that Sweety has not arrived yet.

Ranvir Bhatia, a short, plump man with a shock of curling grey hair and fierce eyes, looks dapper in a white jacket and a green silk scarf around his neck. He seems to be on cordial terms with everyone, greeting each guest as though he were meeting a long-lost friend. He has an excellent memory, drops names shamelessly and narrates wicked stories about important people with the wit and drama of a skilled raconteur. He leads Gayatri away to meet some people on the balcony and Varun is left under the gaze of an unknown woman with a dark eager face, a zealous red bindi glowing on her forehead. She holds aloft a full glass of whisky like a trophy she has just won in a strenuous sporting contest. In her stiff white salwar kameez with an orange dupatta, she could have passed for a sturdy party worker of the BJP. She discloses that she is a professor of sociology at Delhi University.

'I just completed a teaching term and am working on my book now,' she informs Varun.

'How fascinating! What about?' Preoccupied with the opening and closing of the front door to the Bhatias' apartment, Varun is only half aware of what she is saying.

'It is about the New India, the new middle class, their hopes, aspirations and struggles. Do you know that by 2025 we will have eighty million middle-class households?'

'Really?'

'Everybody who has written about them so far has harboured the notion that the middle class is one homogenous group but that is like saying Indian food is chicken tikka masala and tandoori roti. There are so many subcategories. You have the old middle and the new middle, the urban middle and the rural middle, the upper middle and lower middle.'

'And the middle middle?'

The woman ignores his comment.

'My book is really about the new urban upper middle class. This is the generation that coped well with scarcity but grapples with affluence. These are the sons and daughters of honest government officers, doctors, civil engineers and bank employees who, thanks to liberalization and globalization, can now afford annual holidays abroad, three televisions and two cars. But they still bargain for free dhaniya and feel guilty about throwing away empty ketchup bottles.' The woman's swift definitive gestures slice the humid air.

'That's interesting. When we first moved to the US, my wife found it difficult to throw away empty ice-cream tubs. She insisted that I use one to keep my socks.'

The woman does not return his smile. 'See!' She nods triumphantly. 'But my main argument, which I put forward in chapter five, is that the middle class is characterized not so much by economic markers as by their moral make-up.'

It is at this moment that Sweety and Amandeep enter

the Bhatias' home. Varun Sarin, who has never seen her wearing a sari before, holds his breath in the shock of recognition. She seems to him like a forest nymph who holds the colours of the sun and the trees within her. She is open, she is hidden, she is the soft rich moss, she is light floating gossamer. He can see her slim pale arms and the flat dark hand of her husband holding her elbow, propelling her into the room. He feels his skin prickle and the back of his neck and ears grow warm. He can see her rake the crowd with her eyes, find him and then ignore him. Her face is a mask.

Varun's companion does not notice his distracted expression. They have been joined by another man, bespectacled and white haired, with an unlined face, wearing a green khadi kurta and frayed jeans.

'They are all sanctimonious SOBs,' the professor declares. 'They bleat about corruption, create such a hullabaloo over the Commonwealth Games scam, berate that Jharkhand fellow about the crores he made over mining rights, march in solidarity with Anna Hazare and pretend to be in favour of the Lokpal bill, but they will not hesitate to bribe a traffic policeman if he catches them speeding.'

'True, true, Shaswati.' The other man nods. 'But it is only because they, we all, are scared. Scared to death but don't know it.'

'Of course. The poor, the very poor, who are beyond such fear, conduct their lives in the open. They shout, quarrel, drink, beat each other, make up the next day. The men have multiple sexual partners, the women don't hesitate either. Incest is quite common.'

Shaswati speaks with the confidence of someone who is privy to the intimate lives of the people she discusses.

'Have you done any research on this?' asks Varun.

'Arrey baba, it is common knowledge. The rich do the same but with less noise and more style. All sorts of things go on inside those palatial mansions though they are discreet. It is the middle class, as you say, Tapan, who are scared.'

'Scared of what?

The woman's large intelligent eyes bore into Varun, her glare is merciless. 'Of everything. Of life. I have collected some very interesting case studies. Look at these people around you.' She waves a whisky glass at the crowd. 'The women are repressed, the men are trapped. They are all lusting after each other's wives but they pretend to be decent domesticated souls. The well-dressed ladies are seething with dissatisfaction and suffer from low self-esteem but they don't have the guts to have a nice little fling that will sort them out.'

The anticipation, the light-heartedness that Varun experienced a few minutes ago has given way to something else.

Tapan laughs indulgently. 'Really, Shaswati. You have shocked our friend.'

Shaswati does not seem regretful. She wanted to incite, to provoke, and Varun Sarin, looking at her, feels a savage need to do the same.

'What about you? Do you seethe with dissatisfaction and suffer from low self-esteem?' he asks.

Shaswati lets out a booming belly laugh. 'I did. I did.' She leans conspiratorially towards him. 'Then I kicked my husband out, after nineteen years of marriage. And I had my nice little fling. Right, Tapan?'

Tapan puts an arm around her shoulder and they look at each other with affection. Varun, excluded from the exchange, moves away to refill his glass and search for Sweety but finds the way to the bar unit blocked by a group of people exclaiming over a recently acquired tattoo on the arm of a well-built man. His wife, whose name, Richa, is carved into the skin of his forearm in the Devnagari script, trails a proprietary finger across the letters and says, 'He is branded now.'

'What if she leaves you or you get tired of her?' asks Varun. 'Will you be able to scrape it off or do you have to chop off your arm?'

They look at him, expecting to see a smile, a wink accompanying the remark but Varun is serious, waiting for a response to his question. The man makes as if to erase the tattoo and says, 'Fuck! They said you could wipe it off.' He smiles uneasily.

'You'd better be nice to me,' says his wife. 'Or I'll chop off your arm.' She chucks her husband under the chin and the crowd around them laugh in relief.

Varun is left with the comforting thought that the woman might pick a fight later that night. Turning around, he bumps into Amandeep, jostling his elbow and causing a minor turbulence in the glass of orange juice he is carrying. Apologies are exchanged, introductions made. The orange juice is on its way to Sweety and Varun accompanies it, urged on by Amandeep. 'You must meet my wife.' He introduces Sweety to Varun with the air of a man showing off a prized possession. They do not shake hands. Sweety tilts her head gravely and acknowledges his existence. Her bare arm is two inches from his, the little hollow at the base of her neck, the hollow with the mole that he had kissed a few days ago, is seven inches away; if he reached out, he might touch the arc of her waist. When they speak, their breath mingles. Varun focuses the conversation on Amandeep, discovering a common interest in golf. Vague plans are made to tee off together at the Golf Club. Amandeep, jovial after his second whisky, is full of funny stories, the newest one being about finding a fellow Sardar selling pashmina shawls at a market fair in a little village in Switzerland. Varun laughs with the others. Amandeep seems to wear a glowing halo, his ignorance makes him noble, his friendliness makes him gracious, and his obvious desire to please and entertain gives him the stature of a philanthropist.

Later, Varun finds a minute alone with Sweety.

'So, now we know each other officially,' she whispers, attempting a slight smile.

'There is nothing official about the way I feel. You look very beautiful . . . quite sumptuous.'

'For you,' she says softly.

'Thank you. I wish I could take you away from here this minute and make—'

'Shh!' She cuts him off and asks, 'Where is your wife? We haven't met.'

'I don't know. I last saw her on the balcony.'

'Should we go there?'

'No.'

'Okay. I'd better go. Nice to meet you, Varun.' She looks mischievous, suppresses a smile and prepares to move on.

'My pleasure, Sweety.'

Their eyes meet and for a second they hold each other's gaze, blurring everything else around them. This is the culmination of the evening for Sweety, a sudden heady awareness of her own power, a successful transmission of her feelings and its reciprocation. She has offered her beauty, her youth, the supple fullness of her body and he has accepted with gratitude and good grace. It is almost as though they made love.

Later, as they walk back to their apartment, Varun is distracted and does not notice that Gayatri is in a talkative mood.

'For a change I actually had a good time. Thank god I wasn't stuck with those boring women who only talk about maids and kids. I think one of the bankers I met was trying to poach me. He took my email and said that someone from HR would get in touch with me. First Global is a pretty decent bank and the position, head of corporate banking, is quite interesting but I am not sure I want a change now. It has hardly been two years with GD. But Rajiv is getting on my nerves and Jai is going to move in a year or two, so I was wondering.'

'Hmm . . .'

'I have never worked in a bank before. Corporate finance is really what I am good at but the position involves some business development work as well. I am not sure if I will be comfortable with that.'

'Hmm . . .'

'Maybe I should quit working and become a stripper.'

'Hmm . . .'

'Varun, you're not listening, are you?'

'Sorry. I, I just . . . you were saying?'

'Nothing.'

'About banking . . . something . . . er . . .'

'Never mind.'

'Oh, come now, please tell me.'

'Never mind, I said. It's nothing of any importance to you.'

They walk the rest of the way in silence.

19

THE SARIN HOUSEHOLD was in a flutter. Jhumpa, the cook and housekeeper, was missing. Jagdish, the driver, had not reported for work. Bulbul, the maid, raucous and excitable when the news reached her, ruefully admitted that she didn't know their whereabouts. Bulbul and Jhumpa had never been on good terms but they did share a definite interest in each other's welfare: sickness or absence of one meant that the other had to complete the pending chores. Gayatri had been forced to take the day off. Varun had called for a taxi to take him to the airport. He was going to Mumbai for a two-day conference. That left Gayatri to handle the investigations with the security guard.

Investigations revealed that Jhumpa had not been suddenly spirited away. She had packed her bag; her good saris and toiletries were missing. There was no sign of a struggle, and nobody had heard anything unusual. The maid's room had a separate entrance and she had been free to leave without any disturbance to the household. The security guards at the gate claimed not to have seen her.

The security supervisor called on Gayatri. He was a tall, hefty man named Bhim Singh Rathore, who sported a luxuriant moustache that flowed across his face, bifurcating each cheek into two distinct banks. He used to be with the police force and it was rumoured that he had been dismissed for refusing to beat up innocent people from the nearby villages who were routinely rounded up by the cops on trumped-up charges. His enemies, though, claimed that he had been fired for taking bribes from roadside hawkers in return for letting them ply their business illegally on the pavements. At Trafalgar Towers, it was Bhim Singh

Rathore who supervised the safety and well-being of the residents. He took his role as investigator seriously, relishing the idea of some 'police work' instead of merely chasing monkeys and stray dogs from the premises. He was familiar with the world of the returned NRI and expats. Some of them enquired about minimum wages and then paid exorbitant amounts to their domestic help. Once, one of them had complained that another resident had spoken rudely to his maid. They often did not lock up their valuables, forgetting that there were other people in the house. He found their naiveté absurd, often annoying, sometimes touching.

He commenced his enquiry.

'Madam, how long has she been working for you?'

'About a year. Ever since we moved here.'

'Do you have any reference for her?'

'Someone in my husband's office gave me the number for an agency in Delhi. Some agent got her here. Jhumpa had the reference of a lady in Defence Colony where she used to work as a cook.'

Gayatri didn't trust people easily and was meticulous about reference checks for the employees she hired at work. But there had been something helpless about Jhumpa, a secret sorrow that she held back, a defeated stoop to her shoulders that had stirred Gayatri. She had hired her without bothering to enquire too deeply into her background.

'Was she married?'

'She mentioned once that her husband was an alcoholic. He used to beat her up. I think he left her. That is why she came to Delhi looking for a job.'

'Haan, it's the same old story. Does she have any family here?'

'I don't think so.'

'Where is her native place?'

'I don't know. Somewhere in West Bengal, I think.'

'What about her family there?'

'I think she has a child.'

Sometimes Gayatri would come upon Jhumpa gazing blankly into the distance as she stood in the kitchen balcony, seemingly lost in another world. Once she had asked her, 'What's the matter?'

'It is five years since I last saw my only son,' Jhumpa had replied, bursting into tears, and Gayatri had not known how to comfort her. She had left her alone after that, not wanting to take responsibility for troubles for which there could be no satisfactory solution.

'Uska health kaisa tha? Any problems? Mental or . . .

'I don't think so. She seemed okay.'

Jhumpa had often complained about a pain in the stomach, dizzying headaches, a buzzing in the ear and heaviness in the chest. After fretting about these initially, Gayatri had realized that they were only attention-seeking devices taken care of by a kind word and some placebos in the form of 'iron tonics' and vitamin supplements.

'What did she do with her money?'

'I don't know.'

'Did she get any phone calls?'

'No. I don't know.'

'Did she have any visitors . . . male visitors?'

'No . . . not that I know.'

'Is anything missing from your house? Has she stolen anything?'

'I don't think so. I don't keep anything very valuable in the house.'

'Did you shout at her? Hit her or . . .'

'No! Of course not.'

'Madam, kuchh toh hoga. You don't seem to know much about her. A grown woman cannot disappear just like that.'

Bhim Singh Rathore was getting frustrated, Gayatri annoyed. She found his attitude condescending. She wanted to assure him that just as Jhumpa's underprivileged status did not entail a proclivity for stealing, her own economic superiority did not make her cruel or unfeeling.

'What about your driver, madam? Have you checked with him? He might know something,' Bhim Singh Rathore persevered.

'He hasn't come today. His mobile phone is switched off.'

'A-ha! Where does he live?'

'I am not sure. Chakarpur or Chhatarpur.'

'And his family?'

'I think they are in the village, somewhere in the hills. He is married. Has two or three children.'

'Kya un dono ka koi chakkar tha, madam?' Bhim Singh's voice dropped a notch and he did not meet her eyes.

'What do you mean?'

'Was there anything between the maid and your driver?'

'Of course not! Jhumpa was not like that.'

'Madam, you do not know these people. One of the drivers in Exotica ran away with a girl only two weeks ago. She was going to become the mother of his child. I am sure your maid has also run away with the driver. Aisa hota hai, madam.'

'I don't think that would have happened. Rathoreji, we should call the police.'

'Madam, what will the police do in this case? They are not children. You wait for a day or two. If they don't come back, we will see what to do then.' His tone implied that he was the police, the guardian of law and order, the last word in the matter of security for Trafalgar Towers.

After the security supervisor had left, after she had prepared a meal and cleaned the kitchen, Gayatri allowed herself to think about them – Jhumpa and Jagdish. She knew very little about Jagdish. She could barely recall his face, mostly she only saw the back of his head, and their communication was limited to a few words. His driving skills were adequate, he was regular and respectful. That was all that mattered. She could not imagine that this innocuous man was party to an adulterous relationship; it seemed improbable that there was anything between them. Gayatri tried to recall any signs of a growing attachment between him and Jhumpa. Something told her that she had been voluntarily blind, both to the possibility and the actual events. Had they seen each other when he came home to collect the car keys? What happened when she sent Jhumpa to the market in the car to pick up groceries? Did he sneak back home from the office to be with her when they were out? Did they lie together on her bed? She recalled the way Jhumpa had smiled at her reflection in the mirror that hung above their sideboard. She remembered now that Jhumpa had volunteered to pick up vegetables from the market, she even hummed as she stirred the spices over the kitchen stove.

By the end of the day, that Jhumpa and Jagdish could be together was a possibility Gayatri could no longer ignore. She mentioned this to Varun when they spoke over the phone but couldn't elicit a satisfactory response from him. In her mind, surprise had given way to a sense of betrayal. She had treated Jhumpa with kindness, with far more consideration than most people would have for a servant. Varun even thanked her for bringing him a glass of water. And they did not make her stay up late to serve at parties like so many others did. Yet this was how her generosity had been repaid. She should have kept them in their place, like those other ladies did, the smart ones who knew when to be lenient and when to command. They seemed to have inbuilt radar systems that indicated when the help were stepping out of line. Loyalty was a rare quality and generosity needed to be measured too, Gayatri realized. It was all about maintaining the delicate balance between supply and demand. And sometimes, in this process, the lines between the exploiter and the exploited blurred. Gayatri felt as if a crime had been committed on her watch and she was the one being punished.

20

ON THE MORNING flight from Mumbai, Varun Sarin lingers in the hazy place between sleep and wakefulness, drifting from dream to reality without recognizing the distinction between the two states. Once, when he opens his eyes, he sees Sweety bending down to adjust his seat belt. Her breasts smell of lemon, faint lavender and something else he knows but cannot name. He reaches out for her and, a few minutes later, is left with the appalling idea that he might have misbehaved with an airhostess. He has been miserable these past two nights, alone in a hotel room. Even after speaking to her late into the night, he missed Sweety. He imagined her next to him on the crisp white hotel bed. The empty space stung like a slap on the face and the harsh stab of physical desire mutated into a dull pain through the night. He did what he could to assuage the need but ended up feeling even more ill-used and dissatisfied.

In the enclosed space of the aircraft, hemmed in by strangers, far away from the solidity of earth, Varun is safely cocooned with his random thoughts. He imagines that he has been cracked open but he cannot recognize the naked unformed shape that emerges from the debris. He has never thought himself capable of great love or unbridled lust. He cannot comprehend the man he has become, one who combines the cool plotting and planning that their relationship entails with the reckless heat and passion of their encounters. He cannot reconcile the image of a duplicitous man cheating on his spouse with few misgivings with one who can be so vulnerably in the thrall of another woman. Through his own confusion, he feels a great surge of compassion for his fellowmen. Behind their placid façade, he detects the chaotic dance of their private lives. It comes to him almost as a revelation that we all believe our experiences to be unique and yet expect the understanding of them to be universal.

He looks at the inoffensive faces and bodies of the men and women around him. How many of them live with the absence of love in their lives, how many are reconciled to it, how many still search for it and how many have found it? The man sitting beside him snores loudly, his paunch heaving and spilling out of the seat belt. He notices the man's innocent, open-mouthed stupor, the hairy chest visible between the buttons on his crumpled shirt, his broad oily forehead, and wonders if he has a woman waiting for him. He represses the urge to wake up the man and question him about the nature of his life.

If the plane were to suddenly plunge into a free fall, what would they do? Would this man be a hero? Would he, Varun Sarin, find a reservoir of courage within himself? Would he try and save the women and children or would he attempt to preserve himself first? What would he do if he were attacked on a dark street by a knife-wielding stranger? Would he fight or crumple under the attack? He remembers a photo he once saw, on the Internet or in a magazine, of a man who was being set upon by a mob, probably during the riots in Ahmedabad. He can still recall the anguished face, the eyes red with tears and fear as he pleaded with the mob to spare him. He wonders what happened to the man.

Varun knows that he has not yet been tested. In the stories that his grandmother told him, stories mostly from Hindu mythology and history, people were always being subjected to tests by whimsical gods. Harishchandra, Nala and Damayanti, Shibi who offered his flesh to feed a hungry eagle, they all were put through harsh, painful examinations. They all emerged unscathed, met adversity with courage and fortitude. They were not tempted by evil, they endured, they rose to the challenge and were rewarded with immortality, a place in heaven and history. He has never been in situations that called for greatness, for supreme sacrifice, for soul-wrenching choices. He has made tough decisions, he has faced challenges which in retrospect seem trivial but he has never been confronted with the reality of himself. He wonders if what he is going through is a test and what account he is giving of himself. His character is just beginning to form, all that he has been through was only a rehearsal, a preparation for what is about to unfold. At forty-four, he is beginning to realize that what he does not know about himself, about life, is much more than what he thought he knew. He is lost in a maze of questions and there are few definite answers to be found.

The plane lurches through an air pocket, the turbulence stronger than usual, and Varun hears his fellow passengers' sharp collective intake of breath. There does not seem to be any real danger but these are moments when people are reminded that they are suspended in a steel box thousands of miles above land and are at the mercy of both nature and technology. Varun is not contemplating immediate death but he is reminded again of the fragility of life, the transient nature of all human attachments. He decides that he must meet Sweety as soon as he reaches Trafalgar Towers.

He calls her from the taxi soon after leaving the airport.

'Please come now. I have to see you.'

'Where? You know I can't.'

'Just come to the lobby to buy something from the shop.'

He is thankful that Gurgaon is only a short distance away from Delhi airport. He is delighted to see her on the porch when he alights from his car. She seems to be tapping a message on her mobile phone. She is dressed in a blue and white salwar kameez, her hair has just been washed and the damp tendrils curl around her neck. She wears silver earrings, long dangling ones that kiss her collarbone. Her face is free of make-up except for a line of kohl and a glimmer of lip gloss. To his eyes she looks lovelier than ever. He has not been this close to her for a long time and he is immediately aroused.

She holds a loaf of bread and smiles.

'I had to pick up some bread urgently.'

'Yes. One can't ignore these urgent needs.'

'I have been pretending to send messages on my phone for five minutes now. The security guard probably thinks I am crazy.'

'No, I am crazy.'

He is immensely pleased that she is in a good mood and thankful that they are alone. As they get into the elevator, he presses the button for the twentieth floor. Every time they are together, he is only dimly aware of the colours and shapes of the world around him. 'I live on the seventeenth,' she whispers.

'I know. I can't let you go so soon.'

'It's only three more floors.'

'Every floor matters.'

After a few seconds of silence, they look at each other and she mouths, 'I love you.' This is the first time she has said it and it brings her great relief. She feels dazzled, wooed and won over. It has taken only this small gesture of prolonging a ride in the elevator to make her feel loved in the way she has always wanted to be, foolishly, unreasonably and recklessly.

He reaches across and strokes her face. Her eyes are moist. She presses his hand to her cheek.

They have passed the twentieth floor and are on the way down, somewhere between the tenth and seventh floors.

'Come and be with me,' he invites her.

'No. I can't.'

'It's all right. There's no one at home. We'll never get another chance like this.' Varun knows that Jhumpa has not returned, and the movements of the other members of the family are accounted for.

She hesitates.

'Please. I don't know when we can be together again.'

The house is dark and quiet when they enter. She feels like an intruder and though she does not want to, she finds herself taking in the details of his life. He quickly leads her to the guest bedroom, which is clean, anonymous without any signs of recent occupancy. They make love quickly, greedily, with the confidence that requited love brings. She is bolder, awakened to her own pleasure, leading him to the secret places on her body, finding his. They look into each other's eyes as they move together, discovering their own special rhythm and pace, each knowing what the other wants. The act of love seems imbued with a new intimacy.

It seems to Varun that after a peripatetic childhood, after a youth spent mostly in hostels and adult years wasted as a rootless immigrant in a foreign land, he has finally come home. Home is not a place so much as a feeling, the feeling he has found in the company of this woman, a feeling of rightness and peace, a liberation from the roles that all other relationships demand: as husband, father, son, brother, boss. With her, he lives in the moment. The present is all he really has, he is completely himself and is loved for being just who he is.

'This is even better than before,' Sweety confesses. Her head is on his chest and she feels their breathing slowing, settling down. This can happen to me, she thinks. This thing is real. Love exists. It tastes like cotton candy that melts the moment it touches your tongue.

'Thank you, ma'am. We aim to please.'

'I feel different with you. Normally, I am not like this.'

'Like what?'

'You know . . . I don't do much.' She feels shy and hides her face against his neck. He strokes her hair.

'I feel different with you too. I want to do much more. But you, you are a tigress, a magnificent tigress.'

She giggles and absently traces a heart on his chest. 'I like this part.'

'I like this part, and this part and this.' His hands scan her body.

'I didn't mean that. I meant . . . you know . . . I mean . . . we can laugh together afterwards and be happy, talk a bit. That part, the not doing anything part.'

'I know what you mean. I like this part too, but the not doing anything part is not going to last very long.' He kisses her gently and knows that he wants to make love to her again.

The doorbell rings, a sudden shrill squeal that splinters the silence. Sweety freezes. Then panics, pulling her clothes together, trying to pull herself together.

'Oh God . . . Is it your wife? I can't believe it. What will happen now? This is so stupid.'

'Shh.' He holds her tight. 'It's all right. The door is locked. No one can come in.'

The moment is lost. The doorbell does not ring again but she can't stay. She will not listen to anything he says. She has to go. He lets her out after making sure that there is no one around. She leaves without looking back. He goes back to the guest room and looks at the bed, inhales her smell that still lingers on the crumpled sheets and removes three long brown strands of her hair from the pillow. He wishes he could preserve the strands: holding them in his hands gives him a strange sense of satisfaction, a feeling that he has something of hers. When he opens the window and lets them float away, he knows that he has lost something precious. He reaches down to tuck in the edge of the bedcover and finds a loaf of bread beside the bed. The incongruous yellow and orange packet with the thin brown slices is the only sign that she has been here. He takes it to the kitchen and makes a cheese sandwich for himself. He can still taste her skin. He feels a little guilty, guilty that he might have defiled her, bruised her goodness. The pure shining thing that she carries within her might have been tarnished by his rough attentions. He wants to tell her that he is not sorry for what he has done, only sad, sad that it has to be this way. When he calls Sweety a few minutes later, she does not answer the phone. He leaves for work knowing that he will be unable to concentrate on anything else for the rest of the day.

21

BROUGHT UP-TO-DATE WITH the saga of the missing domestic help a few hours later, Varun was less concerned than Gayatri had expected him to be. The possibility that Jhumpa and Jagdish had run away together stirred in him a mild astonishment and he found himself acknowledging a pang of envy at their rash, ill-advised act that could only lead to certain unhappiness. But he could not comprehend the extent of Gayatri's agitation. She on her part was annoyed by what she saw as typical male indifference to matters of domestic importance. He offered to cook dinner and drive her to work till they found replacements but she wanted some other form of comfort that he was unable to provide.

Four evenings after the disappearance, in the brief span of time between dinner and sleep, Varun and Gayatri sat stiffly in bed, trying to watch something on television. Varun thought of Sweety, finding it difficult to believe that he had made love to her in the adjoining room barely twenty-four hours earlier. He had sensed her confusion and felt guilty for complicating her life. Yet, he could no more prevent himself from reaching for her than he could stop himself from breathing. Like the ticker tape that ran across the bottom of the TV screen, she seemed to permeate his thoughts constantly.

His wife's furrowed brow, Varun knew, foreshadowed the dialogue that she was about to initiate. He felt nothing but a slight annoyance. The scraping of her leg against his might have been the cold touch of the sheets, the shape of her body and face evoked no response. He was curiously detached.

'I can't imagine how Jhumpa could do this. After all I have done for her. It's so irresponsible. And Jagdish? He has a family in the village. How could he be so fucking idiotic!'

Varun didn't know what to say. He chose his words carefully. 'We don't yet know that they are together. We shouldn't jump to conclusions prematurely.'

'Of course they are together. What else can it be? That security supervisor, Bhim Singh, came yesterday and said that one of the guards had seen her with Jagdish in our car a few times in the last two weeks. I didn't send her on any errands during the day. This is disgusting.'

'Gayatri, they both are consenting adults. Just because they come from a different social class, it doesn't make this a crime. There is nothing we can do, or should do, about it. I agree they shouldn't have left suddenly without notice. But people in love do stupid, unreasonable things.'

'In love! Varun, you are so naïve. You make them sound like some tragic romantic couple in a Bollywood movie. I can't believe Jagdish is capable of this. I thought he was a quiet, decent fellow. But not only does he cheat on his poor wife, who is busy looking after his kids in the village, he has probably dumped Jhumpa somewhere after screwing her.'

'But—'

'It has nothing to do with social class. I have nothing against them and I am the last person to be prejudiced. Men like him, irrespective of education or background, have no sense of responsibility, no morals, no self-control.'

Varun felt helpless against Gayatri's implacable rage. He recognized some truth in what she was saying but was unable to fathom his own feelings on the matter. He was a little abashed, the words 'men like him' touched a raw nerve. He could not summon the righteous outrage she demanded.

He ventured, 'These things happen' and immediately realized how banal he sounded. He envied Gayatri's ability to see things in black and white, the way in which she cut through information and arrived at decisions quickly, without qualms. Though he could be rational and decisive at work, he found himself increasingly ambiguous in his approach to people, seeing things in shades of grey.

'I will ask someone from my office to get us a good driver soon. Maybe you can ask around for another cook.' This was the best he could offer as a solution.

'Fine.' Gayatri turned her back to him and switched off the bedside lamp beside her. It was a signal that he should do the same.

Jhumpa and Jagdish returned the next morning. When Varun opened the door, he saw them standing together.

Jhumpa seemed to have acquired a new confidence over the last few days, her posture was straight, her features had softened. With a bright-red streak of vermillion in the parting of her hair and a line of kohl under her eyes, she looked almost pretty. When Gayatri came up behind him, they fell at their feet in the manner of newly-weds seeking blessings from their parents.

Gayatri struggled for words. Her knowledge of Hindi was limited, adequate for routine household instructions but not equal to the task of berating Jhumpa for betrayal, for bringing shame and dishonour upon herself, or for scolding Jagdish. She was stunned at their audacity and could only think of banishing them forever from the building, from her life.

'What happened?' asked Varun evenly.

Jagdish looked sheepish. He refused to meet Varun's eyes and shuffled his feet awkwardly. Varun sensed embarrassment rather than shame or regret. Jagdish was a thin, gangly man of medium height. He had a nondescript face with a thin moustache, thinning hair and beady black eyes. He was completely unremarkable, the kind of man who blended into the background and was unlikely to distinguish himself in any way. To carry out his job with some degree of efficiency and provide for his family, to live without a fuss, to die peacefully, this would have been his measure of success.

'We have got married,' declared Jhumpa. She pulled at a black, beaded chain around her neck as proof of her marital status.

'Married! Tum paagal ho? You both are already married. Jhumpa, how could you do this?' Gayatri found her voice finally.

'That does not matter.' Jhumpa seemed to speak for them both. 'My husband left me long ago and will never come back.' She indicated her new husband. 'He will continue to work and provide for his family in the village. He can still visit them once a year. Anyway, they only want his money.'

Varun couldn't help marvelling at how quickly Jhumpa had carved out a new life for herself. Looking at her face, alight with hope but also a quiet determination, he knew that this was not a woman in the throes of wild passion. This was a beaten, broken woman who had been given a second chance in life and was holding on to it grimly with all her strength and ingenuity. He had never really noticed her before. Her presence had been a blur, but now she stood before him as a person with needs, desires and dreams of her own.

'What are you both going to do?' he asked.

'We didn't want to go off like that suddenly but we didn't have a choice. I didn't know if you would let us get married but now that it's over, we want your blessings. You are good people and we would like to continue to work for you.' They stood with folded hands and bowed heads like prisoners awaiting a sentence.

'This is so weird, Varun. I can't believe we are standing here listening to this nonsense. They've behaved irresponsibly and immorally and now they want us to take them back into employment and carry on as though nothing has happened. Just send them packing. I don't want to have anything more to do with them. I can manage.' Gayatri turned away from the door, leaving Varun to do the needful.

Varun remembered something a woman had said to him at a party, something about the poor not being scared. Jagdish's life would no longer be unremarkable, he found himself thinking. He was now a man with two wives, a man who had found love or something like it, a man who was prepared to stand by a woman he had made promises to.

It was Jagdish who spoke. He had it all planned – he was a new man altogether, one who could cut his way through complications and simplify his life. He wanted to move into the servant's quarter that Jhumpa occupied. He currently shared a room with two other men and could not take Jhumpa there immediately. They would stay together and the saheb could adjust their salaries in lieu of rent.

'No way,' shouted Gayatri from the living room. 'There is absolutely no way they are staying here. Are you out of your mind, Varun?'

It was the logical thing to do. Varun did not see any reason why they should not stay together. They were married in a fashion; he appreciated the need for proximity. He also knew this would be unacceptable to Gayatri. He would never hear the end of it if he agreed.

'Jhumpa can stay here for a few days. You need to find a place for her soon. And while you both are working here, you need to behave as you did earlier.'

Gayatri had distanced herself from the proceedings. She did not want to be drawn into a battle with her husband. She knew that he had made up his mind, that he was giving her a way out, a way to save face. She left the room in a huff.

They both fell at his feet. Jhumpa was crying. Varun Sarin felt like a king who had just granted a royal pardon. He had been given the gift of mercy and had used it generously. He wanted to tell Sweety what he had done, he wanted her to approve. She would understand his impulse. He had tried her number intermittently over the past few days without success. When he called her again, the response was the same: 'The number you have dialled is not reachable.'

22

SWEETY SINGH WAS at a kitty party lunch with her friends at the Palms Country Club. What she really wanted to do was to run away to another place. She had been thinking about this for the past few days, ever since that morning at Varun's house. She wanted to go to a desert, a mountain top, an island where there were no people, no phones, no elevators. A place where she could be by herself, where she could sit gazing at nothing for hours. There were times when she wondered if her treachery had been found out. In the greeting of the lift attendant, the sly smile of the security guard, the questioning look of her maid, the searching gaze that her husband directed at her, she detected suspicion. The sly smile became a knowing look, the searching gaze an accusatory glance and her own reflection in the mirror a mocking parody of her feelings.

She wasn't paying attention to her meal, or to the conversation around her. Her mind lingered on the dreams she had been having, strange dreams she couldn't recall except as a tangle of unexpected people in unfamiliar places. Once, she had woken up feeling that she had spent the night in Varun's arms. They had made frenetic love on the grass under a sky littered with stars. There was a red tent pitched nearby and it felt as though they were the only two people in the universe. So vivid was the dream, so real was the touch of his fingers inside her that she didn't recognize her immediate surroundings when she woke up. The sight of Amandeep sleeping next to her seemed unreal, bizarre. Another time, she experienced the horror of seeing Sanya-Manya being swept away in a torrential river. 'Mamma, Mamma, save us,' they screamed but her feet were rooted to the bank. Before she could plunge into the water, they had vanished into the whirlpool.

Sweety wanted to confess. She longed for a friend who would listen to her without judging her and offer some kind of solace. She looked across at the women she was with, mostly housewives like her, with children. Ragini, Roma and Garima were a part of the group, as was Juhi Bhatia. Ragini, who knew almost everyone in Trafalgar

Towers, had co-opted three other women into the group. There were cliques within, invisible lines of connection and rules of inclusion and exclusion that Sweety was not party to. She had been invited by Juhi to be a part of the group two months ago. The relationships among the women seemed cordial on the surface, their concerns were usually innocuous, their gossip more frivolous than damaging. Sweety knew that most of them had an unshakeable faith in their own beliefs, and were reluctant to accept a differing viewpoint.

The women were discussing another neighbour, a lady called Anamika whom Sweety did not know.

'Guess who I bumped into today?' Ragini offered, breathless with excitement. She paused for dramatic effect and continued, 'Anamika. You will never believe where I saw her.'

'At Emporio or Khan Market?' asked Roma. 'She claims that she only shops at those places. The Gurgaon malls are not up to her standard.'

'No, dear. I saw her at Vyapar Kendra,' Ragini revealed with the flourish of a magician unveiling a pair of turtle doves from a hat.

There was a sharp intake of breath and a collective sigh of disbelief.

'She tried to hide behind a pillar but I went up to her and said hi.'

'Oh my god! She must have died of shock,' said Garima. 'I wish I could have seen her face.'

'She claimed that she was there to pick up a suit for her maid but then the tailor came to her with a packet and said, "Madam, aapka blouse mil gaya."'

'What a fraud!' said Juhi. 'She always pretends to get only designer blouses from Delhi.'

'Haan. It is a designer blouse by Ramu Darzi,' Ragini smirked.

'Nahin, you must call him Ram Darziani, designer ladies' tailor,' added Roma with a faux accent.

They laughed loudly, and even Sweety was jolted into joining the amiable dissection of the unfortunate Anamika.

The topic then veered to extramarital affairs. A portly lady called Vimmi spoke of one of her college friends, a woman called Deepa, who had an affair with a married man. Deepa's husband found out about it and she was forced to move out of her house and leave her two children with her husband and in-laws. Her lover did not want to leave his wife, so Deepa was left alone. Her parents refused to support her and cut off all relations with her. The women discussed the absent Deepa as though they had access to her innermost thoughts and motivations. Vimmi, who had been initially sympathetic to Deepa's situation, was quickly convinced otherwise by the others. Between the main course and the dessert, they dismissed Deepa as a slut, an idiot, a nymphomaniac, a woman who deserved what she had got. The ladies happily chewed on the last few pieces of New York cheesecake, but Sweety had lost her appetite. These seven women with whom she had shared some sort of camaraderie, forged over shopping expeditions and lunches at fashionable restaurants, suddenly seemed alien to her. She wondered if they detected any sign of moral deviance in her, whether the conversation had been directed at her as a subtle warning.

Sweety wallowed in her own misery for a while before forcing herself to snap out of it. She reminded herself that she was privileged to have so much in a country where thousands of people lived without food, shelter or clothing. Love was a luxury many could ill afford in the daily struggle for survival. She thought of all the unfortunate women in the world, those who had been molested, raped, abused, stoned, whipped, forced into prostitution or slavery or subjected to daily humiliation in cruel marriages. She was truly blessed. Yet her joy was sullied. She knew that this affair, for she now acknowledged it with the word the world would have used for it, could not have the usual climax of union or heartbreak. Heartbreak was what she lived with every day. She asked herself why something like this should have happened to her. Did Varun have an answer, she wondered, maybe if she could track the root cause of this mystery, she would have found a solution.

As she left the lunch her mind was a mess, but externally she was even more the servile wife and dutiful mother. She would also have to be the accomplished daughter-in-law: Amandeep's family was coming for dinner the next day. This was the first time she would be entertaining them all in her house. She knew that it was not just a dinner; it was a competition, a game in which points could be earned or lost. Amandeep had been co-opted on her side: it was just as important for him to show that he had made the right decision in marrying her, in moving away from the family home. The recent appreciation of the dollar against the rupee had been beneficial to him. Export orders had increased and he was thinking of diversifying into handicrafts, apart from garments. He had given Sweety a generous allowance for the dinner and had replenished the bar with imported whisky.

Sweety had spent two days scouring the malls for appropriate gifts for her in-laws. She knew that she would be the recipient of housewarming presents from them and the return gifts had to surpass those received in terms of price, appropriateness and novelty. She had planned an elaborate menu with three non-vegetarian dishes, apart from the usual dal makhni, paneer and aloo gobi. She would also bake a chocolate cake. Sanya-Manya had been tutored to sing a couple of songs, one each in Hindi and English, that they had learnt in school. The cleaning maid had been paid extra to scrub the fans and the windowpanes and the furniture had been augmented with the addition of a drinks trolley. These distractions had served to take her mind off her own lovelorn state. One part of her marvelled at her ability to dissemble, to bargain at the meat shop and critically appraise the quality of a Noritake dinner set that she planned to purchase while thinking at the same time about the possibility of speaking to Varun without any interruptions.

The dinner was a success. Amandeep's brothers got pleasantly drunk on the Scotch, the sisters-in-law praised Sweety's interior decoration skills and the children polished off the chocolate cake. Her father-in-law remarked positively on the tenderness of the chicken and her mother-in-law asked for a second helping of the roganjosh. Sanya-Manya's songs elicited exclamations of 'so cute', 'so sweet', 'wah beta, shabash'. The return gifts were received with cries of faux surprise and her mother-in-law made the right noises – 'Sweety beta, iski kya zaroorat thi' – as she accepted the small token of a genuine pashmina shawl. When the guests departed at midnight, Sweety felt a glow of achievement and the hearty accumulation of points in her favour. Amandeep was effusive in his praise for her. The alcohol had dulled his senses but sharpened his desire.

When she got into bed, tired but pleased with the way the evening had gone, he roughly removed her clothes and fumbled at her breasts. Sweety had been on her feet the whole day, cooking, cleaning, caring for others. She longed to curl up in a corner of the bed and sleep. Instead, she wrapped her arms around her husband and drew him into her body. She made moaning sounds in her throat and closed her eyes. Under the cover of darkness, she could have been with any man, anywhere in the world.

23

GAYATRI AND JHUMPA were reconciled. To prolong the cold war would have been an acknowledgement of her humiliation by Varun who had, at one stroke, declared himself master of the household. Jhumpa had since then attempted to make herself indispensable to the Sarin household. She appealed to Gayatri's innate sense of justice and her sensibility as a woman who could understand the pain of another woman. She offered to give Gayatri a massage after she returned from work and had a cup of green tea ready for her when she got up in the morning. She had cleaned the baffle filters of the kitchen chimney without being asked and supervised the cleaning maid, Bulbul, with a proprietary air. After a week of curt monosyllabic responses, Gayatri had accepted the fact that Jhumpa and Jagdish greatly eased the daily passage of her life. A visit from Mrs Sarin and her sister-in-law Shweta's family was imminent; she couldn't cope with them on her own. But she had not forgiven Varun for his unilateral decision, for the summary way in which he had overlooked her objections and appropriated all the merits of generosity and forgiveness.

A few days after Jhumpa and Jagdish's dramatic return, Gayatri's mother called. She sounded weak and distraught because of a gastric infection. Though her parents did not ask her to visit, Gayatri decided to take a week off and go to Bangalore. She would combine it with a business trip, a visit to the Goodricke Dickson factory on the outskirts of the city. She would leave Jhumpa and Varun to handle his family in case they decided to visit. The thought of spending some time with her parents while Varun ministered to his mother's needs gave her grim satisfaction. Though it was not a holiday, she welcomed the trip as a respite from her routine. She knew that Varun and Anirudh Sarin, busy in their own worlds, would carry on as usual, the rhythm of their days undisturbed.

A day after his mother had left, Anirudh invited his classmate Nikita Pant over, ostensibly to complete a science project. Nikita, a brittle waiflike creature perpetually flicking her thin brown hair out of her eyes, had told him that she did not want an official boyfriend. Anirudh knew it was not shyness but a fear of commitment that made her insist they should just be friends and hang out together for a while, see how it went. She had gifted him a Green Day CD and a T-shirt for his sixteenth birthday. This was a good sign: clearly she knew his taste in music and his size, and Anirudh was optimistic that they would come to a mutually suitable arrangement soon.

Nikita was already in the apartment when Varun came back from work.

'Baba is in his room with a girl,' Jhumpa informed him. 'They came back from school together. I have given them some Pepsi and biscuits.' She had assumed the mantle of the chief housekeeper and felt compelled to be vigilant in Gayatri's absence.

Varun knocked gently on the door of Anirudh's bedroom. He heard his son's voice call, 'Come in', and was relieved to discover that the door had not been locked.

'Hello, Uncle,' chimed Nikita when she was introduced.

'We have a science project to finish,' said Anirudh.

'Sure. It's almost 7:30. Would you like to stay for dinner, Nikita? You could check with your folks,' Varun said.

There was a brief pause. Anirudh and Nikita glanced at each other and some kind of understanding was reached, for Anirudh nodded his assent.

'Sure. I'll tell my mom. The driver can wait till we finish up.'

At the dinner table, Varun kept up a steady conversation with Nikita. Anirudh, sitting opposite her, seemed content to listen and watch.

'What are you planning to do after school?' Varun asked.

'I am going to study environmental law.' Nikita seemed to have it all planned out. Varun wondered if his son would be as decisive about his future. They had discussed college, taking the SATs and going to the US but Anirudh was still unsure about what he wanted to study.

'I plan to study at the National Law School and specialize in my field later. There is so much work to be done in this area in India. Uncle, can you please pass me the paneer?' She spoke with the air of a habitual guest at the dinner table.

As he watched his son watching the rise and fall of Nikita Pant's nascent breasts, Varun wondered if Anirudh Sarin would get his heart broken soon. He realized that his son liked this girl but he could not fathom her intentions. She seemed more self-assured, confident about her place in the world. After Nikita left and Anirudh got busy trying to look unaffected by her presence or departure, he attempted a man-to-man talk. He wasn't sure what he wanted to convey – maybe a warning, some advice, an invitation to talk, an acknowledgement of their shared state.

'She seems nice.'

'Yeah, she's okay.'

'Girls are different.'

'Yeah!'

'You have to respect them even if you don't understand them.'

'Oh!'

'Be careful.'

'Sure, Dad. I am not stupid.' Anirudh escaped to his room and Varun was left with the feeling that he had not accomplished much. He wished he could be sixteen again, experience the thrill of love without complication or tension. He wanted to capture some of the youthful insouciance, the innate belief that things would turn out well, that life was just starting up. He smiled to himself: Sweety made him feel sixteen. He needed to reconcile himself to the unpredictable nature of their relationship, its crests and troughs, his inability to slot it into any copybook format, their helplessness in the face of what they both now called love.

When he sends her a message later that night – can we talk – she calls him back.

'I am sorry. I haven't been taking your calls.'

'It's all right. I know how you must feel.'

'No, you don't. You seem okay, comfortable with this. I don't know how you can do it, live your life in different compartments. I tried not to call, to forget everything that has happened. I know I shouldn't be calling but I can't stop myself from doing it.'

'It isn't easy but I am not fighting it. We just have to stay with it. So far, I have been mostly happy. Miserable when I can't see you or be with you, but otherwise happy.'

'I had a dream about us.'

'Good one?'

'Yes. We were together on a hill with no one else around.'

'Someday, sweetheart. Someday.'

'Do you think so?'

'Yes. Yes. Do you know what I would like to do?'

'Mmm . . . yes, I think so.'

'That too. I would like to take you to a jazz club in New Orleans, in the French Quarter. Somehow I never went there in all the years I lived in the US. We can have a drink and listen to some amazing music without worrying about anyone else.'

'Can I wear a red dress? I've always wanted to wear a long red dress with red stilettos.'

'Please, please wear a red dress.'

'Can we dance? Close and slow, you know, like in the movies?'

'Yes, we will. Close and slow.'

'It will never happen.'

'Don't say that. It can.'

'I can't even see you when I want to.'

'Let's meet now. My wife is travelling and I guess your husband is too. Maybe just go for a post-dinner walk.'

'We can't. You know that.'

'Yes, yes . . . I know. What will the respectable residents of Trafalgar Towers think?'

'Why, Varun, why? Why did this happen to me? I am not unhappy. I am very attached to my family. Nothing is wrong with my life, you know.'

'Nothing is wrong with my life either. Just because nothing is wrong, doesn't mean everything is right.'

'I don't know. I don't know any more.'

'I love you. That is all you need to know.'

'I know.'

The brief conversation is enough to give Varun the feeling that all is right in the world. When Sweety asks, 'Why, why us?' he is unable to come up with a satisfactory answer. It must be fate, maybe destiny, something he is starting to believe in. He has always been a proponent of free will, he truly believes that there is a decision to be made at every point in time and humans make conscious decisions even though they have an imperfect awareness of their consequences. But when it comes to his own situation, he can't come up with any explanation. He has not thought of consequences, he has not thought beyond the next minute. Love at his age confounds him.

He Googles the words love, attraction, lust and is dazzled by the vast amounts of information on the subject. There are 25,270,000,000 results for love, 270,000,000 snippets on lust. He understands that love, unlike the popular belief that it is a matter of the heart, is the result of chemical reactions in the brain. The effects of increased dopamine and norepinephrine activity, the salubrious result of oxytocin, the emotional reflexes of the limbic brain – these are easier to comprehend than the mystifying question of why he, Varun Sarin, should fall in love with a particular woman called Sweety. Why his body should feel the pull of hers even when she is not present, why their blood should sing to each other when they meet, why something in his soul stirs when he sees her smile. He wants to know and yet he realizes that the primary reason for the attraction between them is its inexplicability, its absolute lack of reason or logic.

It does not reassure Varun that around the world, other people are grappling with the same question. He reads the newspapers with greater attention, trying to glean some insight into the minds of men and women. Every day there are stories of crimes of passion, of a woman and her lover murdering the husband; a doctor, suspecting his wife of infidelity, killing her with an axe and driving all the way to

Allahabad to dump her body in the Ganga; a man throwing acid on the face of a girl who has spurned him. He reads about a middle-aged minister embroiled in a scam on account of questionable dealings on behalf of a mysterious woman, reported to be his girlfriend. Another married politician has left his wife for an attractive lawyer. Both have converted to Islam, given each other new names and new lives, and sworn undying love on 24x7 channels, only to be denounced by the rest of the world. A professor is arrested for molesting a graduate student, a film actor is accused of raping his domestic help, a young graphic designer is murdered for daring to fall in love and marry an industrialist's daughter. Irrespective of age, wealth or power, men are undone by love, lust or a fatal combination of the two. The women suffer, there are few happy endings. The same story is repeated over and over again and no amount of analysis offers any rational explanation.

24

THE WOMEN OF Trafalgar Towers are getting ready to celebrate karva chauth. Most of them will fast through the day until they set eyes on the full moon and then, in the presence of their husband, they will break the fast after making an offering of water to the moon and performing the ritual puja. In the afternoon they will gather on the lawns of Traflagar Towers, shimmering like exotic jewels after hours spent at beauty salons to recapture some of their bridal glory. Their hands will glow with mehendi and their hearts will fill with the pride of being virtuous women. They will admire each other's clothes, complain good-naturedly about the foibles of their men and the gentle tyranny of mothers-in-law. They might even play tambola to pass the time until the men return from work.

Sweety looks forward to karva chauth. On the day of the fast, she receives a fine piece of jewellery from Amandeep, a generous gift from her in-laws, and an opportunity to pamper her body and face for a good cause. It is not compulsory in her Sikh community, but her mother-in-law has been observing the karva chauth fast since her own marriage and it is a ritual enshrined by Amandeep's Hindu grandmother, Beeji. Amandeep's family has their own partition story, which she has heard from his grandmother, a resilient woman who passed away a year ago, at the age of eighty-nine.

The grandmother was born a Hindu in pre-independence Lahore, the only daughter of a wealthy landowner. During the days immediately after the partition, her parents and elder brother had refused to leave their house and lands, believing till the end that the frenzy of Hindu-Muslim riots was temporary and would never reach their own doorstep. Their Sikh neighbours were more pragmatic and made plans to move to India with whatever valuables they could gather. Beeji's parents feared for her safety and sent her along with the Singh family, who treated her like their own daughter. Her family planned to reclaim her once the furore died down. Beeji never saw them again. After living with the Singhs for two years as they moved from a refugee camp to their own home in Delhi, she married their eldest son, Sukhwinder, Amandeep's grandfather. Though she did not formally convert, Beeji adopted all the Sikh customs. She went regularly to the gurudwara, organized paath at home and helped at the langar. The karva chauth fast was a practice she brought to her new family. It was also a thanksgiving ceremony for the gift of her own life, which she owed to her husband and his family.

The story appeals to Sweety. She imagines that the young Beeji, who must have been beautiful, and the dashing Sukhwinder Singh had fallen in love with each other. This is Sweety's first karva chauth away from her in-laws. They plan to visit them in the evening for the feast that follows after sunset but she will spend the afternoon on the lawns of Trafalgar Towers with her neighbours.

Unlike Sweety, Gayatri does not look forward to karva chauth. She has been steadfast in her observation of the fast all through the years of her marriage. As a new bride she was inducted into the practice by her mother-in-law, who was a firm believer. As a good Hindu Punjabi wife, there was no question of not keeping the vrat. It had never been a part of Gayatri's own upbringing; her mother had always been a desultory keeper of fasts since most festivals in the southern part of India are marked by the preparation of special kinds of delicacies, rather than abstinence. In the beginning, Gayatri thought of the fast as a proof of her love, a way to show Varun that she cared deeply about him. She continued to keep the fast every year in the US though the sighting of the moon in October was never as satisfactory. Her mother-in-law was punctilious about calling her to recite the karva chauth story. Gayatri dutifully arranged for a sari to be gifted to her through www.indiangifts.com and received $50 from Varun on behalf of the elder Mrs Sarin. Later, she had come to believe in the detox story she told her American colleagues at work: She fasted because it was good for her health, her body needed a break.

In the last few years, Gayatri had begun to feel a little detached from the ritual. It was something she did because she had to, because she feared that a lapse on her part might coincide with some misfortune befalling Varun and that she would be held accountable. The rational part of her saw no connection between depriving her body of food and the well-being of her husband, but she couldn't argue with a thousand-year-old tradition ingrained in the collective feminine psyche. This year, sensing the growing distance between them, she is all the more determined to observe the fast. She will not have even a sip of water till sunset.

A day before the festival, Sweety calls Varun. 'It is karva chauth tomorrow,' she tells him.

'Ah!'

He knows he has to tread carefully. This is an occasion to reinforce wedding vows, a reminder of the sanctity of the institution of marriage, and he is afraid of any emotions it might trigger in Sweety. He has little faith in most of the rituals of his religion but has learned to respect others' wishes and defer to certain requirements made of him. In the early years of their marriage, he had told Gayatri that he did not care if she didn't keep the fast, he didn't believe in its power and saw no reason for her to starve for his benefit. But Gayatri had been affronted. To her it seemed that he could not appreciate the feeling behind her gesture, that he was ungrateful. Since then, he had participated in the puja's rituals if not its sentiment.

'I am keeping the fast. I always do,' Sweety continues.

'Of course. You must. I mean, you must do whatever you need to.'

'Can I see you in the evening?'

'Are you sure?'

'Yes. I want to see you before I break the fast.'

'I don't want to complicate things. I don't want you to feel bad about this.'

'What is so complicated? I want to pray for the well-being of the people I care about. Who says it has to be for just one person? I want to do this for you also.'

'Okay. I will try to be there.'

'Some of us are planning to come down at about 7 when the moon is up. There is a place on the lawns of Tower 3 where you get a good view.'

'Do you think we should see each other in front of all those people? I am not sure I can go through with it.'

'Sometimes I think it is better if I don't see you. But then I feel miserable because I can't. When I see you I am happy and then, after you leave, I am even more miserable. So silly, na?'

'Welcome to my world, Sweety.'

As the women of Trafalgar Towers wait eagerly for the sighting of the moon, Varun Sarin looks forward to seeing his girl. Karva chauth doesn't seem like such a bad idea after all.

The October air is still warm, with only a hint of the approaching winter. Varun, returning home early, urges Gayatri to join the other couples on the eastern lawns. Gayatri is tired, hungry and a little resentful, but she relents. She quickly changes into a salwar kameez and walks down with the puja tray. There are a few couples on the lawn: the women seem noble, serene, the men abashed. An elderly lady calls out instructions to her daughter-in-law: 'Light the lamp, keep the sieve in front of your face, now, sprinkle the water.' The young girl's hands still bear the mehendi and red bangles of a new bride. She obeys as her husband flutters around with a small camera, capturing yet another image of what it means to be a couple, girdled in wedlock. An elderly lady touches the feet of her husband, younger women giggle nervously and tell their husbands that they will never do it. A couple of them make a token gesture, a

slight bowing and a half-hearted stretch towards the knees
of the man in front of them.

Over the heads of others, half hidden by Amandeep's
back, Varun sees Sweety. She tilts her head just a little and
they look at each other. It reminds Varun of the diagram of
a lunar eclipse from his science book at school: the earth
coming between the sun and the moon, suspended between
two grand arcs. Sweety seems luminous, lit from within,
and Varun can now understand why so many poets and
lyricists have waxed eloquent about the beauty of the moon.
She quickly averts her eyes and bestows a dazzling smile on
her husband, a smile that Varun knows is meant for him.
Two women have fasted for him today, offered prayers for
him and wished him well. The thought is humbling. He
looks around at the beautiful bodies swirling around him
and is grateful for the evening, the moon, the cool breeze.

25

SPECULATION. DREAMING. PLANNING. The pastime of
lovers. As he eats, works, sleeps, plays golf, watches TV,
Varun is starting to wonder about the future. Sometimes
he sees himself with Sweety. An image floats into his mind.
He is with Sweety in a supermarket, they are buying
groceries. They have a gentle argument about the menu for

dinner. He wakes up in the morning and imagines her face beside him, soft with sleep and unshed dreams. When Jhumpa opens the door in the evening, he imagines it is Sweety welcoming him home. She is wearing a loose white kurta, her hair damp after a shower. He holds her against the kitchen wall and kisses her hard. Afterwards, they chop tomatoes together and stir the sauce into a pan of pasta. He now imagines Sweety not in unknown surroundings, discreet hotels or holiday resorts, but in familiar places. He is not content any more with occasional meetings, he wants something that will last longer. A kind of intimacy. He is not unaware of the paradox that it is the forced intimacy of shared beds and bathrooms, the rigours of compulsory cohabitation which marriage entails that he seeks to escape in this relationship. He fails to conjure up an image of the future they may have together but he cannot imagine a future without her presence in some form.

Sweety does not think of the future. Sometimes she is too ridden with guilt and misery to think of anything. She compensates by lavishing attention on her daughters. She visits her in-laws with expensive gifts. She tries to please her husband, fulfilling his smallest demand as a way of compensating for not loving him enough, for not being a devoted wife. She deprives herself of calls and meetings with Varun. When she has performed her penance, her abstinence can be rewarded. When she feels that she has earned the right to treat herself, she plans tactical interventions. They have an understanding that Varun will not call her when her husband is in town; calling him is her prerogative. They function within carefully thought out boundaries. She constantly wonders when they will meet next, how, where. It seems that Varun is content to follow her lead. She knows the patterns of her life best; he will be co-opted into them at her will. She tells him of her daily plan, where he might fit in. He likes that she is demanding of him, of his time, is grateful for the sense of entitlement it signifies on her part. He hopes she will understand if he cannot readily accede to them.

Some days, she calls him with a plan of action.

'We are having our kitty lunch tomorrow at the coffee shop at the new Westin hotel,' she informs him.

Varun shifts the venue of a planned business lunch from his office to the same restaurant. He sits at a little distance from the table of seven giggling women, a table from where he can see Sweety, and he is happy for a while just knowing that they are in the same space together. Juhi Bhatia, who is also in the kitty group, recognizes him and waves. He gets up and approaches their table briefly. As Juhi introduces the group to him, he shakes hands with Sweety and says, 'Of course, we've met. We stay in the same Tower.' In that transient moment, when they look at each other, he knows that what he has been thinking of all morning is true. He really is in love with a girl called Sweety and perhaps she loves him too.

Another time, she calls him over to Galleria shopping complex. 'I have to buy inland letters at the post office. Come there, na.'

'Who are you writing to?'

'My grandmother. She lives in a village near Amritsar and I write to her every fortnight. I make Sanya-Manya write a line or two each or draw a picture. She is almost ninety years old and can't see very clearly. She gets a neighbour to read it out.'

There is something about this that moves him. That she should take the trouble to write on paper in an era of email and texting and post a letter to a lonely old woman several miles away is a sign that he is right, right to love her the way he does.

'Will you write to me?' he asks.

'A letter? Why? We can call or text or even email.'

'I know. I like the idea of a letter, something that has been touched by you, felt by you, that smells of you.'

'If we had met fifty years ago, I might have.' She laughs.

He goes to the Galleria and spots the post office. He stands outside Quill And Canvas, the bookshop next to it, feigning a deep interest in the titles displayed in the window. Just as Sweety comes out of the post office, she is accosted by a lady, another of their neighbours in Trafalgar Towers. He ducks into the shop and starts to browse randomly. He feels like a fool and the opportunity is lost.

On another day, she asks him out for coffee.

'Come to Mega Mall. There is a Barista. Not too many people come there.'

'I wish I could. But you know I am in office. I have meetings lined up for the whole day.'

'Change it, na. What's the point of being the CEO if you can't bunk a meeting?'

'That is the whole point. You can't bunk if you are the one who has called the meeting.'

'Hmm. Your loss.'

'I know. I know. You know I would come if I could manage it.'

There are few opportunities for them to see each other. Varun has contemplated the option of meeting elsewhere. He knows there are people who go away for dirty weekends, who might meet at a friend's vacant apartment or in an anonymous faraway hotel. A rich industrialist he knows always travels with a companion who is not his wife. He also knows that Sweety would never agree; he cannot subject her to the tension of concocting a story or the ignominy of possible discovery in a strange place.

But on certain days, he is desperate to be with her.

'Let's go to Jaipur again,' he says once.

'I can't just take off like that. You do something, na?'

'Like what?'

'I don't know. You are the smart CEO. Mein toh just housewife hoon.'

'A very smart and beautiful housewife.'

'Only you think so. Sometimes I think I should do something, you know. Now Sanya-Manya are in school till 2:30, I have some time.'

'What would you like to do?'

'I don't know. So many women are doing interesting

things these days. Two ladies I know in Tower 3 are artists. They just had an exhibition at the Art Mart in Epicenter. Very nice paintings. Even Ragini from my kitty group is starting a business. She gets suits made from a tailor in Delhi and sells them through exhibitions. Yesterday she said that she is also getting jewellery from Jaipur. You know Roma, your neighbour, she was saying that she is planning to start science tuitions for senior school students. I didn't know she was an MSc in chemistry.'

'What would you like to do?'

'I don't know if I'll be good at anything. I've never worked.'

'I am sure you will be.'

'I want to do something.'

'Good. Think about what you would like to do. I have to let you go now. I have someone coming in.'

'Okay. Bye.'

Sweety has begun to feel that she and Varun have eased into a plateau in their relationship. The thick dust of new love has begun to settle and though her life is neither dull nor boring, she feels the need to do something more. The interior decoration of her house has been completed, she can manage her family's demands, which she realizes can be all-encompassing, her social life is not as exciting as she had expected it to be. She envies Varun his work, Gayatri her financial independence. She fears that she has nothing to sustain her. She needs more than the house, her family and a lover, she needs something that is hers, completely her own.

When it comes to understanding others, Amandeep is blessed with very little imagination and a strong conviction in his own powers of inference. When Sweety tells her husband about her need to do something more, he is surprised, and mildly affronted. It seems that nothing is ever enough for her. She has a good husband, two lovely children, and didn't he readily move out of his parents' house for her sake? What more can she want?

'You have your work, you travel all over the world. I never go anywhere. It's boring.'

'So you want a holiday. Why didn't you say so, Sweety? I have a trip to Bangkok next month. Let's leave Sanya-Manya for three-four days, either with your parents or with Mummy. You'll have a great time in Bangkok.'

'But I don't want a holiday.'

'It has been a long time since we spent some time together. You also need a break from housework. Chalo, this is a very good idea. I will fix up a nice hotel. We can go to Pattaya also.'

'But . . .'

'What? Still not satisfied?'

'Okay. Let's take the children too. It will be a good experience for them and I don't want to trouble Mummyji.'

'Chalo then, this time we'll take them. We'll have a good time. All ladies enjoy Bangkok shopping.'

Sweety knows that she needs to bide her time. She first has to figure out what she wants to do. Then she will start a campaign.

26

GAYATRI SPENT MORE than an hour every night on her laptop in a world which to her was more real than the one she inhabited through the day. She trawled through the status updates on Facebook, dropped occasional comments, checked jokes sent to her on email and chatted with her friends. She had kept in touch with Sheetal and Harini, occasionally corresponded with four other women, who had been part of her life in Fremont. They had supported one another through the struggle to raise children through the constant juggling to manage jobs and families, through the loneliness of being away from their roots. She had been especially close to Harini, Sam's wife. It was Harini who had eased her and Varun into Fremont, providing them with a ready social circle and a list of shops that sold Indian groceries. Harini had been content to be the mother of two children, expert cook, chauffeur, zealous volunteer at the school and stand-in mother for Anirudh when Gayatri needed to travel on work. When Sam and Varun had quit their jobs, they had confided their misgivings to each other while putting on a brave, supportive face for their spouses. It had been more of a shock for Harini, who came from a stock of conventional Tamil Brahmins who looked down on businessmen and preferred the trickle of a steady income to the dubious rash of sudden riches. Luckily they had enough savings and the venture soon yielded results. Harini had stayed back in Fremont with Sam, who took charge of the business development part of their venture, liaising with potential clients and building what he called a robust pipeline. Varun opted to move to India to head the TechKnowlEdge operations as CEO. They still acknowledged each other as best of friends.

When Gayatri came online at 9:30 p.m. IST, Harini had already dispatched her family to their daily routine. They chatted in a private chat room, created a few years ago as part of a project aimed at sensitizing parents to the dangers of unrestricted online activities on the part of their children. The school had encouraged parents to find out what cyber stalking was all about, to understand what to watch out for if they came upon their children having unmonitored chats. In a fit of girlish good humour, Harini and Gayatri had taken on the personalities of two middle-aged white males, Harry and Gary, pot-bellied, beer-guzzling morons who were out for a spot of cyber fun. Later, they had retained their screen names and used the private chat room to gossip about other women and exchange notes on their children and grumble about their spouses. It gave them what Harini called 'cheap thrills'. No one else knew about Harry and Gary.

Gary: Hi, how's it going?

Harry: Good. Sheetal and I had a huge meal at Chat Bhavan yesterday. Missed you. How's V, Rudy? Your parents?

Gary: ☹ I miss you all. Even miss shopping at good old Bharat Bazaar. All well here. Am worried about parents. Amma's arthritis has become worse and Appa might need to have a cataract operation.

Harry: Tough! But you can see them often now. Bangalore is not that far.

Gary: Not that often – maybe twice a year. Difficult to take off from work and they don't want to travel here. May visit soon. Have to take care as only child!

Harry: I know.

Gary: What else?

Harry: Have to tell you something. Am leaving.

Gary: Leaving.

Harry: Moving to L.A.

Gary: What???? Is Sam leaving TecK?

Harry: No. I'm going to L.A. Divya's aunt has an Indian restaurant there. Her husband died a few months ago. She wants someone to help her manage it.

Gary: Divya's aunt has a restaurant in LA?? OMG!! When? Why?

Harry: Megha is going to college. UCLA. Will be closer

there. Ashwin already in MIT, far away. Kids taken care of – so now to take care of me.

Gary: Sam???

Harry: Sam will manage very easily by himself here. Doesn't need me any more.

Gary: Don't tell me you both are splitting up???

Harry: Not the D word – sort of like a separation.

Gary: Why? Did Sam do anything? You know what I mean.

Harry: Don't know. Can't tell. Maybe. Not doing too much with me.

Gary: &@#!!

Harry: After twenty-three years of cooking, cleaning, child rearing and Costco runs, time for Harry to get a life.

Gary: Did Harry meet a Solly ☺

Harry: Bad one! No, not yet. Too old now ☹

Gary: Never too old. Had no idea. Thot you guys were ideal happy couple.

Harry: Ha! Ha! That was you and V.

Gary: Ha! Ha!

Harry: Why? Anything I should know???

Gary: No . . . not doing too much with me either . . . and you know how I feel about this shitty place.

Harry: Come to LA. Will do restaurant business together – you can manage it and I'll do the cooking.

Gary: Wish I could. Rudy has two more years of school. Will tell him to apply to college in CA and then come.

Harry: Am leaving next month.

Gary: So soon? How is Sam taking it?

Harry: Cool. Married to TechK now. Doesn't care.

Gary: Sad . . . but am happy for you.

Harry: Don't think he even knows that I am leaving him. Thinks it is some kind of empty-nest syndrome thing and am going for short break. Will see how it goes.

Gary: Will get used to it.

Harry: Am going to live in small apartment all by myself and eat peanut butter sandwiches for dinner. No more cooking sambhar and rasam. Maybe Sam will start believing that pizzas and sandwiches can be proper meals.

Gary: Good for you ☺

Harry: Hope so. Don't want to come crawling back and do housekeeping for the rest of my life.

Gary: I know. But after such a long time . . . Couldn't you find something to do in Fremont itself?

Harry: No. Will still be stuck if I stay here. Have to go to new place for new life.

Gary: So strange. Can't imagine you and Sam not being together.

Harry: Tried not to rock the boat for a long time but now I need a lifeboat.

Gary: Leaving the sinking marriage boat ☺

Harry: Latest gossip. Surbhi found hubby having affair with blonde secy-type girl in office. Blonde threatened to sue him for sexual harassment. Soooo predictable. Surbhi has gone off to Ahmedabad, leaving him to sort out mess.

Gary: Really!! Surbhi is such a pretty girl. MBA from Berkeley, doing so well with ebay, right?

Harry: All that doesn't matter. Men!!

Gary: Am still in shock. Can't believe about you and Sam.

Harry: Can't believe it myself. Wish me luck. Not told kids yet. Waiting for Megha to settle in college next month.

Gary: You will do really well. Restaurant name?

Harry: Indian Summer ☺

Gary: At least not Taj Mahal.

Harry: Don't tell V anything yet.

Gary: Won't. You take care. Let's skype sometime soon.

Harry: Will do. Take care. Hug Rudy for me.

Gayatri was still in shock after they finished the conversation. It seemed to her that she could no longer believe in the truth or permanence of anything that she saw around her. She had always thought of Harini as a conventional and content housewife, believed that Harini and Sam's marriage was stable, solid as rock, enduring as the ocean. She wondered what else around her was an illusion. Her own life, which she didn't care to examine, seemed like a charade. As she thought about the state of her marriage it seemed to her that all through the past few years, it had been sinking slowly. The mistakes others make are mirrors that show up the glaring faults of our own flawed lives. Yet, in the news of Harini's escape, for that was the word that came to her mind, she saw possibilities. She experienced the first stirring of an idea that there could be another life for her, a life different from the one she reluctantly lived.

27

DURING THE FESTIVE season commencing two weeks before Diwali, Gurgaon resembles a prosperous new bride. The malls and buildings glitter with multicoloured lights, residents string Chinese bulbs on their balconies and these glow on and off in staccato rhythms. Chain stores announce festive offers, sweet shops open extension counters where salesmen briskly pack mithai boxes with kaju katli, burfi and laddoo, small grocery stores stock up on dry fruits and diyas, and cars packed with gift boxes add more colour to the traffic jams. The condominium associations put up Diwali melas where enterprising women sell clothes, jewellery, scented candles and Tupperware dishes. The early winter breeze is cool and crisp as a new five-hundred-rupee note. People spend a lot of money in the shops, lose a lot of money at teen patti, and pray that they may make a lot of money in the coming year. Extravagances are forgiven, excess expected.

The Sarins have decided to entertain at home, a dinner long overdue, intended to reciprocate the invitations of others. They are not habitual hosts of lavish parties. Gayatri prefers informal arrangements where guests pitch in with the clearing up, and where getting together is the main motive, the food and décor incidental. But she has seen that parties in their neighbourhood are more elaborate. The guests comment on the quality and quality of snacks, the origin of the liquor and the variety of the cuisine. They have already attended two taash parties where Varun had played a few hands of teen patti. He is not very fond of the game, but it is a distraction and sometimes he does enjoy the rush of winning a round riding on sheer luck. Gayatri does not like to gamble, she does not know how to play poker and always loses at bluff. The only card game she enjoys is bridge, but in the time and place she lives in, no one knows the game.

Varun Sarin has invited a few people from work and some of neighbours, including Mr and Mrs Amandeep Singh. He has not seen Sweety for many days, their conversations have been sporadic, unfulfilling. On some days, when he is immersed in the rigours of his daily work, he is able to stop thinking about her for a while and it seems as though he might have imagined it all. At other times, the memory is so sharp and clear that he feels her like the ache of a phantom limb. It amazes him that he is able to maintain a semblance of normalcy in his life, that he is able to go about his everyday routine without giving a hint of what lies beneath that placid exterior. He questions the intensity of a love that is subordinate to the dictates of society, a love that is content to languish slowly, function within limits, rather than stand up for itself. On some days, he is happy to let things be, content in the thought that, like water, their love will find its own level; they can wait and see how it goes. Now, the prospect of her trip to Bangkok the following week looms ahead like a storm cloud. He wants to see her at least once before she leaves. That is why the party.

Gayatri has arranged for caterers to prepare and serve dinner on the balcony of their house. Their décor is minimalist; both Varun and Gayatri prefer straight-line furniture in pastel colours and still retain the sensible pieces purchased from Ikea. Home improvement has happened more out of necessity than aesthetic impulses. For Diwali, Jhumpa has decorated the house with candles and flowers.

Two large terracotta contraptions procured from roadside vendors in the Old Gurgaon market bear small diyas inside decorated alcoves; the light from them casts swaying patterns on the walls behind. When the guests arrive, bearing gifts of dry fruits, crystal glasses and aromatic candles, they are greeted warmly by the hosts. The gifts are put away to be recycled the following season. Gayatri, who has had a quick shot of vodka in the evening, is geared up to be effusive, cheery. Varun ensures that his guests have a glass of their favourite poison in their hands. Jhumpa places plates of hot kebabs on the centre table. Jagdish is doubling as bartender. He allows his hands to brush Jhumpa's when she passes him the ice tray and they look meaningfully at each other. Varun Sarin sees them and cannot help thinking that he is a coward. His woman will be in the room shortly and he will not be able to allow himself an unfettered glance at her.

The Singhs walk in together, an hour into the party. Sweety has been dreading and looking forward to seeing Varun. This, she reminds herself, is not her man but a neighbour, the host for the evening, with whom she has to be polite, friendly, without being familiar. She smiles at the hostess, who says, 'Hi, I am Gayatri. You look lovely. Such a wonderful combination.'

'Thank you,' says Sweety, who is wearing a blue bustier blouse with an orange chiffon sari. A chunky choker studded with corals encircles her neck. She looks daring, lovely, but her nerves are splintered.

'Your house is looking very nice,' she tells Gayatri.

'Thanks. All decked up for the season.'

Varun approaches Amandeep, nods at Sweety. A brief 'Hello' is all he can bring himself to say.

The men are soon whisked away to a corner of the room. The card session begins. Another table is set up in the study, where the women and a couple of men play for lower stakes, the non-serious game for those who just want to have fun. Amandeep is a serious player. He wants to win but he plays with the air of a man who only wants to have a good time. Sweety joins a clutch of women she knows and pretends to listen to their talk of the kundan and polki jewellery they have purchased while Gayatri flutters around making sure that the kebab platters are refilled, there is enough ice and the glasses are washed and kept ready for refills.

Gayatri has invited Roma and knowing that it is the done thing, Roma's close friends, Ragini and Garima, have also been asked to the party.

The women are now discussing plans for the Trafalgar Tower Diwali dinner to be held the next day. There are two factions in the organizing committee, different views on the composition of the menu, the allocation of funds towards the décor and drinks. Realizing that there is some subtle politics at play, Gayatri tries to change the subject. She asks Jhumpa to serve the ladies a platter of spring rolls.

Ragini, who lives on the floor above, looks at Jhumpa and whispers to Gayatri, 'Have you got a new maid?'

'No. Jhumpa has been with us since we moved here. Why?'

'Oh! I heard your maid ran away with the driver?' The other ladies move in closer, sensing drama, the impending dissemination of trivial but exciting information.

'She got married to the driver,' replies Gayatri tersely.

'I heard from my maid, Bulbul, who also works in your house in the morning that the driver was already married?' Garima adds.

'Yes.' Gayatri shrugs. She wants to quell any more questions, appear nonchalant. These women, she senses, can offer her no compassion, no solution. She is momentarily repelled by their eager curiosity, the way their noses seem to quiver at the scent of a scandal, the vicarious pleasure they derive by peering into the lives of other people which appear richer, fuller than their own.

'Aaaj driver ke saath bhagegi, kal sahib ko patayegi. Some women have no shame. You should see the way some of them dress. Chhote-chhote tight-tight kapdey, showing everything,' another woman adds.

'You never know with these people,' Juhi pitches in. 'Did you hear that they found a few maids running a prostitution racket from one of the guest houses in Uniworld Town? The caretaker of the guest house was getting a cut in the business.'

'Really?'

'I don't believe it.'

'I am not surprised.'

'Do we have any guest houses in Trafalgar Towers?'

The topic reverts to Jhumpa's love life. Gayatri brings the women up-to-date.

'And you accepted that? And allowed them to stay on? Arrey wah, tum to mahaan ho, Gayatri,' chimes Ragini. 'You are too great. I would have sent her packing. These people cannot be trusted.'

Gayatri detects a hint of sarcasm in the way the woman mention her greatness. She did not feel great at the time; she was only a reluctant participant to the decision on Jhumpa's living arrangements. A part of her agrees with her voluble neighbour. Another part wants to slap these inquisitive, intrusive women. A third part, fuelled by some misplaced loyalty, feels the need to defend a decision seen as a joint one by the rest of the world.

Sweety, who has heard some of the story from Varun, is sympathetic to the cause of Jhumpa and Jagdish. She feels the curious empathy that those in difficult love feel for others in a similar situation.

'Poor thing! Bechari kahan jaati. People in love do stupid things,' she finds herself saying. 'It was really good of you to allow them to continue working here,' she tells Gayatri.

Gayatri, surprised and briefly bolstered by this unexpected vote of confidence, confers a grateful smile on Sweety.

'Sweety, tum toh badi romantic ho!' exclaims Roma. 'What has your husband been up to?'

The rest of them laugh good-naturedly. The topic of Jhumpa's affairs temporarily set aside, they move on to languid complaints about the loss of romance in their married lives.

When Sweety needs to use the washroom, she is led by

Gayatri to the one adjoining the guest bedroom. When she sees the bed, the same cream sheets on which she had made love to her host, Sweety feels giddy. On this bed, in this room, she had put her mouth on a man's naked body and he had entered hers with passion and tenderness. The same man who is now serving whisky to his guests and nodding at her as though she is a stranger. All this lying, this deceit, pretending she does not know the man who held her in his arms, the strange solidarity she feels with his wife, the plastic faces of the other women who eye her bare shoulders, the gloating faces of the men, the impassive face of her lover who also pretends not to know her, the pointless nature of their relationship, all these thoughts churn together in her mind. She feels her stomach heave and something sour and metallic rises in her mouth. She is violently sick in the washbasin.

Her husband is engrossed in the game and gestures an assent when she whispers to him that she needs to go home. She does not tell Varun but makes her excuses to Gayatri. 'Stomach upset,' she says, 'and Manya, my daughter, has been a little unwell. I have to go. Please. I had a good time.'

Varun sees her leave and wants to stop her. But he is accosted by a man who wants more ice in his whisky. 'What happened?' he asks Gayatri.

'Oh, that lady had to leave. She wasn't well or maybe her child wasn't well. I didn't catch her name.'

'Sweety.'

'What!'

'Her name is Sweety.'

'Oh! For a moment I thought you had lost it – calling me sweetie. Sweety suits her. She is quite pretty in a fair, Punjabi way. Do you know her?'

'Hardly. I play golf occasionally with her husband at the club. When do you think we should serve dinner?'

'By 10:30. I don't care if the others serve dinner only at midnight. It's better if we get it over with quickly. Those who are interested can continue playing even after.'

Something has been sucked out of the evening: the lights seem dull, the colours on the women's clothes fade and blur. Varun feels deflated. He fills his glass with more Scotch and laughs at Amandeep's jokes through the evening.

Sweety reaches home and throws herself on the bed. She wants to cry, to bawl like a child, kicking the bed, punching the pillows. This is not how it should be. Love should be liberating, light, strength-giving. Instead, she feels all her energy draining from her. She goes to the children's room where Sanya-Manya are asleep. As she sees their tranquil dreaming faces, she feels the love flow through her like cool water. She sees them now as people, not just her children. Though they look alike, often fooling even their relatives into mistaking one for the other, she knows them completely. She knows that Sanya has a little mole on the right side of her neck and Manya a small scar from falling from the Jungle gym when she was two. She knows their moods, their characters: S for Seedhi Sanya, the straight one, the good girl who takes life seriously; and M for Masti Manya, the gregarious child who is single-minded in the pursuit of 'fun'. These are her little girls who love her unconditionally, depend on her to show them the way to live, to teach them lessons in courage and truth. She cannot let them down. The love for a man, any man, feels light and hollow before the weight of motherhood. She touches Manya's face, she feels the heat spreading into her palm. The child seems to have fever.

28

SWEETY SINGH AND her children do not accompany Amandeep to Bangkok after Diwali. Manya has a viral infection. Amandeep has already scheduled meetings with buyers and suppliers; there is a trade expo in Bangkok that he cannot afford to miss. He has reluctantly carried on, reassured by Sweety's insistence that she can manage. Gurgaon has excellent medical care and both sets of grandparents are nearby in case of any emergency. Children get sick all the time. Sweety is secretly relieved that she does not have to go on the holiday but this is not the price she had wanted to pay.

This, however, is not any run-of-the-mill sickness. The Crocin syrup, the tulsi-ginger-honey concoction Sweety prepares, the besan ka sheera that her mother-in-law urges her to give the child, none of it is of any use. After four days of high fever, a perpetually runny nose, a racking cough and bouts of vomiting, Manya is diagnosed as having contracted swine flu. Gurgaon has been struck by a swine flu epidemic. Schools have shut down and children are sequestered indoors. Sanya is sent away to Green Park to stay with her grandparents and cousins. Sweety is left to handle a weak, sick child, made more irritable by the loss of her twin. Manya's natural exuberance has worn off and Sweety aches to see her lying listless, a small shrunken shadow on the bed. The doctor has prescribed Tamiflu, advised plenty of fluids and rest, and assured Sweety that it's not a severe case. But Sweety is left with a sense of impending doom. There are reports of a couple of people dying of swine flu, an old man and a baby, both already made vulnerable by age and poverty. A terrible fear and helplessness hang over the city.

Sweety stays up through the night by her daughter's side, praying. She is not overtly religious; God is a mild, benign presence in her daily life. Sweety has been schooled by her mother to perform the japji sahib every morning and on some days when she remembers, she recites the rehras in the evening. She goes to the gurudwara occasionally, believes in the power of the Guru Granth Sahib, but does not perform any other rituals associated with her faith. In times of crisis, though, God becomes a potent being, capable of granting or withholding favours, and she offers frequent prayers in supplication at such times. Now, as she recites the 'Ek Onkar' prayer several times, she recalls the meaning of the words, feels their wisdom, the message they reveal to her.

> *Sahas si-aanpaa lakh hohi ta ik na chalai naal.*
> *Kiv sachi-aaraa ho-ee-ai kiv koorhai tutai paal.*
>
> Lakhs of clever tricks, but none of them will go
>   with you in the end.
> How can you become truthful, how can the veil of
>   illusion be torn away?

It seems to her that she has been living in a veil of illusion, her life is all trickery and deceit, none of which matters in the long run. The happiness she has derived from love, the pleasure she feels at another man's touch, all of it is false. If anything happened to her child, she would be to blame. This is retribution for her wayward behaviour. She has violated a sacred code and has to be punished in a way that will hurt her the most. God has ways of making people see the truth, this is her chance to redeem herself and save the life of her child.

She calls Varun the next day.

'How is Manya?' he asks.

Sweety had sent him a message saying that she was not going to Bangkok because of her child's sickness. His euphoria at the news had given way to concern when he learnt about Manya's health. She is Sweety's child and anyone she cares about matters to him. Every time he sees her children, he feels a strange connection. 'They are hers,' a voice mutters inside her head. 'They have her blood, her eyes, her hair, and belong to her in a way you never can.'

'Not good. Her fever went down yesterday but it was up again this morning. The doctor says it will take at least another five-six days.'

'She will be fine. I am sure of it.' Varun feels helpless. He wishes there is something he can do. Sweety's misery infects him.

'I don't know. I am so worried. She is very weak. Cannot get up even.'

'Everything will be all right. Do you have help? Is there anything I can do?'

'My mother will come tomorrow. The maids are there also.'

'Hmm. You are very brave and I think you are doing a great job.'

'No. I am not. This is all my fault. Varun, we have to stop.' Sweety hears a hysterical note in her voice, she knows she will regret the words later, but she cannot hold herself back.

'Stop what?'

'Stop seeing each other.'

'We don't see each other. It has been a very long time since I was with you.'

'I know. But . . . but the feeling is there, that we can.'

'So you want to stop feeling? Is that possible?'

'I don't know. But we have to.'

'Why? Why now?' Varun feels something cold, clammy slide down his body, a feeling that someone he knows has died. He had never thought about the end, that this would end.

'Don't you see, I am being punished. Manya is so sick. She is not getting better.'

'So you think there is some cosmic cause-and-effect relationship playing out here, that there is some connection between what you do and your child's sickness?'

'You sound as though it is a stupid idea.'

'It is. I can't imagine where you got it from. So you think if we stop whatever little we do, it will make things better? You think that there is some great being in the sky who arbitrarily doles out rewards and punishments? That if you make some great sacrifice, your daughter will get better. That is ridiculous.'

He sounds harsh, judgemental. Sarcasm has always been his shield against fear, against potential disappointment. He is scared of losing her. He does not have it in him to compete against that great and powerful thing called motherhood.

'It is not ridiculous. You don't know about these things. You have lived abroad for so long that you have become . . . become—'

'Become what? An atheist, an idiot?'

'No. You won't understand. You don't know how I feel.'

'You are right. I don't. I can't imagine how you can even think that you can walk away from us so easily. This . . . this doesn't happen to people every day.'

'It is not easy, Varun. It will be very difficult.'

'Then don't do it.'

'I have to.'

'Then go ahead. Stop. I'll do whatever you want me to. Why do you even bother to ask me?'

'Don't be like this.'

'I am like this.'

'I am not talking to you if you are going to be like this.'

'That is what you want, right? To stop talking.'

'I am hanging up.'

'Go ahead.'

Varun realizes that he has not come off well in the interaction. He had wanted to be compassionate and understanding. Instead, he has squabbled with her like a child, a petulant child on the verge of a tantrum. He wishes he had handled the situation like a mature, sophisticated man, given her time to get through the sickness of her child, assured her of his support. That is the way he deals with his employees and customers who know that Varun Sarin can be depended on to keep a cool head during tough situations. He has no option now. He will not call her back.

Two days after Sweety's call to Varun, Amandeep returns home and Manya Singh turns the corner. As he sits by Manya's bedside, he tells her that they will soon go for a holiday to Thailand. She can feed a baby tiger at the zoo and have parrots nibble seeds from her hands. Then maybe they would also go to Hong Kong where she and Sanya would have the most wonderful time on all the rides in

Disneyland. His voice is soothing, he rocks her gently and says that she is papa's brave little girl. She has to get better soon.

Manya's fever comes down and she asks for a piece of Dairy Milk chocolate. The doctor pronounces her to be out of danger. The child is still weak but her spirit recovers quickly. Sweety feels vindicated. While she had some hesitation in taking the blame for her child's illness, she has no doubt that she deserves some credit for her quick recovery. Her sacrifice has not been in vain. Urged by the elders in her family, she arranges for thanksgiving prayers, a paath at her house, a kirtan followed by a langar where friends and neighbours are welcomed and fed. While others pray for the health and happiness of the family, Sweety prays for the strength to stick to her resolve.

29

IT IS A harsh winter in Gurgaon. The premature snowfall in the hills has driven down the temperatures. The dull fog that settles in during the first week of January, disrupting flight schedules and befuddling motorists, has now advanced to early December. The evenings darken by five and children are forced to stay indoors and amuse themselves. Heavy woollen blankets have replaced the lighter Jaipuri razais and there is a sudden surge in the demand for oil heaters. The new expats wonder why their homes do not have central heating. The poor scour the garbage dumps for any combustible material they can burn at night to keep warm. NGOs step up the drive to collect warm clothing from the well-to-do, to be distributed to the needy. Newspapers report the death of three homeless people on the Delhi roads.

The long, bleak spell has cast a pall on Varun. He has called Sweety a couple of times but stopped doing so when she did not answer or return his calls. He cannot bring himself to blame Sweety for anything but stupidity. He blames himself for rendering himself so open, so vulnerable, and only hopes that she is hurting as much as he is. He had expected her to contact him but she seems to have vanished off the face of the earth so completely that on certain days he doubts she existed at all. He finds it hard to believe that he can miss her presence so keenly. Even a month after that fatal phone call he cannot stop thinking about her. Once, he had called her from another number just to hear her voice. She must have sensed his presence on the other side for after a few seconds, during which all he could hear was her sharp swift breath, she disconnected. Even the few hellos she said were potent. It brought back memories and he was left with a strong sense of disbelief that something so precious, so powerful was lost to him for ever.

Varun immerses himself in work. There is a new development there which diverts his mind. Systech has made an unforeseen but attractive offer to buy TechKnowlEdge. Systech is an Indian firm that competes with Infosys, Wipro and TCS in the information technology space. It started off as a small software company specializing in removing bugs from other software, and had grown into a hydra-headed firm with divisions in software development, network management and consulting. It was listed on NASDAQ, had posted excellent profits and was looking to expand its workforce and offerings to clients. On meeting the Systech CEO, Sanjay Shanbag, at a conference, Varun had been impressed by the man's ambition and passion. He himself seemed to have lost both. When he and Sam started TechKnowlEdge, they were not looking to sell it quickly and make some easy money. Varun had wanted to create something that would last, that would be identifiable as his legacy. He never wanted to conquer the world; only to stake his claim to a part that would always be identifiable as his. Now he is not so sure. He wonders if he can be responsible for the careers and aspirations of two hundred people, if he is a credible role model as the CEO of the firm, if he really wants to continue doing this work for the rest of his life. The venture capital firm that had initially funded TechKnowlEdge believes that it is the right time to sell. Sam is undecided. Systech has offered them both the option of staying on to lead the Decision Analytics division, which is what TechKnowlEdge would become. There are rumours within TechKnowlEdge about some changes; the employees are restive, the customers anxious. His own future appears uncertain. He is impatient with others, less tolerant, more distracted. Varun reflects on the irony of waffling over the fate of a firm that helps in decision making and risk management.

On a gloomy Wednesday morning in January, when Anirudh wishes his parents 'Happy Anniversary', Varun looks surprised, Gayatri, a little abashed. For the first time since his marriage, Varun has forgotten his wedding anniversary. Gayatri remembers it but did not want to mention the fact when it seemed obvious to her that it had slipped past Varun's memory. The wedding anniversary rituals have changed over the years. At some point of time, he and Gayatri had stopped giving each other anniversary gifts; it had seemed foolish and they had run out of ideas. They still go together for what Gayatri terms a 'fancy' dinner at a place that requires reservations to be made in advance.

Reminded of their seventeenth wedding anniversary, they wish each other stiffly.

'Do you want to go out for dinner?' asks Gayatri

'Do you?' counters her husband.

'You seem quite busy these days, so if it looks difficult, it is not a problem.'

'No, it is not difficult but I thought you also seem to be working late.'

'Hey, we can order in at home. Maybe we can do a Thai or Chinese takeout,' suggests Anirudh.

His parents fall in with the idea.

Anirudh senses that everything is not right with his parents. Intuiting as only children often do, he feels that they both are more unhappy and disengaged than they have ever been earlier. Some of his classmates in Fremont had single parents and he had seen the outcomes of acrimonious splits between husband and wife. Though he still does not think that his parents would ever reach a stage of divorce, he is uneasy.

He is doing better in his own relationship. On the day of his parents' anniversary, Anirudh Sarin is feeling as romantic as a sixteen-year-old boy can. He has managed to establish a connection with Nikita Pant that can no longer be termed as just friendship. She has been acknowledged as his girlfriend among his classmates and though there is no overt declaration of any emotional attachment, they hang out together. Anirudh has his father's ability to adapt easily to his circumstances and his mother's determination to make the best of whatever task is undertaken. He is sporty without being overtly athletic, conscientious about studies without being studious, a bit of a geek, intelligent but a little lazy about pushing himself. He has not yet found his governing passion in life but has become a keen and accomplished guitar player of late. Over the past few months, his voice has matured to a pleasant baritone and he can belt out a few numbers with practised ease. After a soulful performance of a Coldplay song called 'Yellow' during a class party, he has become popular with the girls in his school. This has caused Nikita to quickly take advantage of her right of first refusal and she has let it be known that Anirudh's attentions are welcome. They hold hands and there is the promise of more delights to follow. They hang out together after lunch and have started sharing the details of their lives with each other.

'What gift can I get for my parents' anniversary?' he asks Nikita at school.

'I wrote my parents a poem for theirs,' suggests Nikita. 'They really liked it. You know, they have everything they need so you should do something that will be special for them.'

'Whoa! I can't write a poem.'

'Why don't you sing a song. Did they have a song, you know like, we have our song.'

'We do?'

'Yeah – "*Yellow*"! Don't you remember? I was wearing a yellow dress at that party when you sang it first.'

'Oh? Yeah! Right! But I don't think they have a song.'

'Just sing one of the oldies, from their time.'

Anirudh suspects it might not be a very cool thing to do but he likes the idea. He has ordered the anniversary dinner from China Club and, as they wait for Jhumpa to lay out the food, he invites his parents to hear a song that he dedicates to them. He has chosen an old number – '*Annie's Song*' by John Denver, something he hopes they can relate to. Varun and Gayatri sit on separate sofas with encouraging smiles. Hearing his son's young-old voice swell with '*You fill up my senses'*, Varun can think only of Sweety and wonder at the aptness of the song. Memories of Sweety wash over him and fill him like a sleepy blue ocean. He marvels at how she continues to fill his senses even after all this time. Gayatri marvels at how mature and thoughtful her son had become. She is deeply touched by his gesture of singing rather than the song itself. She feels a little vindicated in her role as mother. She has produced a fine young man. When he finishes his song, they both clap loudly and are lavish in their praise. For a few moments parental pride supersedes all other emotions. As they hug him, forming a tight family circle, Anirudh Sarin feels that he has done his bit. Maybe things were not as bad as he thought.

30

AFTER THE RECOVERY of Manya Singh, after the glow of her sacrifice has faded, when her daily routine had assumed a semblance of normalcy, Sweety Singh realized that her life had changed forever. She could never go back to the way she was a year ago, a state of ignorance, not blissful but at least benign. There was perhaps an unconscious yearning, faint stirrings of a desire for something nameless, formless. It had been substituted with a painful, tangible longing for something that threatened to disrupt the easy tenor of her days. She had not foreseen how much she would miss the fleeting presence of Varun in her life. She had seen him once, as she was stepping out for some chores. She had only glimpsed his back as he waited for his car at the porch of Tower 2. There was something endearing about the way he stood, slouched, disinterested. She noted the way his hair was cut short, exposing a thin band of skin between his neck and collar. She noticed the way his hand gripped the black laptop bag, noticed the fine strong fingers that had gripped her body a long time ago. She resisted the urge to walk across and put her arms around him, to rest her head against the cool blue back and say, 'I'm sorry.' The moment passed and he stepped into his car.

The self-enforced separation had only served to increase the fervour of her feelings. She thought about him constantly, included him in her daily prayers and hoped that he had achieved something close to happiness even without her. The nights when she was alone were the worst, for she lay unsleeping on the bed with a visceral ache that began in her groin and slowly spread to the rest of her body. She feared that with the passing of time, the memory of her brief trysts with Varun would fade, the pleasure she derived from imagining and reconstructing the time they had together would vanish. On some days she reproached herself for her hasty decision, sometimes she was angry with Varun for reducing her to this state. Even as she tried to stay away from any contact with him, she could not believe that this state of separation could last forever. It had taken its toll on her, on her appearance. When she looked into the mirror, she saw a different woman. The colour on her face had drained, her hair appeared dull and there were dark shadows under her eyes. She felt listless on most days; it was as if her life force was ebbing away. She was dying slowly and no one around her seemed to notice it.

Sweety feared she would go mad if she didn't find something else to occupy her mind. One morning, as she picked up the newspaper, something caught her eye. Along with the menus from Dominos Pizza and Wok-a-Mamma, and the pamphlets advertising Organic Foods, Hot Yoga Classes and Prakash's Pest Control that fell out from between the paper, she saw a leaflet announcing 'A chance for Happyness'. The pale yellow paper with childish drawings of a smiling yellow sun and dancing stick figures was from Happy Kids, one of the leading playschools in Gurgaon. Happy Kids was offering a three-month course on teaching preschool children. After the basic course, there was an option of an advanced course for those keen on becoming teachers at Happy Kids. The timings were good, she could be back home by the time Sanya-Manya returned from school. She told Amandeep that it was a temporary course, that she would learn how to teach children, something that would be so useful for her to help Sanya-Manya. She hoped it would help her as well. Amandeep, whose trips abroad had become more frequent, had begun to feel a little guilty about leaving his family behind, leaving Sweety to cope with the rigours of bringing up the twins. He had also noticed that his wife was looking a little pulled down, a fact she attributed to the strain of Manya's illness. He gave his consent, insisting that she should stop it immediately if it was too tiring.

On the first day of the session, she entered the cheerful red-blue-yellow building that housed Happy Kids with a sense of anticipation and foreboding. The smiling shining face of Mrs Bharadwaj, the principal of Happy Kids, greeted her, and she immediately felt her spirits lift. The classes were to be held on the premises of Happy Kids so that there was an opportunity to observe other teachers, see the way children interacted with each other and become familiar with the atmosphere of a playschool. Sweety Singh had been to Little Handprints where Sanya-Manya had studied, an older playschool closer to where they lived in Green Park, but her interactions there had been limited, her interest in the surroundings cursory. Now Sanya-Manya went to a 'big school' in a yellow school bus and she only visited Camelot World School on important occasions.

Mrs Bharadwaj invited the women who had enrolled for the course to introduce themselves.

'Myself Vinita Bansal,' said a middle-aged lady. 'Mere bachhe badey ho gaye hain and they are away in hostel for higher studies. My older son is studying in US and my younger one has got into IIT. My husband is so busy with his business. I am alone at home and maine socha ki kuch useful karna chahiye.' Each of these women had a story.

Four of them had just completed their graduation and were whiling away time till they got married or decided what they should do with their lives. Two were newly married wives of executives who had been transferred to Gurgaon, well-qualified young women who had given up jobs to move with their husbands. They were waiting to get appropriate jobs and the course offered a learning opportunity while they waited. Eventually, they would be mothers, they said, and this course would help them handle that. There were also four mothers who wanted to be more than homemakers. They were serious about the course and wanted jobs at good playschools once they finished, jobs they could handle while being mothers. Then there was Sweety, who did not reveal the real reason why she had joined the course.

As they were getting ready to start, another woman rushed into the classroom in a jumble of bright colours and baubles. She was a tiny little thing with a head of frizzy hair and a pair of bright black kohl-rimmed eyes. There was something light, bird-like, about her; she sat down on the chair next to Sweety as though ready to take flight at any moment.

'I am Ambika Mohanty,' she announced. 'I am doing this course because it is good time pass.

'Just joking,' she quickly added, noticing the shocked looks on the faces of the other women. 'I love children and want to work with them.' Everyone nodded approvingly.

'Right answer,' she whispered to Sweety who smiled back

at her. During the short break, another lady asked her the inevitable questions: 'Are you married? What does your husband do?'

'I was married. Abhi mere husband nahin hai.'

Instantly, the curiosity gave way to sympathy that was due to a young widow. 'So sorry,' muttered some of the women. 'I mean I have an ex-husband. I am a divorced single parent,' Ambika clarified. The sympathy changed to embarrassment as though the onlookers had been witness to something private and mysterious which they longed to know more about but were forbidden from exploring further. Single parents were an exception in the world Sweety was familiar with.

Sweety found the classes interesting. Learning something new now gave her a thrill that she had not experienced in school or college. She and Ambika got into the habit of sitting next to each other and spending the breaks together. To her, Ambika Mohanty came across as terribly brave, surprisingly cheerful and coolly unconcerned about what the world thought of her. Ambika found Sweety to be merely curious, not judgemental. She sensed there was more to Sweety than her pretty face; her eyes held secrets. They connected.

Ambika had an eleven-year-old daughter, Aneesha, who lived with her along with Ambika's mother. 'We have three generations of hormonal women living under the same roof,' Ambika told her. 'It can get quite crazy.' By their second meeting, Sweety had learnt Ambika's life story.

Ambika Jain, the daughter of a wealthy diamond merchant from Surat, had threatened to run away to Mumbai and become a film actress if her family did not accede to her wish to pursue a college education in New Delhi. In a community where most girls were married off by the time they graduated, Ambika was first a rebel, later an outcast who was mentioned by her extended family in hushed whispers, as poor Sejal's daughter who ran away with an Oriya boy. She had come to live with her mama-mami in New Delhi and study literature in Venkateshwara College. It was there that she had met Abhijit Mohanty, studious, sensitive Abhijit, who was from a different world, whose charmed recital of Andrew Marvel's 'To his coy mistress' had stirred Ambika to such an extent that she had yielded her virginity to him in the back seat of Mr B.P. Mohanty's government-issue Ambassador car. Abhijit had wanted to study literature but opted for an economics major during the second year, a choice more in keeping with his parents' wishes that he too pursue a career in the civil services like his father.

'How shocked the hoity-toity Mohantys were when Abhijit announced that we were getting married even before we both had graduated,' Ambika said with a satisfied laugh when they met for lunch at the food court in Metropolitan Mall. They had an hour to kill before the children came home.

'Even I got married very early,' offered Sweety.

'We didn't want to, but I got pregnant and Abhi was quite in love with me those days.'

To Sweety, Ambika's story had the quality of a fairy tale even without the mandatory happily ever after with Price Charming. The Mohantys had been quite decent, Ambika said, allowing Ambika and Abhijit to stay with them after the wedding while Abhijit pursued his master's from Delhi School of Economics and prepared for his civil services entrance exam. Her own family had disowned her. She had not seen her parents for nine years until she was summoned by her father as he lay dying of prostate cancer in a Surat hospital.

A few years into their marriage, she and Abhijit had realized their incompatibility; the lust and ardour that had sufficed during the stages of courtship did not survive the rigours of premature parenthood. Abhijit had not cleared the civil services exams in his first attempt, which failure he attributed to the distractions of his marriage and the nocturnal habits of his baby daughter. They had begun to drift apart and Abhijit had embarked on an affair with a more compatible classmate who was also a part of his IAS study circle. He cleared the exams in the second attempt and made it through the final selection, as did Jaya Tripathi, his lover and now batchmate. It did not make sense to him or to Ambika to continue in a marriage that gave them little joy and no comfort. They had separated two years ago but Ambika had continued living with her in-laws even when Abhijit was away on training. They had grown fond of her and were devoted to Aneesha, who had been brought up mostly by the senior Mrs Mohanty.

'And now?' asked Sweety.

'The divorce came through a year ago. After my father passed away, I persuaded my mother to come and live with me. My younger sister lives in Ohio and she didn't want to go there. Abhijit's parents didn't want us to move too far away because they wanted to stay in touch with Aneesha. That was one of the conditions of our divorce settlement. So we sold our family home in Surat and bought an apartment in Gurgaon, not in Delhi but close enough. Aneesha can visit her grandparents during the weekend, meet Abhijit when he is in town. She will probably have a stepmother soon when Abhi and Jaya get married. Right now they both are posted in some back-of-the-beyond place in UP.'

'How do you feel?'

'Now? I am cool with the whole thing. I don't hate Abhi or regret anything that happened. I met Jaya once, she seems quite sensible. I need to find a job I can hold on to. I have tried many things but nothing seemed interesting enough. Luckily, we don't have financial problems. Abhi provides for Aneesha's expenses and I have some money that my father left for me and Ma. But I need to find something useful for me to do.'

'You seem happy,' Sweety wondered aloud.

'Yes. I think I am. I believe that in many ways my life is beginning only now.'

As she spent more time at Happy Kids, Sweety felt more calm. It soothed her to see the little children. In their shining innocent faces, she saw hope; in their unquestioning acceptance of their surroundings, she experienced a sense of comfort; in their ability to live completely in the moment, inspiration. In Ambika Mohanty she found a friend.

It seemed to Sweety that Ambika had come into her life for a reason. She had been used to women who abided by the rules; if they bent them, it was done furtively. They did not break them and flaunt it to the world. Her own outlook now seemed narrow, the exposure she had received to the ways of the world had been limited, her options always circumscribed by the expectations of others. She had broken with tradition by cleaving away from the joint family but that was only a mild uprising. Ambika Mohanty's story contained a message for her if only she could decode it. She wondered if she could tell Ambika her story. She found her kind enough, though a little self-absorbed, sometimes carried away by her own coolness. Would Ambika be able to understand what she was going through?

31

THE SARINS WERE meeting an old friend, a batchmate from their days together in business school – S.S. Anand who, for no apparent reason, had been called Dolt since his engineering days. An IIT rankholder and batch topper who made partner in an international consulting firm in record time, Anand was far from being a Dolt. Now in his forties, he was ironically proud of his nickname. 'Better to be called Dolt than Ass,' he joked. They had not seen each other in eighteen years. Dolt had been living in London for the past few years, had dropped the initial S in his name and acquired a blond British wife. They had been sporadically in touch on email but had never managed to meet.

Dolt had recently connected with Gayatri and Varun through Facebook. He had sent them a message stating that he was in India and asking for their whereabouts. Gayatri had instantly replied, 'We must catch up if you are going to be in Gurgaon or Delhi. Do call me.'

Gayatri was pleased that he had reached out to them. She has never mentioned it to Varun, but twenty years ago she had suspected that Dolt would have initiated a relationship with her if it had not been for Varun Sarin. He had been a bespectacled lanky boy in those days, quiet, studious, known to be brilliant but reserved. Though he had never said anything, Gayatri had known with the intuition women have that he had a soft corner for her. During the initial days, they had hung out in the same group and had travelled together on the train to Bangalore, which was also his home town. After the news of her and Varun had become public, he had withdrawn and she sensed in him a kind of reproach, a feeling of having been let down. She had not thought about Dolt much – Varun had seemed more dashing, more popular, and she had been carried away by the first romantic liaison of her life.

Now, sitting across from Dolt in the restaurant at the Taj Mansingh in Delhi, Gayatri was pleasantly surprised to see that he had vastly improved with age. The spectacles had vanished, he had filled out and was now a well-built, distinguished-looking man. The strong Tamil accent had been replaced by the clipped tones of a BBC newscaster. Material success had given him an air of confidence. He was articulate, even suave, and chose the wine with the air of a connoisseur. He greeted them effusively, thumping Varun on the back and shaking Gayatri's hand with vigour.

'Thanks for coming out to see me. You both look just the same,' said Dolt.

'You look different,' remarked Gayatri. She sensed that she was responding to him as she would to an attractive man, a stranger. She had dressed with a little more care, choosing a flattering colour and putting on more make-up than she normally did.

'Thank God for that!' smiled Dolt. 'I was a typical scrawny nerd those days.'

They spent a few minutes discussing the whereabouts of various classmates, discovering that they had not been in touch with many of them. They discussed the economies of India, US and UK, the job opportunities in these countries and marvelled at the way they all had grown and changed over the past few years.

'The economic growth that this country has seen has

been quite phenomenal,' proclaimed Dolt. 'I was driving through Gurgaon yesterday and was amazed to see the buildings, the expressway. So, you guys are living in the Millennium City? How is it in Gurgaon?'

'Good,' said Varun. 'Bad,' replied Gayatri at the same time. They all laughed uneasily. Gayatri felt the need to explain herself.

'I mean, the growth is all so superficial. It is just a clutch of tall buildings among a cluster of villages. If you get into Gurgaon, you can see that the infrastructure is really bad. The roads have these huge craters that can damage your car, people are still throwing garbage on the streets, too much traffic, no public transport, no greenery. Large pockets of poverty in between all the so-called wealth.'

'Well,' added Varun, 'I guess it will take time. But we are getting somewhere. I think people are more concerned now about their surroundings. There was a recent drive to plant a million trees there. I saw some volunteers trying to handle the traffic at busy junctions. The place where we live is not so bad.'

'Yes, our condominium is okay,' conceded Gayatri. 'It is a self-contained little island where one tries to shut out the reality of the world outside.'

'So how have you been?' enquired Varun, trying to steer the topic away from Gurgaon.

Gayatri could see that Dolt and Varun were sizing each other up, looking for signs of success or failure. The fact that Dolt was staying at a very expensive hotel and buying them dinner, that he wore a Rolex watch and designer shoes had been offered up for evaluation. Varun was dressed in a casual linen shirt and trousers. He wondered what Dolt would make of him. He was glad that he was a CEO, an entrepreneur, and out of the usual corporate rat race where a designation and the market value of the organization were the markers of a person's status.

'What are you doing in Delhi?' Gayatri asked. She found it difficult to call him Dolt. She could hardly relate this man to the shy boy who had carried her suitcase at the railway station.

'Meetings. Mostly with some people in the government. I am thinking of setting up something here. I have already put in my papers at McKinsey but will continue for another three months to wrap up a study. Sarin, maybe you can give me some ideas about doing business here. It is quite difficult to get appointments with some of these officials even when you want to put money into the economy. I think I am going to have to deal with the famous Indian red tape and corruption.'

'What type of business are you planning?'

'Renewable energy. That is going to be the next big thing. You know that we will soon run out of oil and coal reserves. It is just a matter of time. I have some investors who want to start a venture in wind and solar energy. Do you know there is this scientist at MIT, an Indian, who has figured out a way to commercialize solar energy which is ten times less expensive that what we have today? If this works, it

could change the face of the country, of the world.' Anand
spoke with passion, the zeal of a new convert to a noble
cause. For a minute, Varun envied him, this drive which he
once had, the desire to build and create something. He
wondered what Dolt would be doing two years from now.

'Where are you planning to set it up?' asked Gayatri.

'Down south, I guess. There are already some projects
there that are doing well. What I am really keen on is
creating a community there, partnering in local development.
We are thinking of setting up a model township around this
project, a school, a hospital, employment opportunities for
the youth.'

'Changing India one village at a time,' remarked Varun.
Realizing immediately that he might have sounded cynical,
inappropriately dismissive of another man's dream, he
quickly added, 'It sounds great. Have you identified any
specific place?'

'Well, we are evaluating a couple of places in Tamil
Nadu, near Coimbatore. I am thinking of being based in
Bangalore for a while when we get started.'

'Really? Is your family still there? Remember those long
train journeys we used to make every vacation?' Gayatri
piped up.

'I remember, Gayatri,' he said softly. 'My mother is
suffering from cancer. She's on chemo. I've been trying to
get her to come to London but they don't want to move out
of the house. My two sisters are settled in the States. But
she doesn't want to go there either. Anyway, the doctors in

India are quite competent. But my father is finding it tough to manage by himself in Bangalore.'

'I am sorry to hear that,' Varun and Gayatri said together. For a minute, they felt a sense of kinship, a shared acknowledgement of the fact that they were at the stage of life when they had slipped into the role of caretakers for their own parents, and the prospect of losing one of them loomed on the horizon every day.

'I figured this was a chance to come back, sort of pay my debt to the old man and to society.'

'I know what you mean,' said Varun.

'What about your wife, kids?' Gayatri needed to know.

'We don't have kids. Fiona is understandably not too keen on coming here. So, I don't know. We will figure out something.' He shrugged, looking a little discomfited, and Gayatri was left with the impression that all was not well with his marriage. She would never have imagined Dolt falling in love and marrying an English girl. How had the shy boy picked up the courage to propose, for he must have proposed, to a girl from a completely different world? It was mystifying, and the mystery made Dolt more attractive, as though he had secret charms only a few were privy to.

'My parents are still in Bangalore. They are not keeping too well. I am planning to go there soon,' she offered.

Varun was surprised. 'Has anything happened recently?' he asked Gayatri.

'No,' she replied quickly. 'Appa's cataract operation is due. I should visit soon.'

'Yeah. It is tough. Growing old, I mean. Tough for them, tough for us. I don't have kids so I've told Fiona, if I get too sick, just shoot me.' Dolt laughed and they all laughed together as though it was a particularly funny joke but Gayatri could detect an undercurrent of something else. Something that hinted at sorrow. She felt a sudden pang of empathy, she wanted to reach out and tell Dolt, 'It's all right.'

They finished their dinner and promised to stay in touch. 'Great to catch up with you guys,' said Dolt.

'Really good to see you, Anand,' said Gayatri. 'We should catch up if we are in Bangalore at the same time.'

'Sure, that would be great,' said Dolt. For a moment he looked at Gayatri as though searching for something more to say, and then, with another vigorous handshake, he was off.

As the Sarins drove back along the broad smooth roads of Lutyens's Delhi back to Gurgaon, Gayatri wondered if she would see more of Anand in the future. The prospect carried a pleasant tingle of anticipation.

'Dolt has done well for himself,' Varun remarked. 'He looks quite prosperous.'

'Hmmm . . .'

'I think he had a crush on you back then.'

'Really? What makes you say that?' Gayatri feigned ignorance. She was amazed that Varun had noticed it, puzzled that he had never mentioned it all these years and curious about the reason for broaching the topic now.

'Come on! Don't tell me you didn't know. He used to look at you as though you were a . . . an appetizing piece of idli.' Varun's tone was light and they managed a laugh together.

Gayatri rolled down the window of the car and allowed the cool night air to ruffle her hair. She liked the wide roads of Delhi, the semblance of order in the carefully tended roundabouts and the absence of traffic at this time of the night. Varun fiddled with the car radio and toggled between stations. 'Let it be,' said Gayatri, as an old Kishore Kumar number filled the air. '*Aa chal ke tujhe main leke chaloon, ik aise gagan ke taley . . .*' She recalled those days in school and later college, carefree days when she didn't have to worry about the future, when she was eager and excited about what lay ahead, when the knowledge that she could secure the attentions of two men had given her a strange thrill.

Dolt would have been the perfect match for Gayatri in her parents' eyes; an intelligent boy from a good family and from the same community. She wondered how her life would have unfolded if she had married him instead. Where would she be? Would she be happier? The course of her life had been determined by her choice of spouse. Everything that had happened over the last seventeen years had been linked to that single event.

For a change, husband and wife had the same thought. If Gayatri had reciprocated Dolt's feelings, if he, Varun Sarin, had not married Gayatri Murthy, what would his life have been like? Would he have met someone like Sweety, would he have waited or would everything have been just the same, except that Gayatri would have been replaced by a woman with another name?

32

AFTER A GAP of more than three months, Varun and Sweety meet each other during the Holi festivities at Trafalgar Towers. The weather is pleasant, the lawns of Trafalgar Towers are bordered with colourful patterns of phloxes, carnations and pansies, the biting winter wind has given way to a cool spring breeze. In these past weeks, Varun has been mostly miserable and bitter with occasional spells of stoicism.

It is an effort for him to put on an act, to behave as though all is well with his world. He fakes it at work, does not bother to do so at home. He cannot bring himself to forgive Sweety. He has never bought into the reason she had given for her behaviour and feels deeply, unreasonably wronged. He often wonders if he had been a mere palliative for a bored housewife, an instrument to fulfil her sexual fantasies.

He cannot stop thinking about her. The few memories of the time they had together are already frayed with overuse, like a child's favourite toy that he is loath to throw away.

He can still recall the way she smelt the first time he made love to her in Jaipur, the way her skin felt beneath his tongue that second time, in his guest bedroom, the way she smiled up at him as he gazed at her from his balcony.

Logic tells him that if he invests enough time and energy in reconstructing his relationship with his wife, he will be assured of a decent return. They might be able to recapture something of the easy comfort and friendship they once shared even if they cannot resuscitate the romance. But he cannot bring himself to make the effort and neither does Gayatri make any overtures. The situation at work continues to be uncertain; a team of analysts is evaluating the assets of his company and he awaits the results without eagerness.

Varun does not care much for the Holi festivities. He does not grudge others their fun but will not indulge in the celebrations himself. Two of their neighbours have invited him down for some beer in a corner of the lawns reserved for the elders and more sedate folk. He has allowed himself to be led there, wondering all the while if he will see Sweety. For Gayatri, Holi is a barbaric festival, merely an excuse for the baser animal instinct in the male of the species to rear its ugly head. She has not played Holi ever since she was unceremoniously dunked into a slush pool on the college campus amidst the alcohol-induced Holi celebrations there. Nothing will induce her to join the other citizens of Trafalgar Towers on the lawns as they drink bhang and smear each other with herbal gulaal. She locks herself in the bedroom with a book and shuts out the din of the world outside. Anirudh has been invited by Nikita Pant to a Holi party at her Chhatarpur farmhouse along with some of their classmates. He is enjoying his first-ever Indian Holi celebration, one he will remember for the rest of his life because of the thandai-laced kiss that Nikita bestows on him shyly in the gazebo on the sprawling lawns.

Sweety's children and husband are ardent Holi revellers. Amandeep has decided to participate actively in their first community Holi celebrations. He has bought pichkaaris for Sanya-Manya and is insistent that his family enjoy themselves on the occasion. Sweety has always been moderately enthusiastic about Holi but this year she does not want to be a part of it. Amandeep believes that husbands and wives need to enjoy the same activities and derive satisfaction from active involvement in each other's pastimes. That is what marriage entails, anything else would be disloyal. He will not have Sweety sequester herself away from the merriment. Sweety reluctantly changes into an old white salwar kameez and oils her hair and skin in preparation for the colour that she will allow others to smear on her. She wonders if Varun will be there.

A part of the lawns at Trafalgar Towers has been transformed into a waterhole where a group of young girls and boys scream and howl with unrestrained joy. Some are sodden with colours which have mingled with the mud to give them a rich brown hue. A music system blares out the perennial Holi songs interspersed with the latest Bollywood numbers. A group of men are enticing a few women to frolic in the mud pool with them. Amandeep is part of this gang. Most women find him a little loud but harmless. This is the one day in the year when married men can hold the hand of an unrelated woman and touch her hair, her face, without fear of reprisal or misunderstanding. There is a certain thrill about this licentious subterfuge, the fine balance between provocation and protest that the men and women maintain, the inferences they draw about who can do what with whom and just how far can they go within the new boundaries that have been drawn for the day. Sweety has escaped from their clutches under the pretext of checking on her children and is wondering whether to head back to her apartment.

Varun sees Sweety as he heads back home from his corner of the lawn. Three bottles of Fosters, one glass of bhang and the mild March sun have made him lightheaded. He almost fails to recognize her beneath the daubs of purple, yellow and green that cover her face but her eyes blaze a familiar honeyed hue and he is immediately struck by how happy he can feel just by looking into them.

'Happy Holi,' he says.

Sweety is flustered. She has not thought about what she will say or do if she sees him. She is dimly aware of the presence of her husband nearby. She returns the greeting without looking at him.

'I am looking for Sanya-Manya,' she offers as an explanation for her presence. She wants him to know that she did not intend to meet him. It is only a coincidence.

The children spot their mother and come running towards her with clumps of colour in their hands. They look like imps, alien multicoloured imps, not the demure well-dressed girls that Varun knows. They throw the colours on him, scream 'Happy Holi, Uncle' and 'Mamma, we are playing some more. Abhi nahin aayenge', and run off to join their friends. Sweety is left behind with Varun.

Varun strokes her face and runs his fingers through her hair with imaginary colours. He is surprised by his own boldness and only marginally reassured that no one will think anything amiss if they see him touching her in this way. He can hear his heart beating rapidly, he might explode any minute. All the doubts, anger and resentment of the past few months have dissolved in this moment. How could he . . . how could he ever feel anything but tenderness and desire for the woman who stands before him. It doesn't matter what she feels for him, what she thinks about him. She is well, alive, in front of him and that is all that matters. It could be days, months, even years before he sees her again but this is something he will take with him to the grave. He tells her this silently, in his head.

Sweety looks at him, feels his smile, hears his unspoken words and knows they are doomed.

33

GAYATRI MURTHY WAS trying, unsuccessfully, to meditate.

'Breathe in, breathe out. Feel your breath.' The calm voice of the facilitator washed over her.

I can't feel anything. I don't believe I am doing this. Why did I agree to this training program? Transformational Self-leadership. Typical management mumbo-jumbo. Just because Jai's boss went through this. Maybe it is going to be some stress management and yoga course. At least, if they teach me some effective aasans to get rid of my fat belly, it will be worth it. Can I open my eyes? I wonder if Rajiv is meditating. I am sure he is trying hard. If there is a best meditator award going, Rajiv will be gunning for it.

Stop. Focus on the breath. Breathe. Breathe.

We are still only in the first half. One more day left. At least if it had been in some exotic resort, it would have helped. But they had to do it in Manesar. Only a little better than doing it in Gurgaon itself. I might as well have stayed home and relaxed. Don't stress. Don't stress. We are not supposed to stress. Relax. Relax.

How can I relax? There is so much pending work at the office and I have to get the house ready for guests. I can't believe

Varun's mother is visiting again with four more relatives as a bonus. Why does she have to go to Vaishno Devi at this time? There will be a stopover on the way back again. How will I cope with five of them in the house? Every meal will have to be a grand banquet. We will be constantly making parathas and frying pakodas. Hope Jhumpa doesn't fall ill. She was complaining that she was feeling sick. How can she be sick and eat so much? She looks like a well-fed horse. God! I hope she hasn't got herself pregnant. That would be too much. How will she work if she ends up with a baby? It doesn't matter if you are a maid or memsahib, once you get married and have a kid, your career is over.

If I had continued at InSec, I would have been a director by now. Instead, like a fool I quit and went with Varun to the US. Moving countries when I was already four months pregnant! Those horrible three years in Chicago, cooking, cleaning, washing, looking after Rudy with no help at all. If we hadn't moved to Fremont, I would have run back to India. After finally getting used to the US, I have to end up in Gurgaon – again because of Varun. How can Varun happily continue to live here? He doesn't seem to hear the constant dripping of water on the AC from some apartment on top. It is so bugging. And every Saturday, our neighbour downstairs has to party till three in the morning by playing that horrible loud bhangra-type music. No point complaining to anyone. Please adjust, they say, as though we are bloody party poopers. I can't bear it any more, living in this ugly, uncouth place.

'Breathe, breathe. Focus, focus. Bring your awareness

back to your breath. Let your thoughts float through. Watch them as though you are watching a movie screen.'

It is such a long time since I saw a good movie. How much I used to enjoy them on campus, and the discussions afterwards. Varun and I haven't done that in ages. We haven't done anything together in a long time. We haven't slept together in so many weeks. I can't remember the last time. Not that I miss it too much. I think I am growing old. Should I dye my hair? When will menopause start? It is so unfair. Men don't have to worry about any of this. Varun is not bothered about anything. These days I have no idea what goes on inside his head. Not that I care. He can do whatever he wants. This whole marriage has been about him. My needs have never been important. Always his job, his career, his family.

'Take a deep breath. Whenever you are ready, open your eyes.'

I don't want to open my eyes. I am so tired. Why can't I just sleep? I have to book another session at the spa this weekend to recover from the training. Last time, the Balinese massage was so good. I think everyone has opened their eyes. I am so tired.

By the end of the day, Gayatri felt a little different. She had paused in reflection, examined her values, fears and needs. She had been moved by the story Rajiv has shared of his alcoholic father and ambitious mother, a lonely childhood made traumatic by the constant pressure to prove himself. She saw him differently now and her animosity had reduced to some extent. Another man, whom she had dismissed as

aloof and withdrawn, had spoken haltingly about his attempt
to end his life after his marriage broke up. The facilitators
for the session – a tall slim man called Sorabh, who had a
low soothing voice, and Vikram, who was full of innocent
ebullience – urged her to open up. But Gayatri was content
to introspect and listen, she gave of herself sparingly. She
began to feel that people were not as they seemed, their
opaque ordinary lives held secrets; beneath their banal
exteriors existed drama, sordidness, sorrow, and an amazing
resilience. Her own life, offered up for examination, seemed
tepid, her concerns trivial: she had not been the recipient of
great love or terrible hate. Yet she had begun to feel that
there was more to her than she had thought.

She had a few minutes of coaching time with her
facilitators. When they talked about emotions, she said, 'I
feel so angry all the time.'

'Why? What is the source of that anger?' Their eyes were
kind, their tone encouraging.

'I don't know. I just don't like where we are staying now.
Gurgaon is horrible. I wish we had never moved.'

'You are angry that you were forced to move?'

'Yeah. I guess so. I mean, Varun knew I agreed only on
the condition that we were moving to Bangalore. His work
is always more important than what I want. Not just now,
all through these years.'

Vikram held her hand and closed his eyes as though he
was in a trance. 'I am sensing a lot of anger against your
husband. I can see your aura is turning red when you think
of him.'

'I guess so. It is his fault.'

'Is it? What is your payoff when you blame him?'

'What do you mean?'

'What do you gain by blaming him and feeling angry with him?'

'Gain? I don't gain anything. I feel really pissed off. I mean, our marriage sucks, I hardly get to see my parents despite being in India. I am stuck in this place and I don't know if anything is going to be different in the future. Varun doesn't give a damn.'

'I want you to think about this, Gayatri. By blaming your husband for your current situation, you are preventing yourself from taking any responsibility for changing it.'

Gayatri was silent. Reticent by nature, she was aware that she had already given too much away. Yet she felt a strange sense of relief and anticipation. As though she was on the cusp of some discovery. She remembered someone she had met long ago in Fremont, a woman, a colleague at work, who had attended some course, Art of Living or something like that, during a vacation in India. 'I am a changed person,' she had declared. The woman had looked the same, talked in the same way. The change was something subtle, so deep that only she was privy to it, but she had started smiling more often. The smile was different.

The next day, Gayatri attended the sessions on 'Discovering Your Purpose' and 'Giving Meaning to Your Life'. She could admit to herself that her current state of discontentment with her surroundings and disenchantment with her immediate family was proof enough that she was not living the life she wanted. She felt that something was eluding her. Just when she was within reach of some meaningful insight, it slipped from her grasp. The second day ended with another meditation session. She wanted to do better this time.

This time I am going to get it. No, stop. Don't force it. This is not a competition. Relax your mind. Just relax. Breathe. Focus on the breathing part.

That is much better. I almost slept off. I feel more relaxed now. Actually it wasn't so bad. Maybe I should practise this every day. But when? If I really want to, I can. I wish Amma would learn this. She is so worried all the time. It will help her relax more. Take care of her BP. What if something happens to her or Appa? He is seventy-seven now. I wish I could take care of them. As the only child, it is my duty. Varun is so particular about sending money to his mother, calls her every other day, moved all the way to India just to be close to his family. It is not fair. Stop. That was a negative thought. Think positively. Positive.

What did they say? You are your biggest block. Why can't I do it? Just because I am a girl, not a girl, married woman now. So I have become a part of another family. What crap! Men have made these rules and we women happily perpetuate them like idiots. I am the only child. I also have a responsibility. I know Appa has been putting off that cataract operation until I can spend some time with them. How much they have done for me! Every time I go home, Amma insists on making my favourite food, buys me a sari, never complains. They never ask

*for anything for themselves. If only we had moved to Bangalore.
All because some stupid lease for Varun's company didn't work
out. No. Negative, reactive behaviour again. Stop. Don't blame
others. Take responsibility. You have a choice.*

*Breathe in. Breathe out. Breathe in. Breathe out. Breathe in.
Breathe out.*

*Positive thoughts only. Think of what can be, not what has
happened. I am the possibility. I am the possibility. God! I have
been brainwashed. I am chanting this like a mantra. I am the
possibility. Why is it not possible? I can still move to Bangalore.
Varun is not going to miss me. Rudy will manage quite easily.
He could even move into boarding at Hillview for a year. After
that he will anyway go away to college. I am sure there are jobs
in Bangalore. Maybe Anand can give me a job in his renewable
energy project. It might be exciting. Goodricke is not bad but I
won't feel bad leaving either.*

*Breathe in. Breathe out. Empty your mind. Relax. Breathe
in. Breathe out.*

*I have always blamed Varun for my situation. If I really
wanted to, I needn't have agreed to coming to Gurgaon. What
is the point of sitting here and feeling miserable? At least I can
be of use to two people who need me the most. Maybe this is my
purpose. Wow! Was that a breakthrough insight? I feel more
relaxed now. I'll start looking for a job in Bangalore right away.
Then quit Goodricke and move. I can always visit Gurgaon
every weekend, or every month. I hope this works out. I feel
good about it.*

Breathe in. Breathe out. Breathe in, breathe out.

Ommmmmm. Ommmmmm. Ommmmmm.

34

AMBIKA MOHANTY HAD invited Sweety for a girls' night out. They had, over the past few weeks, forged a relationship based on mutual needs: a desire on Ambika's part to talk, to share, to impart a degree of worldliness to Sweety. Sweety was a willing learner, for she wanted to explore, to discover, even be 'corrupted'. She also wanted to forget Varun for a while.

Ambika and two of her friends from college met once a month for a 'wild night out'. They usually went to a club or a lounge bar in Delhi though of late Ambika had been trying to induce Kalyani and Saeeda to come to Gurgaon and sample the nightlife in the suburb. She wasn't comfortable driving on the Delhi roads alone at night. She knew it wasn't safe, especially for a single woman.

Kalyani, an interior designer whose husband was in the merchant navy, was single for large parts of the year, while Saeeda, a successful lawyer, was usually between relationships.

It had taken some persuasion on Ambika's part for Sweety to agree to the outing. Her initial response had been to demur.

'Come with us, Sweety. We'll have a blast. Do you have

to ask your husband for permission?' There was a teasing note in Ambika's voice that stopped short of a taunt.

Sweety knew that she would need Amandeep's approval for the jaunt but she said, 'No. He is travelling this weekend anyway. But I don't want to leave the girls alone.'

'Stop making excuses, Sweety. Don't you have a full-time maid? Or you can leave them with your parents. I have a child too, but that doesn't mean I have to sit at home every Saturday night.'

'Okay. I'll see.'

Thinking back on the conversation, Sweety realized that while she was married and almost thirty years old, very little had changed when it came to her personal freedom. Her parents had brought her up the way sensible middle-class parents of daughters do. In high school and college, she had envied the richer girls in her class, girls who had an air of disturbing self-assurance about them, who wore poker-straight streaked hair and skirts that rose above their shiny knees. They spoke of discos, boys and holidays in places she had never even heard of. Sweety had not wanted to be part of that world, yet had a fervent desire to be admitted into it. At least temporarily, to taste those forbidden pleasures, till the time came when she herself could dismiss them as shallow and pretentious.

Once she got married, she had been subject to the injunctions of her in-laws and husband. By falling in love with Varun, she had already stepped out of the 'Lakshman rekha', the inviolable boundary that a woman dared not breach. Going out with the girls at night might be a relatively innocuous activity but it would have to be approached with a degree of tact and subterfuge.

When Amandeep phoned from Bangkok, she told him about being asked out for dinner with her friend from the course, Mrs Mohanty, mother of an eleven-year-old girl. She made Ambika sound like a respectable middle-aged teacher. Having just sampled some of the delights of Pat Pong – a sex show with naked women doing indescribable things with their orifices and small implements, and a close encounter with a couple of topless dancers, delicate lady-boys with liquid eyes and large breasts whose gracious offer of a night of pleasure for a reasonable price he had regretfully refused – Amandeep was feeling virtuous. He was willing to indulge Sweety's simple desires. He knew that their current maid had proved to be reliable with the girls and he was certain that Sweety would return home at a reasonable time in the night.

'We'll show you the hot spots of Delhi, Sweety,' Ambika suggested. 'Let's have melon mojitos at Smokehouse Grill and dance on the tables, or we could go to Ai and do vodka shots.'

Sweety had never tasted alcohol. Her parents were teetotalers and alcohol was not allowed in their house, though some of her mother's relatives were partial to imported Scotch. She had a bitter childhood memory of being fooled into taking a sip of whisky by a cousin, a boy of fourteen or so, who had been fond of playing pranks. He had procured a small bottle of Bagpipers, probably from Sweety's uncle's stash, and had pretended that it was a particularly special imported cola. The stinging, unpleasant taste, the prospect of punishment and subsequent damnation had deterred her from experimenting with spirits. Amandeep enjoyed the occasional Single Malt but would not have appreciated his wife's flirtation with alcohol.

Sweety preferred to stay in Gurgaon for the night out. She knew people in Delhi and was wary of running into someone known to her in-laws. Her connections in Gurgaon being new, there was little chance of any news reaching Amandeep.

'I've heard there are many places in Gurgaon where we could go. I want to be near home, just in case,' she insisted.

'Okay. I'll get the girls to come here. That way I don't have to drive to Delhi, for a change. We can try Vapour or TC or Attitude. They usually have good music.'

On Saturday night, huddled on a plump red leather sofa, amidst the clatter of a convivial crowd and a live band with two young Manipuri girls crooning crowd-pleasing songs, and mildly tipsy after a tall potent glass of Long Island iced tea, Sweety Singh listened to the chatter of the three other women, who seemed to have arrived from a different world. Kalyani and Saeeda had a patina of sophistication, an air of worldliness, a sense of being utterly themselves and above all others. Dressed in a pair of skinny jeans and a shiny black top, Sweety had thought herself fashionable but her prettiness seemed childish and pale before their bold stylishness.

Kalyani said, 'I am dying for a smoke.'

She was a woman of voluptuous proportions, clad in a tight, short red dress that accentuated her abundant breasts. She flaunted a tattoo of a red rose below her collarbone and a flourishing K within a heart on her right ankle. Her voice was loud, her gestures expansive. Her body had a sheen of fecund good health, a ripe earthiness that exuded an invitation to partake of the treasures that lay beneath the surface. Most men could not take their eyes off her and she knew it.

'We have to step out.' Saeeda shrugged. 'I don't want to go through this crowd again.' Saeeda was tall and thin, with an ethereal otherworldly air that belied a sharp mind and tongue. With her elegant bones and pageboy haircut, she could pass for a model but she was a terror in the courtroom – champion of abused, underprivileged women and openly contemptuous of men, though secretly wary of their crude swagger and aggression. She had brief unsatisfactory affairs, usually with handsome weak-chinned men whom she left after six months or so.

Kalyani and Saeeda were pleasant enough with Sweety but she sensed that she was on probation. They accepted her as Ambika's friend but were too absorbed in their own world to make any extra efforts to draw her in. Sweety was content to watch and listen.

'How is work, Kal?' asked Ambika. They had to shout to be heard over the din of the music and other people's conversations.

'Just got a project, doing a farmhouse for a richie rich client.'

'Are you also doing the richie rich client?' Saeeda enquired with a smile.

'Not yet. Bloody wife deals with me. Always tags along for meetings. I think I need a sugar daddy in my life right now. Wifey wears a solitaire the size of an egg and here I am trying to make both ends meet on a second officer's minuscule salary.'

'Where is Pradeep now?'

'Probably somewhere in Russia banging some hot Ukrainian chick.'

The women laughed. They sipped their drinks and looked around.

Ambika apprised her friends, whom she hadn't seen for a while now. 'Did you get a boob job?' she asked Saeeda. 'They look bigger.'

'Do they?' responded Saeeda, pleased. 'No, I am trying other artificial means. New push-up bra from La Senza. Do I have a cleavage?'

Her friends eyed her breasts closely.

'Yes, you do, darling. Not as great as mine but better than before,' declared Kalyani.

'Remember when we went lingerie shopping last year? You were so flat, they were almost like mosquito bites,' said Ambika, giggling.

'Bitch,' murmured Saeeda. 'Isn't she a total bitch?' she said, turning to Sweety, who sat marvelling at these women, the camaraderie they shared. She didn't think she would ever be able to talk this way about men and the intimate parts of her body.

She was a little flustered at the question but soon realized that Saeeda was joking. Ambika laughed good-naturedly.

Saeeda looked around. 'No one interesting enough to be picked up. Last month I hooked up with one at a salsa social, a good-looking surd. He had some really good moves on the dance floor which I thought would be indicative of how he might perform on other floors.'

'Then?'

'The Khalsa should stick to salsa, darling.' Saeeda laughed.

'They all look like corporate zombies here,' declared Kalyani. 'The only moderately good-looking ones are probably the local Jat lads but when they open their mouths . . .' She threw her head back and guffawed.

'Your suburban men are quite sad, Ambika,' Saeeda pronounced her final verdict.

'They are not my men, girls. I am not a Gurgaonite. We should ask Sweety,' protested Ambika.

Sweety had gulped down her glass of LIIT and was on a high. There was a pleasant buzz around her which made her feel bolder, giggly.

'I don't know of any eligible men – only boring married ones,' she complained.

'Ah, so you think married men are boring?' Saeeda fixed her with a steady look. She had a habit of subjecting people to sudden cross-examinations. She did this not out of ill will but from a desire to help them see things differently. Her friends found this irritating but they had come to understand that her intentions were noble.

'Yes. All of them.' Sweety giggled.

'Including your husband?' Saeeda persisted. Sweety was not thinking of her husband. She was angry with Varun. Since their meeting on Holi, he had not attempted to contact her. She was affronted that he had got over her so soon. She had seen something in his eyes that day, something that had caused her to hope and despair in equal measure. She had half-expected him to do something reckless, imagined him banging on her door and asking her to run away with him. She had wanted desperate confessions, impassioned declarations of 'I can't live without you'. She did not know how she would react if such a thing happened, but she found the mere possibility of it appealing. Instead, there had been a stony silence. She wondered if he had reconciled himself to life without her, to life as a bored, boring married man.

'All boring married men,' repeated Sweety solemnly. She was well into her second drink.

'Girls, let's not be boring.' Kalyani stood up. 'Shall we dance?' Before the others could stand, she had gyrated towards a small clearing in the crowd on the dance floor.

As if on cue, the band started on a version of '*I will survive*'.

'They are playing our song,' shrieked Kalyani. She dragged the other women to the dancing area. The Gloria Gaynor song had drawn more women to the floor. They formed assorted groups and danced to the tune, belting out the lyrics in loud lusty voices. Sweety wasn't familiar with the song but she found a new desire within her to dance, to put her body, now sluggish and heavy, through some exercise. She moved easily first, then with absolute abandon. 'I have all my life to live, I have all my love to give,' she shouted as the women around her did the same in a sudden charmed chorus of sisterhood. The song gave way to another and some of them retreated.

Sweety and Ambika returned to their drinks.

'It has become such a cliché,' said Ambika. 'Dancing to this song as though it was written just for us. Still, we do it every time.'

'I enjoyed it.' Sweety smiled.

On the dance floor, a short man in a tight black shirt had inserted himself between Kalyani and Saeeda. He seemed to be oblivious to his surroundings but his eyes zeroed in on Kalyani's cleavage. She noticed him at the same time and, in a swift movement, drove the thin edge of her high heels into his brown loafers, causing him to twitch and grimace with pain.

'So sorry, bhaiyya,' she apologized with a mock contrite expression. 'Hum ne aapko nahin dekha.' The man muttered something and retreated and Kalyani winked at Saeeda who mouthed, 'Fucking asshole' and shook her head in a dismissive gesture.

Sweety joined the others on the dance floor. The women

danced together, mimicking dance moves from the movies and making up other steps.

'Having fun?' Ambika shouted into her ears.

'Yes. Lots. Thank you,' Sweety shouted back. She felt lighter, a happy convert to the wonderfully therapeutic properties of alcohol and music.

35

BACK HOME FROM the training session, Gayatri started meditating in the morning. Though she found it difficult to focus and her mind kept wandering, she persevered in the hope of mastering the art someday. In the meantime, it gave her the space to think, to allow for new realizations. The thought that she might leave her family and go to Bangalore was a seed implanted in her brain, which she watered and fed slowly. She had never been given to impulsive decisions and there were too many variables to consider here.

As Gayatri sat down at her desk at night and started going through her Facebook account, she was more distracted by her own life than those of others. She knew she couldn't ask Varun to move to Bangalore, it wouldn't be fair. She also knew he would not miss her. She wondered if his withdrawal and seeming indifference were a response to her resentment and obvious unhappiness at the current state of her life. Had she turned into a complaining nag over the past few years, taking out her anger on him? Had he turned to someone else? She was daunted by the thought of them going their separate ways. Surely seventeen years of togetherness were worth preserving even though their relationship had hit a rocky patch. They must have been happy together even if now she could barely remember any such moments that could be captured and pinned into an album.

Maybe that night in Venice, five or six years ago. It had been Gayatri's idea to visit Italy. She would never call herself romantic but the notion of Venice, a city that seemed buoyant, perpetually afloat, the idea of canals instead of roads, seemed infinitely romantic to her. In her early teens, she had been a fan of Amitabh Bachchan and, like the other girls in her class, had imagined that she too would one day meet a tall brooding man who would gaze intensely into her eyes. She had liked a song from one of his films that was set in Venice, a soulful love ballad to which a gondolier contributed a few words in Italian which evoked a sense of unbearable longing and desperate love. She had grown out of that phase but the image still exerted a strong appeal.

They had started their Italian holiday in Venice to coincide with Gayatri's birthday. The first day had been a disaster. Venice appeared to be a city in a state of slow decay, the plaster and brick exposed in places, some of the buildings long since abandoned, the water in the canals dark and grim. It seemed to be in the throes of a long-standing terminal illness, desperately hanging on to life. There were tourists everywhere. Their hotel room was small and stuffy, and Anirudh constantly complained of a stomach ache and boredom. The gondola ride was uneventful; their gondolier was a surly fellow without a song in him. After a long day, during which they had got lost and twice ended up at the Piazza San Marco, Gayatri had decided that it was the worst birthday of her life. They sat on the steps at the side of the Piazza in the disappearing evening light, tired and morose, trying not to blame each other, yet unable to suppress a feeling of disappointment. There were hardly any people around. Only a few pigeons still strutted about aimlessly.

Then the lights on the Piazza came on, rows of glistening yellow shimmers that twinkled with possibilities. The glowing basilica and the bell tower looked like something out of a fairy tale. Anirudh forgot his stomach ache to demand a large gelato and was quickly immersed in its sweet delights. A band in the adjacent Café Florian struck up a tune and Gayatri's mood immediately lifted. It was a medley of tunes from *The Sound of Music*, which they greeted with grateful smiles of recognition.

In a surprisingly spontaneous gesture, Varun held out his hand and Gayatri stood up and pirouetted to the strains of '*I am sixteen going on seventeen*'. They laughed as she sang, 'I am thirty-five, going on forty-five.' Varun held her at arm's length and pretended to scrutinize her face before

saying seriously, 'No, you still look about . . . thirty-four!'
She threw a mock punch at Varun, Anirudh looked up
from his gelato and laughed, and suddenly all was right
with the world. The three of them held hands and, walking
in no particular direction, miraculously found their way
back to the hotel. At night Varun made love to her urgently,
silently, with a passion that she could not recall him
displaying ever since.

Gayatri knew that he was not a difficult man to live with.
He treated her as an equal, a partner, unlike some of the
other men she had encountered. He was not fussy about
food and domestic matters. He gave her space and freedom,
he had never been possessive. But he did not share easily of
himself and rarely consulted her in matters that did not
have a significant impact on her. She could not but admit
that despite a certain closeness and comfort, they had never
achieved a shared sense of being, which was so necessary
for a marriage to be complete. They rarely used the word
love and she herself was wary of talking about her fears and
feelings. Nor did she see him taking the first step and
saying, 'This is not working out.' The mere admission
might set their relationship on a course that could endanger
its continuity. She did not want to lose him, but what they
had seemed like half a life. Even as she contemplated the
idea of moving to Bangalore, she wondered how she could
still keep her marriage alive, if it was even worth holding on
to in its current state.

Varun Sarin, though living in his own distant world,

noticed a change in his wife. He couldn't pinpoint what it was but sensed a certain softening in her demeanour. It was as though she had exhaled after holding her breath for a long time. She had lost her edginess; the snap and crackle that had defined her for the past two years had given way to an air of preoccupation. He speculated that she might be having an affair, then dismissed the notion as a projection of his own state of mind. He wondered if she noticed any change in him. It would be ironical if she caught on now, when he and Sweety had not spoken or met for so many days that it might as well be over between them.

36

IN THE MIDDLE of the summer holidays, Sweety Singh found time hanging heavy on her. Sanya and Manya had been enrolled in summer camps to keep them engaged. They attended acting, art and dance classes for three hours and came back home tired enough for an afternoon nap. The three-month basic course at Happy Kids was almost over and Sweety was wondering if she should opt for the advanced course and go on to make a career in primary school teaching. She had a month to decide. Amandeep had decided to escape the Delhi heat as often as possible and his travels within the country and outside had become more frequent. Her brother, Bobby, was home for the summer break and she had visited him at her parents' home. She had made the mandatory visits to Green Park too, but nothing seemed to fill the interminable gaps in her life.

She had been in touch with Ambika, who had been urging her to sign up for the advanced course and enrol for a BEd degree after that. She painted a rosy picture of their future together as colleagues, charged with the responsibility of moulding innocent young minds. They had fallen into the habit of meeting for lunch twice a week and Sweety looked forward to these meetings as a necessary deviation in her routine. Each time they met, she had to suppress a need to confess, to unburden herself and seek some solace.

That week, an hour before they were scheduled to meet for lunch, Ambika called. 'Sweety, have you heard? There has been a bomb blast in Delhi. Near the high court.'

The news shattered the calm of the day.

'No. When? I'll just switch on the TV,' she replied, walking to the television.

'It's horrible. Another terrorist attack. I've been trying to reach Saeeda, you know, my friend whom you met that night. I don't know if she had to go to court today. Her mobile is not reachable.'

'I hope she's all right. This is terrible. Just when you think everything is okay, something like this happens.'

Even though people had become inured to bomb blasts, shootings and terrorist attacks in public places, each time something similar happened in Delhi, it was a shock. There had been a bomb blast at the Sarojini Nagar market a few years ago and it had left Sweety shaken for a few days, for it was a place she frequented.

She made the calls to her family and ascertained that they were all well. She experienced a feeling of relief, and with that an awareness that her own concerns were trivial, her life's purpose shallow. Then, like most of her friends and neighbours, she prepared to carry on, unscarred by the event.

Three hours later, while Sanya-Manya were napping peacefully, Ambika called to tell her that Saeeda had been injured in the blast. She was not supposed to have gone to court that day but she had forgotten some important papers in the chamber of one of the judges. She had been entering the premises when a sudden blast had ripped through the air. She had lost a part of her leg, a side of her face was badly burned, she was in the hospital. Ambika had wanted to rush to Delhi to see her but Saeeda's mother had advised against it. Ambika rang off, crying, incoherent.

Sweety Singh, sitting on her children's pink bed in between her daughters who had fallen asleep with their arms around her, was ripped out of her cocoon. She was appalled to hear about Saeeda's injury. It seemed senseless, cruel, that the self-confident woman who had danced gracefully in six-inch heels would have to spend the rest of her life without a leg, handicapped, wheelchair bound. After their night out, Ambika had divulged to Sweety how

Saeeda's father had abandoned Saeeda and her mother when she was a child. He lived in Mumbai with his second wife and a new family, doing something connected to the film industry. They had not been in touch for years. Though the 'bastard' was rich, he had apparently never given Saeeda or her mother a single paisa. That Saeeda, brave, so-ready-to-face-the-world Saeeda, should be stricken in this way seemed unfair.

Sweety had spent most of her life without questioning the nature of reality or the world she inhabited. The queries about life, its meaning and purpose that had perturbed philosophers for centuries had not troubled her. She had her own moral code, her own formula to figure things out, and it had worked for her so far. She had never doubted her religion, her parents or the society she lived in. Now, she found herself doubting her mother's favourite adage, *jaisi karni, waisi bharni* – you reap what you sow. The world did not operate on a simple cause-and-effect relationship with rational explanations for everything that happened. If only there were a measuring scale, thought Sweety longingly, by which peace, prosperity or happiness could be doled out according to an individual's goodness or need.

Looking at Sanya-Manya, Sweety felt a rush of anxiety about the fate of her children, her powerlessness to do anything about it. How worried she had been when Manya had contracted swine flu. How absurd she had been to believe that she had influenced her daughter's recovery, to think that God had heeded her sacrifice and allowed her daughter to recover. You do not bargain with God. The powers that be make their own decisions, their reasons always remain obscure. It was mere superstition on her part, a pathetic attempt to salvage the situation, to attribute some cause-and-effect relationship to two completely unrelated events. She had blamed and punished a man who loved her, who was not at fault. She had been feeling so noble all this while for what was, in reality, mere stupidity.

Perhaps it's the shock of the terrorist attack, the sense of how precarious her own sense of security is, the awareness of the short-lived nature of happiness or the realization of the futility of all deliberate action, her remorse at her own foolish promise or the deep sense of empathy she feels for Saeeda, an empathy that overflows to all mankind, a heightened sense of connection with each and every human on the planet. Or it may be that she was concerned about his welfare, that she missed him too much. Sweety reaches for the phone and dials Varun's number for the first time since their conversation three months ago.

Varun is in the middle of a meeting with a team of analysts who are updating him about their evaluation of TechKnowlEdge, a crucial meeting at which he has so far been focused, asking probing questions and answering their queries with authority. When the Blackberry in front of him hums to life and flashes the name SSingh, he is disoriented for a moment. When he registers that it is Sweety who is calling him, his first thought is that something is wrong, that Amandeep has somehow discovered his wife's infidelity, that he is at this very moment rushing to his office with a loaded gun in his hand and Sweety is calling to warn him. He does not answer the call. The rest of the meeting is a disaster. He barely hears what the analyst is saying, he cannot concentrate. After ten minutes, he excuses himself, steps out to the washroom and calls Sweety.

Sweety, who has not thought of what to tell him and has been sitting for the past few minutes in a stunned silence, blabbers into the phone the first thing that comes into her head.

'There has been a terrorist attack in Delhi, a bomb blast. My friend Saeeda has been injured.'

Despite the terrible news, Varun is hugely, somewhat inappropriately relieved.

'Where are you? Are you okay? Is everything all right with your family?' he asks.

'I am fine, at home with the children. He is travelling. And you?'

'At work here, in my office in Gurgaon.'

'Can we talk later?'

'Of course. I'll call you when I wrap up in the evening.'

It is as though he has come home after a long journey, as though she has never been away.

37

EVERY FEW MONTHS, Varun Sarin, CEO of TechKnowlEdge, firm believer in the power of knowledge, advocate of statistical modelling methods, expert in decision-making software, addresses a batch of new hires in his firm, keen-eyed graduates in statistics, econometrics, engineers and computer programmers.

His usual speech started with a question *What is the difference between decision and choice?*

He highlighted the cool superiority of a well-crafted decision using all the information at your disposal versus the hot-headed emotional choice, which was reckless, based on fickle momentary impulses. In a given situation, there could be many choices, but there was only one right decision. This perfect decision, financially, legally, morally irreproachable, was an elusive one. It did not reveal itself easily, it came only to those who knew how to transform random chunks of information into knowledge, who could mine that knowledge for an insight, the insight that illuminated the way to the final action that needed to be taken. Organizations had to make decisions constantly: where to spend the marketing money to get the biggest return, how to reduce the underwriting risk, how to control inventory and meet the ever-increasing demands of customers. There was constant uncertainty. Markets could collapse, there could be a terrorist attack, an earthquake or a tsunami, a prominent political leader could get his head blown off. Uncertainty was the greatest source of stress and fear.

He then described the orderly black rows and columns of an excel spreadsheet, the simple beauty of statistical formulae, the unequivocal truth of the binary language, the ones and zeros in clear black and white: all these were the intelligent man's tools to bring order to a chaotic, random world. Finally, he defined TechKnowlEdge's noble mission: removing the stress and fear from their clients' lives. They were not just writing codes or creating models or mining data, they were saving companies, making people's lives immeasurably better. The new hires were as moved by the earnest passion in his voice as they were by the content of his speech. They went about their work with a greater sense of purpose.

Later, as he lay in bed, unable to sleep but keeping very still so that his sleeping wife would not be disturbed, it seemed to Varun that his entire business was built on a false premise. In the real world, nothing could be predicted. There was no model that could forecast the way the human mind worked. He had no idea why Sweety had decided to stop all interaction with him and then decided to resume just as randomly. It brought alive the fact that he had little control over his own mind, he was powerless to stem the stream of thoughts that ran through his head, he could do nothing about his dreams. The biggest decisions or choices that a person could make – whom to love, whom to marry, how to live, when to die – seemed beyond the pale of logical reasoning, outside the scope of normal planning. A distant event, a word, a glance could trigger off a chain of thoughts that could lead to a decision that in retrospect would seem idiotic. What he, his company, were attempting to do was as futile as throwing a pebble in the face of a hurricane in the hope of altering its course.

The one thing he was sure of was that he did not want to lose Sweety again. He'd had a short but satisfying conversation with her earlier in the evening. She had been agitated, a little incoherent, but just to hear her voice had been reassuring. He did not doubt her feelings for him but there was too much clutter in the way. She was bound to be swayed by circumstances, he knew. He also knew he did not want to be governed by her whims ever again.

There was only one way to get control. They would need to be together. The details would have to be worked out. It might take a little time, it would entail temporary dissonance but once all that was sorted out, they could be together without fear, without restraints. This thing they had, this love, was more powerful. The rest of the world would come around, things would fall into place. Adept at scenario planning, Varun Sarin could picture it all quite easily in his mind. They would have to leave Trafalgar Towers. He would sell TechKnowlEdge. Sam and the venture capitalists would defer to his decision. They were keen, so was Systech. It was only Varun who had been dithering, buying time, asking for more clarity on the deal, though he knew it was fair and generous. He smiled in the quiet darkness, thinking that they would never know the real reason for his decision to sell.

With his share of the money, Sweety and he could do anything. Anirudh, already almost an adult, would understand. Another year at school and he would be off to college, maybe Stanford or Berkeley. Varun had a vague notion of going back to California. He was an American citizen, he would find something to do there. He had good contacts among the venture capital funds and angel investors. He liked the image of him and Sweety driving through Napa Valley in an open-top convertible, her brown hair flying in the wind. In his mind, they looked young and utterly carefree.

Sure, there were some gaps in this scenario. Telling Gayatri, for one. And Sweety's husband. Would her daughters accept him? Did he really want to be father to a pair of six-year-old girls? But the gaps could be filled in later. For now, he decided to initiate the chain of events to sell the firm and tell Sweety of his plans. A week or two at the most to break the news, perhaps a few months more after that to deal with the bleak reality of a divorce. Within a year, Sweety and he could actually be together, openly, legally. At forty-five, the thought of starting afresh, getting a second lease of life, was frighteningly attractive.

38

AFTER A FEW weeks of preoccupation, Gayatri had almost made up her mind. She had not told anyone of her plans but now she needed a sounding board. She logged into the chat room to talk with Harini.

Gary: How r u?

Harry: Great. LA is lovely, all show and sham, but lovely still. Yesterday, we had some Hollywood folk for dinner at the restaurant. Blonde babes with huge silicone implants and lip jobs. I am beginning to see beauty in plastic.

Gary: Good for you.

Harry: Moved into my apartment last week. Nice change not having to worry about anyone else.

Gary: Sam?

Harry: Ok. Have fixed up an auntyji to cook for him thrice a week. The same one who had cooked for Vibha when the twins were born. And Sam has Boxer for company. He has finally figured out how the pooper scooper works!

Gary: Otherwise?

Harry: Keeps asking, how long? When will you come back? Seems like he is missing me.

Gary: And?

Harry: Keeping options open. Heard they are selling?

Gary: Who?

Harry: Sam and V! Don't you know?

Gary: I know there was some talk – an offer from Systech. But didn't know they had decided.

Harry: Don't know about final decision but Sam thinks they will sell. V has to give green signal.

Gary: Not like he's going to consult me.

Harry: What's up with u?

Gary: Am thinking of following your example.

Harry: What?????

Gary: Want to move to B'lore to be with Amma and Appa.

Harry: Short break or . . .

Gary: Long.

Harry: And V and Rudy?

Gary: They will be here. Domestic stuff is set up. Plan to look for job in B'lore. Hate this place anyway. Will start by taking two weeks off for Appa's cataract operation and then stay on.

Harry: What does V think?

Gary: Not told yet – will not mind. Can manage, like Sam ☺

Harry: Have I been bad influence ☺

Gary: No. Been thinking for a while. This training I went for helped me to clarify things.

Harry: So?

Gary: So? What do you think?

Harry: Good. We women don't take care of our own families enough. The way Sam panders to his amma is nauseating. Always loads of his vague village cousins land up for holiday and need to be carted to Mystery Spot, Golden Gate Bridge, shopping, and fed Indian food and filter kaapi for every meal.

Gary: Exactly! So u don't think I am being selfish.

Harry: Not at all. Noble cause. Just go. But consult V. He is quite sensible.

Gary: Ha!

Harry: Why?

Gary: V in own world these days. Don't think he will notice if I am there or not.

Harry: Maybe after u leave, he will come running to Blr? Absence making heart grow fonder??

Gary: Don't think so. More like familiarity has bred contempt ☹

Harry: How is Rudy?

Gary: Good. Busy in his own world – soccer, studies, guitar classes. Has a girlfriend.

Harry: A-ha! Serious?

Gary: Don't know how serious they can get at their age. He doesn't confide in me but don't think it will last too long.

Harry: We are not ready for mom-in-law role yet! Ashwin also has a girlfriend.

Gary: Who? American?

Harry: Indian – thankfully. Met her once. Maharashtrian. Seems nice. Am hoping he will get engaged. No point in telling the kids anything. They will do exactly as they please.

Gary: We are the only ones caught in between. Am also going to do exactly as I please.

Harry: Absolutely. You take care. And let me know when you are off. Shd make a plan to come to LA for holiday.

Gary: Sounds good. We shd call Sheetal and 3 of us can take off to Vegas for a dirty weekend ☺

Harry: Yes!!

Gary: Ok, tc. Catch up soon.

39

IT IS ALL in the details, the tying up of loose ends, the precautions, the double locking of doors, the small lies, the sins of omission and commission, the unbearable

anticipation, the ever-present fear of being found out. Varun
Sarin has come to know the blueprint of an illicit assignation.

It is 8 p.m. on a dry July night. Usually Gayatri and
Anirudh would be present in the house at this time. Jhumpa
would be preparing dinner and the house would be
humming with the sounds of a family going about its routine.
But this summer, Anirudh has joined his friend Ved at the
Pandes' summer retreat, a rambling house set amidst apple
and apricot orchards in the Kumaon hills. The invitation
was extended to the Sarins too, but Varun and Gayatri
muttered something about work and allowed Anirudh to
spend two weeks with his friend.

Gayatri is in Bangalore to attend to her father's cataract
operation. Varun has not noticed that she took more of her
belongings than she would need for a two-week trip. Before
leaving, she embarked on a cleaning spree and gave away
mysteriously large, full bags to the cleaning maid and the
houseboy who came to collect the trash. She handed over
the running of the house to Jhumpa, gave precise
instructions to Varun about the milk, the newspaper, the
gardener who came in to water the plants twice a week, and
other matters of domestic importance.

Jagdish has found a home, a small two-room portion of a
house in the Chakarpur village nearby. Jhumpa has already
shifted there. Varun had given Jagdish a loan to buy a
second-hand scooter to overcome the problem of public
transport in Gurgaon. He sees them arrive one morning,
Jhumpa perched on the pillion, her hand firmly around

Jagdish's midriff, another clutching the sari around her. There is something touching about the scene, so heartbreakingly commonplace and so right that for a moment he thinks, this is what happily-ever-after looks like. He watches them as they pull into the driveway and turn into the two-wheeler parking lot. They come to work every morning and leave together in the evening, an ordinary working couple. The arrangement suits everyone. And for now, Varun is alone.

He knows that he has been given an opportunity, it would be criminal to waste it. He would like to take Sweety out to dinner, sit across a table and talk, watch the candlelight flicker across her face, and look deep into those eyes and savour the prospect of what might follow. There is a Pan Asian restaurant, Eest, at the Westin Hotel nearby, with private dining areas safe from the prying public, a place with a dim elegance that lends itself to a quiet meal for two. They would be like any other dating couple.

Sweety refuses his invitation. She cannot afford to be seen with him, you never know who will get the wrong idea – or the right idea. So he asks her over to his place. Still coping with the remnants of remorse, Sweety finds it impossible to refuse. Perhaps she will be able to explain herself to him better. Sanya-Manya are spending the day, and night, at Green Park with their cousins and grandparents. Sweety has muttered an excuse about staying back to get the RO system repaired: the service engineer was expected some time during the day and since clean drinking water was a priority, it could not be put off for later. Her husband is away in Bangkok, the maid has retired early to the servant's room. There seem to be few impediments to their meeting.

When Sweety rings the bell, Varun almost runs to the door and, after a quick look to see that there is no one else in the corridor, lets her in. She is wearing a pair of grey track pants, a light T-shirt and sneakers. Her hair is pulled back in a ponytail, her face scrubbed clean, devoid of any make-up. It is almost as if she wants him to see her for who she really is, without any cosmetic accoutrements.

'Were you out for a walk?' he asks.

'No, I thought, just in case anyone wondered why and where I was going . . . I thought . . .' She trails off, a little abashed. 'Maybe afterwards I might walk.'

'Smart girl.' He smiles and leads her to the living-room sofa.

He sits next to her, looking at the contours of her face, into her eyes. She gazes back. He tucks a strand of hair that has escaped from her ponytail behind her ear. The gesture is intimate, yet disturbing, and Sweety feels something constrict in her throat.

'I . . . I am sorry . . .' she begins but he puts a finger on her lips, holds her face between his palms and kisses her.

'I missed you,' Varun says. 'All the time.'

Sweety nods. There is nothing to be said. She trembles, there is a surge of emotion within her as though she is going to be swept away. There is nothing she can do about it, nothing she wants to do about it. How easy it is, easy to be held, to be led again to the same bedroom, easy enough to offer herself, so easy to take this man, at once a stranger and so familiar, into her own body. It is a validation of what she has always suspected, it's what the purple-covered romances that she read in college had proclaimed: the body leaps to its own conclusions, the body recognizes what it needs and takes it, relegating the mind, even the heart, to a secondary role. The body is treacherous, shameless, and ultimately always proven right.

It seems to Sweety that she has two selves. Mrs Amandeep Singh, dutiful wife and mother, a circumspect woman who says and does what is expected of her. And this woman, who is capable of abandoning all thought, rejecting all notions of propriety, who is just a body seeking and giving pleasure. This act of the body is the first real act of autonomy in her life.

Slowly she comes back to reality. Despite the air-conditioning, they both are slick with sweat, the narrow gap between their bodies alive with the heat of their lovemaking. He kisses her closed eyelids. When she opens her eyes, her lashes curl against his cheek. They smile at each other and whisper the three little words, the impact of which time, distance and overuse cannot diminish. She kisses his face, every inch of it, and they say it again and again.

'I wish we could be like this forever,' Sweety murmurs.

'I know. I would love to wake up every morning with you

and see your face every night before I sleep,' he says. Then an idea, a moment to be grasped, taken at the flood: 'Marry me,' Varun says. It does not come out right; there can be no right way to propose to a woman who is already married. She does not seem to have heard. 'Let's get married,' he repeats.

'Nice joke.' She smiles a little wistfully.

'I am not joking. Sweety, darling, can't you see how good we are together? I can't lose you again.' His voice is more insistent now.

Sweety realizes that he is serious. 'How can I, how can we? It isn't possible.' She has never considered it. It is enough that they can talk, meet like this once in a while.

'Of course it's possible. It won't be easy, it won't be quick, but I'll take care of all the details. You just have to say yes.' It seems to him that it can happen, it is entirely within the realm of possibility. If she says yes, they can conquer the world together.

'But ... our families ... how can we?' The mood has changed for Sweety. She sits up and puts on her clothes. She is in a hurry to get back to a familiar world.

'Do you love me?' he asks as if that is the most important question in the world.

'You know I do. Why would I be here like this? But Sanya-Manya and—'

'Sweetheart, the children will of course be with you, with us. We can go somewhere else, anywhere you want. I can take you to the US. We can start a new life together. I am sure you've guessed that my wife and I, well, we haven't exactly been getting along very well recently. My son is old enough to adjust to any changes in our life. Once your husband knows, I am sure he won't want to prevent you from being happy.'

'But ... he ... I don't ...'

'We've been very lucky so far. But I know it's not very safe to continue to meet like this. I don't care too much about what they say about me but I don't want your reputation to be spoilt. It's best that we do something about it. I have no doubts.'

Sweety can only marvel at how logical he sounds, how persuasive his little speech is, how easy he makes it seem, how normal, as though it only needs a neat and precise incision to separate her from her old life and transport her into a new one. Her mind still befuddled, her body still tingling and tender, she does not know what to say.

'I'll think about it,' she says, and leaves.

Maybe it is the afterglow of sex, a testosterone surge, the flow of pheromones that love bestows on its recipient, but Varun Sarin feels optimistic about the future. The parting this time holds a promise.

40

GAYATRI WAS IN her room at her parents' home in Jayanagar, Bangalore, a three-bedroom bungalow with a small green square of a garden and a patch of yard at the back. The house stirred to life early in the morning and she woke up at 6 a.m. to the familiar chant of '*Suprabhatam*' on the music system. Then it was time for some meditation and a morning walk around the colony.

Bangalore had changed considerably over the last few years. The once sleepy garden city had become a technology hub. Brash young people from different parts of the country thronged the streets. The traffic on the main arteries of the city had reached nightmarish proportions and tall apartments had invaded the skyline. Yet, despite the addition of a few more houses and two new multi-cuisine restaurants, the colony where she had grown up was quiet and their house, located on a side street, was still sheltered from the bustle of people and vehicles. The 4th Block market had changed marginally with the addition of ATMs and a handful of new shops, but when she went shopping for vegetables with her mother, it seemed to her that the intervening years fell away and she became a young girl from twenty-five years ago.

Her room, which had not been occupied for over twenty years, had changed very little. It was like a shrine to the teenage Gayatri, preserved in the way the living quarters of famous people are, a museum to house memories. The framed poster of George Michael, the object of her single adolescent crush, still hung embarrassingly on the wall. The books that lined the shelf on the top of her desk were an eclectic mix of Enid Blyton, Agatha Christie, Ayn Rand, Salman Rushdie and Germaine Greer, books that spanned the length of her youthful reading habit. On top of the shelves were the trophies she had won through her academic life: a row of tarnished plaques, greying cups, and a bouquet of medals that dangled from an unseen peg. The curtain had been changed, the bedcover was of a lighter shade, but both had retained the character of the original cloth. She had never stayed in this room after her marriage. During their family visits they were housed in the guest bedroom, which had a large double bed, though Anirudh sometimes slept on the narrow cot in her old room.

Gayatri had taken her father to the eye doctor and a date had been fixed for the cataract operation. Her parents seemed to have aged considerably since the last time she saw them. But her mother claimed that her knee was much better and hobbled about the kitchen enthusiastically, trying to prepare Gayatri's favourite dishes. Despite the fact that she was there to take responsibility for her parents, in this room, she felt carefree, as though she were a child again, absolved from making any significant decision. She felt more relaxed already. The almost visceral sense of discontentment with her surroundings had vanished, as if someone had put a soothing hand on some of the creases in her life, though she knew that there were still a few pressing matters to be ironed out.

She had to confront the imminent dissolution of her marriage and the possible end of life the way she had known it all these years. She knew that she had been a coward, pretending to go away for a short break when she had no intention of returning. She knew that she was running away from a conversation that she and her husband had never had. She could not find the words to say what she wanted to, she could not even articulate it to herself. She wondered now if Varun and she had been mostly happy with spells of discontentment or mostly miserable with stolen moments of illusory happiness. It seemed unreal that a marriage could end like this – no explosive outbursts, no shower of sparks, no sudden slam of a door banging shut. Just a slow process of decay that started at an unidentifiable moment, as difficult to pinpoint as the exact minute when day gives way to night and everything around is plunged into darkness. It surprised her, this quiet fraying of their relationship, the absence of any strong feeling, the way everything seemed to have disintegrated, leaving only silence and emptiness. She felt no resentment towards her husband, the constant feeling of inexplicable anger had vanished. She felt scoured from within, clean but raw.

When she called Varun a week after her departure, she

was not sure what she would say. Their conversation was, as usual, transactional, perfunctory, sticking to the essentials, exchanging the cold details of daily living. But this time they both sensed that there was a need for further discussion; they could hear the clamour of unsaid words in their heads, waiting to be let out.

'So, what are your plans?' asked Varun. He needed to know. He was in the ridiculous position of a married man who had proposed to another woman, who was also married. He did not know how to break the news. For the past week he had been hoping vaguely that something would work out. He was still optimistic about a future with Sweety but something held him back from the final step of dismantling his marriage. He wished Gayatri well, he had nothing against her. In the last few days, he had held several decent, sensible conversations in his head, conversations that concluded with both of them remaining friends and agreeing to move on amicably.

'I am thinking of spending more time here. The operation is tomorrow and we'll see how that goes. I am wondering if I should be based here for a longer time,' Gayatri ventured tentatively.

'How long?'

'Six months to a year, maybe. I think they will need me around. They are finding it difficult to manage everything on their own. Amma might have to get a knee-replacement surgery done as well.'

'Hmmm. I agree, it's important for you to be with your parents. We can manage.'

Gayatri was surprised at Varun's quick assent. He seemed genuinely concerned, and understanding. She also detected a note of relief in his voice. While she was relieved too, reassured that he would not oppose her plans, the fact that he could happily manage without her was strangely unsettling.

'It's not working, is it?' she blurted out.

She was suddenly aware that she was speaking of their marriage like a third person, another body between them, its immunity worn out a long time ago and now afflicted with a mysterious terminal illness.

'What?'

'The marriage, you and me.'

'Why do you say that?'

'I am sure you know, Varun. The last few years, especially after we moved, maybe even before that, things haven't been the same. I guess I am to blame a bit. I was really upset about the move to Gurgaon.'

'You know we discussed that, and only after you said that you were okay did we move to India. And you know I had no idea that the Bangalore lease would fall through because of some technicality. I—'

'I know all that. I am sorry. All this while I think I have been blaming you for a lot of things which are not your fault. I haven't taken responsibility either. Anyway, now I am not angry with you or anything. I just feel . . . I don't know. I guess I am wondering if this is working for you.'

Varun had not given much thought to the state of his

marriage. He realized that he had been so consumed by his pursuit of and passion for Sweety that he had shut out the nature of his relationship with his wife. He had detached himself from the business of his marriage as though he had nothing to do with it. He had merely continued with a living arrangement that had been convenient so far.

'No, it's not working,' he admitted. 'I don't know what went wrong. It's not just the move, it's something more fundamental.'

It had to be broached, the next step. She had started on a path she could not go back on.

'So what do you want to do?' she asked him.

'What do you want?' he parried.

'I guess it would be a good thing for both of us to take some time off from each other. Sort of like a trial separation and see how it goes.'

Varun had been granted a reprieve. He accepted with alacrity.

'Yes. I think so. I guess you need to be in Bangalore for some more time. So it makes sense. What do we tell Rudy?'

'That is the most important part. He is still very young. I think we should give it a year before we decide one way or the other. By that time he will be ready to go to college and I don't want to disrupt his preparation for the exams. So for now, we just tell Rudy that I need to stay longer in Bangalore to take care of my parents.'

'Yes. That makes sense.'

'I'll call and tell him later.'

'Sure. What about your job?'

'I am looking for some options here. I've spoken with a couple of placement consultants and have a meeting with Dolt next week. He mailed me about a possible assignment with the energy project. It sounds quite exciting.'

'I am sure you'll get something good soon. Let me know if you need anything.'

'Sure.'

There was a pause while they waited, waited to register if all that had happened over the last few minutes was true. They were not in the habit of words, so the silence stretched thin.

'Varun . . .'

'Yes?'

'I wish we had talked earlier. You know, talked properly.'

'Yes. So do I.'

'Is there . . . any chance . . . I mean, should we try—'

'Try what?'

'No, nothing. I'll speak to you later then.'

'Okay. Bye.'

Gayatri felt discomfited as she hung up. The conversation was a case of too little, too late. She was glad that it hadn't been acrimonious or unpleasant. But she was a little disturbed at how easy it had been, how little reluctance there had been on Varun's part when she mentioned the idea of a separation. It was almost as if he had been thinking about the same thing.

She would have liked to probe further, to dissect the

issues in their marriage, to extract some admission, some revelation from him. She would have liked to do a complete diagnosis, to poke about a bit, see what had gone wrong. But Varun seemed to have already decided that whatever they had between them was truly dead. He didn't even seem interested in a postmortem. Ironically, it was she who had pulled the trigger and put the dying creature out of its misery.

In a sudden flash of insight, she realized that there was someone else in his life, another woman of whom she had been oblivious so far. There had been no signs, she was not the kind of wife who went through her husband's mobile phone bills or asked for details of his whereabouts. She knew it in her bones, just as she knew that her marriage was no longer something she wanted to hang on to. She did not know how far he had gone but realized that in attempting to cut the ties that bound them, she had also given him a long rope to act upon any impulse that he may have felt. It did not bear thinking about, and she would get to know soon enough. Meanwhile, there were things to be done – rounds of hospitals and doctor's appointments. Jai would be in town tomorrow, to talk to her about staying back in Goodricke. Anand, who had responded enthusiastically to her query on employment opportunities, would try to get her to join him in the renewable energy project when they met next week. She would call Harini later that night and tell her what had happened. She knew what her first words to her friend were going to be: 'I did it!'

41

SWEETY SINGH WOULD never know this, but if Amandeep Singh had not been the regular recipient of a variety of wonderfully relaxing massages at the hands of the soft-skinned Leya at the Heavenly Massage Parlor at Sukhumvit Soi 16 in Bangkok, and if Ambika Mohanty had not received an invitation to attend the wedding of her ex-husband with Jaya Tripathi, her own life might have been completely different.

Ever since Varun had proposed to her, she had been in a whirl, barely functional, frequently preoccupied, somehow getting through the routine of the day. She did not doubt that she loved Varun. Their last encounter had proved that quite conclusively. But in the clear light of the day, the patterns of real life seemed quite different and her meetings with him took on a distant, dreamlike quality. She couldn't imagine living elsewhere, removing herself from the comfortable home she had created. Nor could she imagine living a lifetime without Varun.

When she met Ambika for lunch two days later, they both were sombre. Ambika had visited Saeeda at her home. To see her friend in a wheelchair, her face partially bandaged, still weak and pale, had disturbed her badly. She had become painfully aware that life could change in an instant. Ever since, she had been wondering what she would have done if this had happened to her. What would happen to Aneesha if something happened to her? To add to her misery and confusion, there came the news that Abhijit Mohanty was actually, finally, getting married to Jaya Tripathi. Though Ambika had expected it all along, though she had frequently proclaimed that she was cool about it, the sight of the wedding invitation, its auspicious red and gold colouring, its air of respectability, the addition of Aneesha's name to the card along with close members of the Mohanty family and the omission of her own, had punctured the balloon of her coolness. She didn't love Abhijit any more but he was the first and only man in her life. Their own wedding had been a rushed ignominious affair, attended only by a handful of the Mohanty clan and none of her own relatives. There had been no wedding invitation: the Mohantys could not bear the thought that guests might speculate on the small bulge in the bride's sari and the depravity of the groom. The fact that she was single while he had already waltzed into the arms of another woman was deeply galling. The knowledge that this was the woman with whom he had an affair while they were still married was the final blow. She poured out her bitterness and anger, her helplessness in the face of life, the unpredictable injustice of it all to Sweety, who only half-heard her.

Sweety Singh needed advice, a sign, a nudge in the right direction. This, combined with a need to steer Ambika away from her problems, to assure her that other people's lives were not short on misery, made her bring up her affair with Varun. She extracted a solemn promise from Ambika to keep her secret. She refused to name the man – it would not be fair to him. She needed Ambika's help so much, she said. Ambika, who was so wise, who had already sorted out her own messy life, would be able to help her.

Her confession had the desired effect. Ambika moved from anger to curiosity, from being victim to interrogator. A great desire to take charge of her inexperienced friend's life, to save her from the mistakes she herself had made, came over her. What a relief to be able to give advice in a situation that did not affect you in any way! She was the guide, the shepherd, this was one lamb she could save.

'I don't know what to do,' Sweety murmured.

'You can't leave your family, Sweety. That's obvious.'

'He said he would take care of the girls. I am not leaving them.'

'Can you trust him?'

'What do you mean? Of course I trust him.'

'Come on, Sweety. What do you really know about him? You say he has been married for seventeen years. If he can leave his wife for you, what is the guarantee that he won't leave you? He is what, in his mid-forties now? That's almost fifteen years older than you are, much more experienced.'

'How does his age matter? I don't think it makes a difference.'

'Don't be naïve. That's the age when men want to

experiment, you know. He is just a typical middle-aged man having a typical middle-aged crisis. Look, I am sure he says he loves you, but at the end of the day, men are in it only for the sex. He is not getting any action from his wife and here you are, young and pretty, so obviously he falls for you.'

'He is not like that.'

'What about your husband? Does he know anything?'

'No, I don't think he does. He travels so much. He is never there for me. He just wants someone to manage the house, look after the children and make him happy when he is home. He doesn't even know what I want. He doesn't care. We never really talk at all.'

'You think other marriages are any different? Do you think it will be any different with this other guy? Do you think things will remain the same between you?'

'I don't know, Ambika. I . . . I thought you might—'

'What? You thought I would tell you to run away, get a divorce, that it would be cool?'

'Uhuh . . .'

'Sweetheart, divorce sucks. It's never easy. You'll be running around in the Haryana courts, your husband will not let you go easily, especially if it's a case of adultery, and there is the issue of custody of the kids. Trust me – you don't want to go through all that. I am not saying I am miserable and regret what I did. But would I still like to be in love and be Mrs Abhijit Mohanty? I guess the answer is yes. Bloody hell! It really hurt me today to know that my ex-husband is getting married to someone else.'

'But I love him. I don't know how we can go on like this.'

'Love is great, sweetie. I know it can be the most amazing feeling. But it's not everything. Just think what this will do to your daughters, your parents. If you go off to the US with this man, you'll be cutting yourself off from everyone. What if he starts beating you up when you get there? You won't have anybody on your side.'

'I never thought of that. I can't imagine he would ever do such a thing.'

'Okay, I am sure you know him well. But people change. I used to think Abhi and I would be in love for ever. At least with your husband, you know exactly what you are in for.'

'So what do I do?'

'I think you should call it off before your hubby finds out and it gets messy. You should join the advanced course at Happy Kids. I am planning to anyway. I think financial independence is so important for a woman. So get a job, stay married and buy a dildo.' Ambika smiled.

'I wish it were that easy.'

'It's easier than the other option, trust me. Do you have to decide now?'

'Yes. I can't keep him hanging any more. But tomorrow is Sanya-Manya's birthday party. I have to get through that first.'

'Break it off as quickly as possible. And you must not have any contact with him afterwards. Otherwise you will always be torn between your family and this man.'

By the time they parted, Ambika was feeling uplifted at the thought that she had been of some use. It gave her a sense of worthiness, signified a return to conventional morality and common sense. She had been unable to offer any solace to Saeeda, but with Sweety she felt that she had achieved something. She liked Sweety, she wouldn't have wanted to lose the one friend she had made in Gurgaon.

Sweety was left more perplexed than before. It was strange to see Varun through another person's eyes. She had never thought about the difference in their age, had never doubted his motives, had not wondered about the kind of future they might have. Though she could not visualize him hurting her in any way, the details of the life they might build together were beyond her imagination too.

For now, she had a birthday party to get through. Nothing could spoil that. It was the most important day of the year for her children, who were completing six. This was the first time she was organizing the celebrations on such a scale. Previously, everything had been done under the benign but firm guidance of her in-laws. In her current state of mind, it would be a small miracle if she got through this one without any disaster.

The party had been organized at the Multipurpose Hall in Trafalgar Towers. While Amandeep hovered around, taking pictures and chatting with the visitors, it was Sweety who saw to it that all the arrangements were in place and events unfolded as per schedule. It was a flurry of pink balloons and princess frocks. Twenty-three hyperactive children went through the mandatory games of musical chairs, dance and statue and passing the parcel. A boy poured Pepsi over a little girl's head, Sanya hurt her knee and cried for half an hour, three children dropped their plates, all of them fought over the pickings from the khoie bag.

After the children left, the relatives stayed on for dinner – her parents; her brother, who was a favourite with his nieces; and the entire set of her in-laws. The families posed for pictures in various permutations and combinations: Sanya-Manya with their cousins, with each pair of grandparents, with uncles and aunts, with their parents, with each side of the family. Amandeep hoisted his daughters, one in each arm, their arms around his neck as they screamed, 'Papa is the best.' Each snapshot reinforced the sacred ties that bound them for life by blood and by marriage, the glorious family structure that nothing could topple, no outsider could destroy. Everyone had a place, a position, a role they had to play for the rest of their lives.

It was almost midnight by the time she retired, exhausted beyond measure. She slowly combed her hair and smoothed a night cream on her face. She could see Amandeep looking at her speculatively from the bed. He seemed awake, fresh after the long day, almost as if all the action had energized him.

To forestall any move on his part that would require her to respond, Sweety remarked on the incredible level of her fatigue. 'I am so tired. My feet hurt so badly from just standing and running around. I can't believe how sleepy I am,' she said, yawning.

Later, when it was all done with, it was with some surprise that Sweety would recall that her husband had ignored her veiled plea. If he had waited for her to switch off the lights and then hefted his body onto hers, she might have made a different decision.

But Amandeep Singh, who had become a firm believer in the therapeutic properties of massage, and was unwilling to restrict his enjoyment of the process to the parlours of Bangkok, had other ideas.

His experience of massage had been relatively innocuous. He had never gone all the way and had no moral compunctions about dismissing the alleviation of a temporary arousal during the process as a part of the package. A massage, he had come to realize, was not just a way to soothe and relax the body but also to awaken it to its potential, to its own sensuality. Leya, his favourite masseuse at the Heavenly Massage Parlor, usually started with the foot massage, a perennial favourite in Bangkok. It was this world of touching and stroking and caressing that he wanted to introduce to his wife; he dreamt of experiencing the same under her soft hands. He realized that Sweety, who had always been compliant though a little shy with him, needed to be eased into the pleasures of the flesh, slowly. There was a new world they could explore together.

When he asked her to sit back on the bed, Sweety, too tired to desist, obeyed. As he gently took her feet on to his lap, she felt a sudden shiver of surprise run through her. The sight of her swollen pink-tipped feet in her husband's hands moved her strangely. She had not expected this gesture of concern. She watched his face, which was furrowed in concentration as he tried to recall how Leya had rubbed his feet, and she noticed how he gently caressed the ball of her toe between his thumb and forefinger. She listened to his innocent prattle on the beneficial effects of a massage, how she would feel much better after it, how it would bring them closer as husband and wife, how they must plan a visit to Bangkok during the next vacation, and knew with an awful certainty that she could never leave this man.

This was the great sacrifice she would have to make – the sacrifice of her love. She would live the simple life of a martyr, forsaking material pleasures for herself, living only for her family. Her earlier attempt at sacrifice had been a dress rehearsal. This would be the real test but she would triumph. Nothing could be more noble than a life lived for others. People would come and go like the beach sand under her feet but she would be firmly rooted on the shore, holding on to the hands of her husband and children, gazing ahead firmly in the face of towering waves. A feeling of languor came over her and her eyes closed despite herself, as she was carried away to another consciousness. Amandeep Singh looked at his wife and realized that his maiden massage session would not have the happy ending he had hoped for. Sweety was already fast asleep.

42

VARUN HAS SET the wheels in motion and waits for events to unfold. He has conveyed the news of the sale of the company to his employees, highlighted the multiple opportunities that are likely to arise because of the union with Systech, the long-term careers they can hope for, the enhanced job security that it will entail in these troubled times. It goes better than he expected.

He has spoken to Sam, who has been offered the role of vice-president for business development in North America by Systech for all their divisions. He is still considering their offer, but Varun senses that his heart is not in it. He might just take a break and go to LA for a while and then figure out what to do. Harini is there, helping Megha settle down at UCLA. Typical Indian parents, that's what we are, Sam laughed, worried about our young daughter, following her to college. If Varun is interested in moving back, they could think about starting something else. They still have good contacts, they have a decent sum of money. The possibilities are endless.

Varun thinks about the possibilities. His proposal to Sweety had been a little reckless. He had not really thought about a lifetime with her. It had been enough to examine the possibility of starting a life together. For a few moments, he wonders if he can sustain it. Then there is the matter of the age difference. Sweety is barely thirty now. While he was hankering after Julie Fernandes, she was a newborn baby. When she turns forty, he will be fifty-five, an old man edging towards oblivion. But Sweety makes him feel young, he reasons. He read a feature once, in a magazine, about a couple in their sixties who had decided to get married, each for the second time, each knowing that it is in the twilight of life that you really need companionship.

He wonders about the possibility of children. He and Gayatri had never pursued the option of another child. Gayatri, who had got back into her groove only when Anirudh turned five, had not been ready to consign another five years of her life to the upbringing of an infant. She was wary of daycare and wanted to be a hands-on mother, at least till the child was old enough to talk and express his needs. Varun might have liked a daughter but his feelings in the matter were not strong enough and he did not push the idea, knowing that the real burden of childcare would be Gayatri's. Now, the idea of a child with Sweety is exhilarating. A daughter with honey eyes like the mother, their legacy to the world, a testament to their love. If they do have a child together, she will be irrevocably bound to him. For ever.

Varun can wait no longer. When Sweety answers his call, all he can say is, 'So, what have you decided?' He already knows her answer. The way things have whirred and clicked into place is a sure indication of their future together.

'I can't,' she whispers.

'Can't decide?'

'No. I can't do it. We can't be together.' Her voice seems to come from very far away. He is not sure if he has heard her correctly.

'Look, Sweety, don't worry about what people will think or say. I'll handle everything. It's your life, our life, the only life we have. We can't waste it.' He hears the pleading note in his voice and for a minute cannot recognize it as his own. True love, he has heard, involves a complete sublimation of the ego, a dissolution of the sense of self, and now he understands what that means. He is ready to make his case, to beg.

'It's not that. This is not right. I can't separate the children from their father. I can't destroy my family.'

'What about us? Do you love me?'

'Of course I do. I will always love you. But love is not everything in life.'

To Varun, love has of late seemed to be *the thing*, the most powerful thing. He has been privy to a universal truth, together they have seen heaven, and it is foolish, wasteful, to throw it all away. He cannot believe that she might feel otherwise. This was not part of his plan.

'Do you really think that we can carry on now as though everything is normal, can you live as though this means nothing to you?'

'No,' says Sweety. She sounds wiser, older, almost as if she were a mother trying to make an errant child understand the ways of the world, the good manners, the rules of social behaviour. 'We have to stop. There is no other way.'

'Did you tell your husband? Did you discuss this at all?'

'No, I couldn't. He . . . he is a good man. I can't hurt him.'

'Does he love you like I do? Do you feel the same way about him?'

'Don't ask me these questions. You know how I feel. But I can't be selfish and only think of myself and what I want.'

'Do you know how many people even get close to what we have? We are meant to be together.' He cannot believe that his dream is slipping away, he cannot think of anything else to say.

'I don't know. If we were meant to be together, wouldn't God have made it happen? I mean, since both of us are already married, maybe this is not supposed to happen. It is not in our destiny.'

'Sweety, my darling, don't you see, we can make our own destiny. We can take a decision, make our own future.'

'No, we can't. A future where we make everybody else unhappy is not the future I want for us. We will never be happy that way. We have to give it up.'

'Is this one of your idiotic superstitions, another stupid sacrifice?'

'No. It is not stupid. It is the sensible thing to do.'

'I see. So now you have become very sensible. What was all this to you? Was I just some stop-gap arrangement, some, some, time pass when your husband was travelling, a silly little hobby you picked up?'

'Don't, Varun. Don't make it sound so, so cheap. It wasn't like that.'

'And now you are dumping me because you are bored and want to go back to your sensible life.'

'How can you say that? You know that it isn't true. Varun, please, I don't want to fight. This could be the last time we are talking.' She is crying now and the sound of her wretched sobbing, the childish gulps and sniffles, calms him, blunts the edge of his anger.

'Sweetheart, please don't cry. I am sorry. I don't want to fight either. What do you want me to do? I'll do whatever you want.' It seems to him that this is what he is meant to do. He will do whatever it takes to make her happy.

'Please go from here, leave Trafalgar Towers. If I see you here, if I know I can talk to you, I won't be able to stop. I am not that strong. I am going to delete your number after this so that I won't be tempted to call you.'

'I see. This is the end then.'

There is something cold and final about the words, like the last words in old books, nothing after that, only a blank page. It feels like the end of the world.

'I don't know. I only know that we mustn't go on like this any longer.'

An inadvertent sigh escapes Varun. 'All right. We'll do it your way. I'll leave, we'll stop talking, but I will always love you. Nothing will change that.'

'Me too. I will always love you too. Please believe that.'

'I believe you. I have to.'

'Sorry, I have to go now.'

'Yes, go on then. Goodbye, Sweety. Take care of yourself.'

They believe in the sentiment but both Varun and Sweety know that always is a silly little word. Life is unpredictable, full of twists and turns, sudden upheavals and small miracles. Things happen, things no one can foresee or expect or prevent.

Once they have disconnected, Varun Sarin replays the conversation countless times in his head. He wonders if there is something he left out, something else he could have said. Should he have dropped the phone and marched up to her house and taken her in his arms, made her realize that there was no other way? Should he have met her husband and then . . . Should he have been more persuasive, should he have grovelled at her feet, threatened to kill himself, to kill her? What could he have done other than accept her word as law? The second life he constructed for himself in his mind has crumbled over a five-minute conversation, leaving nothing behind. He realizes that there is no real evidence of his relationship with Sweety. All the calls and messages have been deleted as a matter of practice, they have exchanged no gifts, they have no photographs of each other, there is nothing tangible to touch, feel or recall what had been.

He walks over to his balcony, from where he had watched a woman walking in the morning aeons ago. The evening sun has finger-painted the sky a light pink. He feels a deep chill. Through the sounds of children playing in the park below, the honking of vehicles entering the building, the call of birds, the cacophony in his head, he perceives a stillness, a quietude he recognizes as the silence of loss.

43

VARUN WAKES UP next morning, alone in his bed, alone in his house. He has not slept well. He makes himself a cup of coffee, picks up the newspaper from outside his door and goes to the balcony for the early morning ritual. It is only then that the reality of his life comes back to him. He no longer has a company to call his own, his wife has left him, the woman he loves does not want to have anything do with him. Despite the ordinariness of the day, despite the familiarity of his surroundings, everything is different. He tries to find a word that would describe exactly what he is feeling but draws a blank. He wonders what account he can give of himself after the past year. He would like to believe that he has grown to be a better person, that through another human being he has established some sort of connection with the world around him, a connection that makes him more aware, that gives him a certain kind of knowledge, and yet he suspects that he might only have revealed himself to be weak, cowardly and selfish.

The day stretches before him like a punishment. He cannot drag himself to work, cannot bring himself to do anything. The idea of just being, sitting in a kind of stupor in one place, without thought, without effort, is strangely appealing.

But it does not take much for the rhythm of life to take over. The cleaning maid has to be let in. Not long after, Jhumpa and Jagdish arrive. Jagdish collects the car keys and Jhumpa bustles into the kitchen, wondering aloud what she can make for breakfast. The household whirrs into action and Varun needs to play his part in the daily drama. He tries to eat his breakfast of toast and scrambled eggs. It is a chore, the food is devoid of taste or flavour. He decides to skip taking a shower and continues to sit in the balcony, pretending to read the newspaper, the black letters blurring in front of his eyes. He goes through the conversation of the previous day again and it seems surreal, like a scene from a film.

On an impulse, he calls Sweety's number. There is no response. He cannot give up. He tries several times. Then he receives a message. 'Please, please don't call me again.' In the double please, he reads a finality. These are the cold words of an epitaph, a confirmation of what he knows is true.

He had not felt this way during their previous hiatus. That had seemed like an intermission, there had been a lingering hope that they would at some point of time resume where they had left off. But it had been that break, the misery of the days spent away from her that had made him take steps to ensure it would not be repeated, to propose a course of action that had led to the exact opposite of what he desired. Varun Sarin smiles at himself. His life, he himself, are quite absurd. He decides to do her one last favour.

He picks up his phone, his last link to Sweety. His fingers trace the 'Contacts' key, then SSingh. He lingers on the name a while, caresses the screen with his thumb. And then punches 'Delete'. He has not committed her number to memory. When he checks his contact list and searches for SSingh, it is no longer there.

Even as he expunges all physical traces of her, Varun knows he will spend the rest of his life looking out for Sweety, in the elevators of Trafalgar Towers, in the streets of Gurgaon, in the airports of the world, in shops, theatres, parties, everywhere he goes, he will search for her among the faces in the crowd, experience a faint stirring at the sight of anyone resembling her and then a crushing disappointment and a resurgent hope for the next time. He will not have it any other way.

'Hey, Dad, what's up?'

Varun turns around, startled to hear Anirudh's voice. His world has been shattered, its very foundation uprooted, but he must pretend that all is well. He needs to maintain a façade of normalcy. He remembers that Anirudh was due to return today from his holiday in the hills. The Pandes must have dropped him off and someone must have let him into the house. The glass of the French windows and the heavy drapes that sequester the balcony from the rest of the house must have prevented Varun from hearing the sounds of his arrival.

He looks at Anirudh, framed by the large balcony window, as though seeing him for the first time. This tall young boy-man, this person in frayed blue jeans and a white T-shirt, a chunk of hair flopping on his forehead, is his son, his only claim to immortality, his only real contribution to the world, the only *always* in life. Varun reaches out and hugs him. He feels an urge to share his life with this boy, to pass on some wisdom. In the past year, he has learned more about himself than he would have expected to. Love has been a revelation, a form of enlightenment. Someday he might tell his son, 'I once loved a woman very much and it changed me in ways I still cannot recognize.'

Anirudh, surprised at the unexpected gesture from his father, asks, 'Dad, is everything okay?'

Varun nods. 'How was your holiday?'

'Great.' Anirudh grins. He looks relaxed, slightly tanned, and for a minute, he resembles the small boy Varun had hoisted on to his shoulders during their long walks together.

Anirudh describes the Pandes' ancestral house, the scenic treks in the hills. The food was awesome, the scenery was mind-blowing, he had taken some amazing pictures with his new camera. Varun only half-hears him. He knows that he has not been the ideal husband, he has proved himself inadequate as a son and brother, he has probably failed as a lover. Has he been a good father to Anirudh? Looking at him now, Varun can understand a little of the importance of the happiness of children, the need to preserve their innocence for as long as possible. Soon he will send his son out into the world, hopefully armed and confident for the battles ahead. But he will never be able to prepare him fully for life.

'I am glad you had a good time,' Varun says. 'I must send a note to Ajay Pande.'

'Yeah. They are really cool people. Ved's cousins from Mumbai were there too. His cousin Veena is also in Grade Eleven, so we all hung out together and had a good time.'

Varun detects a slightly different note in his son's voice, a flash of a self-consciousness that makes him wonder about Veena.

'How is Nikita doing?' Varun asks.

'Good. She is holidaying in London with her cousins.'

'Are you both still . . . er . . . dating?'

'Yeah, I guess so, sort of. It's not like it's serious. When she comes back, we'll see how it goes.' Anirudh shrugs. He seems more confident than before and Varun feels a pang at the absolute insouciance of the young. His son seems far more mature than he was at his age. Perhaps there are lessons he can teach his father.

'Mom called,' says Anirudh, changing the subject.

'What did she say?'

'She needs to stay back in Bangalore to look after Thatha and Patti. It will take some time. She wanted to know if I would like to move to Hillview boarding for a year. I am cool with that. I know some of the guys in my class are in the hostel and they say it's pretty okay.'

'Sure. Whatever works.'

'Are you guys okay, you and Mom? I mean, you are still together, right?'

'Yes. We are okay. Your mother has to be there and I have other stuff to do. Guess we'll see how it goes.'

Varun hears an almost imperceptible sigh of relief.

'Cool. Dad, I was thinking, I have a month of the holidays still left. Maybe I could travel around a bit? I haven't seen much of India. I went to a village near Ved's place and it's amazing. Those guys have very little money, they live in tiny one-room houses but they are great. They used to insist on feeding me and Ved every time we visited.' Anirudh's face lights up with the recollection.

'Do you and Ved want to go together?'

'No, Ved has been to most places. He just wants to sack out here. I guess I am old enough to travel on my own?'

'You know,' says Varun slowly, 'I haven't seen too much of India either. Can I travel with you? I could take some time off and I would really like to spend more time with you. You'll be off to college soon and . . .'

Anirudh Sarin, sixteen going on seventeen, sees something in his father's eyes. For a moment he feels the weight of his father's age. There is a sense that he himself has grown up.

'Sure, Dad,' he says quickly, cheerfully. 'We could draw up an itinerary and figure out where we want to go. We could check out some off-beat places, not just the touristy stuff. Maybe we can drop in at Bangalore and see Mom before we get back.'

'Yes, that would be good.'

'After we come back, we can check out the hostel and see if there is a vacancy. If there isn't, I might need to wait a bit. You will be around, right?'

'Yes. I will be around.'

'Mom was saying you've sold TechKnowlEdge. So, what are you planning to do?'

The question catches him off guard. Varun pauses as he tries to think of a response.

'I don't know,' he says slowly. Though his mind is blank, he experiences a sudden feeling of lightness, as though he has made a great discovery.

'I really don't know. I have absolutely no idea.' He smiles at his son. 'Maybe we should start by getting a map.'

Acknowledgements

SOMETIMES IT TAKES a village and a community to get a book out.

A heartfelt thanks to

Gurgaon – current home and unlikely muse;

My friends and neighbours at Westend Heights who have contributed to this book in many ways – Rohini, co-conspirator and creative consultant, Rima, Reema, Shallu, Puneet, Simran, Sangeeta, Bideesha, Ritu, Shobana, Ameena, Suhasini, Ruchi, Parul, Aditi, Shabnam, Anita, Reena, Mira, Amrita – for the parties, bus stop talks, morning walks, insights, inspiration and invitations, for grace under pressure, for timely support, for being amazing women who do it all;

Of course the men and kids behind the ladies;

Amit and Shweta Diwan, 'model' neighbours for sportingly agreeing to be on the cover;

Ruchi of the fourth floor who generously offered her balcony for the cover shot;

Rohini and Madhav Mohan, Bhavesha and Sandeep Sharma for their gracious hospitality in California during the summer of 2010 and for giving me a glimpse into life in the Bay Area;

My wonderful co-facilitators with the McKinsey Network for 'being' there, for epiphanies and transformation – Atul, Joe, Leela, Pramila, Preeti, Sonali, Sudha, Uday and especially Vikram and Sorabh for letting me put them in the book;

Vaishnavi for reading the draft and saying all the right things;

The great people at HarperCollins – Karthika, for 'getting' the book, the pruning and polishing; Shantanu, meticulous editor, for the male p.o.v; Shuka and Amrita for the cover; Lipika, Ratna, Neha and the marketing team; Krishna, Sameer and the sales team, who are all so enthusiastic about making this book work;

Mom, first reader, constant supporter who wants me to write funny stuff now. Dad, whose presence is always there;

My sister, Niranjana, formidable reader, in-house reviewer, for taking the time out to read the manuscript;

My little family – Rajesh, for the title, the photos, for everything. Kaavya, the best part of my life. One day, I will write books that you can read and soon you can read the ones that I have written.